SALLY PIPER

THE GEOGRAPHY OF FRIENDSHIP

Legend Press Ltd, 107-111 Fleet Street, London, EC4A 2AB
info@legend-paperbooks.co.uk I www.legendpress.co.uk

Contents © Sally Piper 2019
First published in 2018 by University of Queensland Press, PO Box 6042,
St Lucia, Queensland 4067, Australia I uqp.com.au

The right of the above author to be identified as the author of this work has
been asserted in accordance with the Copyright, Designs and Patents Act
1988. British Library Cataloguing in Publication Data available.

Print ISBN 978-1-7895501-8-4
Ebook ISBN 978-1-7895501-7-7
Set in Times. Printing managed by Jellyfish Solutions Ltd
Cover design by Sarah Whittaker I whittakerbookdesign.com

Sally Piper's debut novel, *Grace's Table* (2014), was shortlisted for the Queensland Premier's Literary Award – Emerging Queensland Author category and she was awarded a Varuna Publishing Fellowship for her manuscript. Sally holds a Master of Arts in Creative Writing from Queensland University of Technology. She has had short fiction and non-fiction published in various print and online publications, including the first *One Book Many Brisbanes* anthology, *The Sydney Morning Herald*, *The Weekend Australian*, WQ plus other literary magazines and journals in the UK. She currently delivers workshops and seminars for the Queensland Writers Centre and mentors other writers on their 'Writer's Surgery' program.

Visit Sally at
www.sallypiper.com

or follow her
@sally.piper.writer
@SallyPiper

For my friends,
those women who walk with me.

SAMANTHA WALKS WITH A KIND OF idleness with intent; daydreaming in motion. She swings one leg in front of the other like a pendulum, foot hitting ground, heel, toe. Some steps fall short, others long; some light, others heavy. Her feet are small, but they have a nose for their own balance.

The rest of her is large, but out here it doesn't matter. Because everything around her is large too. Especially the mountains. They are grand and permanent. The wide-girthed eucalypts that travel up their flanks are slick-barked and gnarled. Their limbs reach up and stab silver lines into the blue sky.

When Samantha passed through here as a younger woman she'd wanted to know how it all worked, how the land and sky and flora and fauna were connected and dependent and in tune. She'd wanted to understand their symbiosis as if knowing meant she had something to contribute, something worthwhile to add to the landscape. Now, in her forties, she knows better: not everything can or need be understood, and there is no relevance to her being here. She has nothing to offer this place beyond her attention. And for once she's content with her insignificance.

Last time Samantha was here she'd fluctuated between fear

and inadequacy. This time it's mostly inadequacy. She barely noticed any of the beauty around her previously. She'd felt too threatened, looking behind her as much as in front, always trying to see the hidden. She tripped and stumbled, in both character and feet. Beneath her backpack her skin had chafed and pilled with sweat and friction. She'd felt vulnerable every time she put that bloody thing on, knowing she couldn't run with it, and again every time she took it off to make camp. Night brought another set of worries.

Now she feels no such threat or vulnerability, though the terrain remains brutish in parts and her backpack – modern and lightweight in comparison to the one she'd worn years earlier – is still heavy with gear. But it wasn't the terrain she'd feared, or even the restrictions of her pack. She'd feared him.

Samantha looks up from her feet and takes in the surrounding forest once more. Eucalypts mostly. Little has changed about the nature of these trees in the last twenty or so years. They still shed dreadlocks of bark and their silvery-green leaves still talk in the breeze. Their branches tick and creak and birds still perch along them, observing more than chattering now that the day is long past dawn. Everything and nothing is as she remembers it.

What is the same, though, is that once again she's following not leading.

Nicole walks in front, just as she had before. And Lisa is in the middle.

They haven't seen each other for years, but here they are, falling into the same old pattern as though there's no other worth considering. Maybe it's more to do with the place they're walking through. Maybe the land has designs on them – maybe it always had – robbing them of the power to choose alternatives.

But Samantha's never been much good at free will. If she were, she wouldn't even be here.

No introduction had been necessary when Lisa had called her, even though they hadn't heard from one another for over twenty years. Samantha would recognise the authority in Lisa's voice anywhere.

'Samantha. I need to see you.'

The significance of the call had sat peculiarly with the banality of what Samantha was doing at the time – at the sink scrubbing the burnt bottom of a pot she'd used to cook bolognaise sauce. She'd seen *No Caller ID* displayed on her phone's screen but accepted the call with a sudsy finger anyway. She always does. She remembers the casual way she pressed the mobile against her ear with her shoulder so she could keep working at the pot as she talked, as though it might be her mother's daily call. But on hearing Lisa's voice, that complacency left her. Her hands stalled in the sudsy water and her neck, cricked to one side, tensed.

'Lisa.'

That's it. That's all she said after all those years. But she hadn't been able to think of anything else to say. Which is peculiar too. Once the two of them hadn't been able to stop talking when they were together. *Talk the leaves off trees*, Samantha's mother used to say of them, *drive birds from the branches*.

But they'd been a lot younger then. Just girls, really. Silly, reckless girls.

'How did you get my number?'

'I rang your parents. They're still listed in the *White Pages*.'

Of course they were.

'Can we meet?' Lisa asked.

Samantha's body responded to Lisa's request with startling familiarity: her heart thrashed against her ribcage and a metallic noise started to clang inside her head. Once again she was listening to the sound of fear.

'Nicole's agreed.'

Nicole, too. Obviously Lisa was still as persuasive as she ever was.

'Please,' Lisa pushed, gently, cautiously.

Which threw Samantha even more. The Lisa she used to know was never cautious.

'Okay.' Samantha heard herself say it while every other part of her – her heart, her gut, her sanity, for God's sake – shouted for her to say *No!* Because nothing was okay, and hadn't been properly okay since.

But not good old obliging Sam, the girl – and now woman – who'd always said *Yes* to this friend, regardless of how unreasonable or stupid or dangerous her request.

Samantha asked herself then, and has been asking herself ever since: *What have you changed about yourself? In all these years, what have you fucking changed?*

But they'd been close once – all three of them were – girls brought together in high school, misfits amongst those who believed they weren't. So naturally, and inseparably, they'd become friends. Now though, they've built their lives many suburbs apart.

Samantha agreed a place to meet and soon after ended the call.

She didn't hear Harry walk into the kitchen behind her after she put her mobile back on the bench. She was too distracted trying to restore sense.

'You all right?'

Stolid uncomplicated Harry. A man who'd barely noticed any of Samantha's mood shifts in the past several years of their long marriage, suddenly decided to tune in to that one moment of unease. Go figure?

'This fucking pot, is all.'

She must have shocked him, if his sharp intake of breath was anything to go by.

'Must be bad,' he said. 'Want me to bring in the gurney?'

Any other day she might have laughed. But not that day.

She'd felt him shrug and soon after heard him leave the room. For once she'd been glad of his lack of persistence.

Samantha put her back into scouring the pot again while that accusing voice – Lisa's voice – whispered criticisms in her ear.

This mountain is a bastard of a thing. Sure, the long switchbacks take some of the steepness out of it, but not nearly enough for the level of fitness Samantha brings to the task, which is next to no fitness at all.

Nicole pushes ahead, just as she did last time. But there's no need for them to stick together now so Samantha doesn't even try to keep up.

It's been less than an hour since they left the car park and already the back of her T-shirt is soaked under her pack and she can feel moisture trickle down between her breasts. Maybe her easy sweating is another of those physiological responses – like the clanging sound that started in her head when she heard Lisa's voice on the phone – a cautionary warning of the body reminding her to take care. As if she needed reminding.

She'd arrived at the car park ahead of the others. She half expected to see his car still parked there when she pulled in, abandoned, unclaimed. For years Samantha has imagined the panels of it rusting away in the salt air, the red paint blistering in the sun, long grass growing out around perished and airless tyres. But it wasn't there of course. Too much time has passed.

Samantha's face feels hot and she knows she has the flushed look of the unfit. She looks down and sees a crescent of moisture on her T-shirt under each breast and a wet ring round her navel. She was never the dry one at school either. She was always the heavy-set girl with dark moisture lines on her PE uniform, even during the warm-up. By the end of the netball or hockey game her uniform would be soaked.

She stops and rakes her hair up off her neck. She holds it on the top of her head with the flat of her hands, elbows out wide, walking poles swinging at her sides. The breeze is warm, but it still cools her bare neck.

She stays like this and watches Nicole as she moves along the trail above. Still athletic, Samantha thinks. Not especially tall, but sturdy and muscled and dogged. She sees that Nicole approaches what they're doing now with purpose not pleasure.

She strains ahead like a horse heading for home. Or is it that she intends to get what they've started over with as quickly as possible? Samantha wouldn't blame her if she were.

Lisa, on the other hand, moves with the kind of determination Samantha remembers her for. When Samantha was younger, she'd always admired Lisa's long legs. They were fast, endurance legs; legs that refused to give up. They knew what they were striking out for.

Lisa stops now and turns to face Samantha, feet planted wide, thumbs loosely tucked under the chest straps of her pack.

'How're you going? All right?' she calls back to her.

'Uh-huh.' Samantha releases her hair and the heat immediately starts to build beneath it.

Lisa turns again and Samantha watches her still-enviably lean legs as she presses away.

'Take a break as often as you like,' she calls.

Samantha doesn't answer. To say *Yes, I will* or *No, I'm fine* sets her up for either commitment or lie.

'I'll wait for you.'

And neither does Samantha want Lisa to have to wait for her. She wants her to believe that she can do it this time. Samantha wants to believe it of herself.

She takes another shortcut through a switchback, hoping Nicole won't notice. She doesn't like cheating, but limited fitness demands efficiency. Samantha should love the freedom of this slow and repetitive movement. She should love the way it lets her dismiss the usual domestic clutter, thoughts about household chores and the bookkeeping tasks of a plumber's wife. But she doesn't.

She remembers a time she'd have relished the peace. The time she walked out on the children early one evening. Fled really. Slammed the door behind her. Didn't care that she'd left three boys under eight in the house on their own. Didn't care that they had no understanding for what drove their mother into the twilight. It was very *film noir*. A dramatic domestic escape.

It was the climax of what had been an escalation in tears, tantrums and squabbles throughout a school holiday afternoon. Too many calls of 'Mu-um! He! Hit! Me!' Too much whining. Too many demands. Too little relief.

A switch had flicked inside her. It wasn't a case of knowing she had to walk away or she'd harm them. It was about self-preservation and nothing to do with the safety of her children at all.

She'd walked out on the hard footpath in sandals, each step a sharp slap against the concrete.

She hadn't known what she was walking towards, only what she was walking away from. Eventually she reached a point, many blocks from home, where she stopped abruptly on the footpath. To anyone who saw, it must have looked as though she'd come up against a pane of glass. She'd turned then and headed back the way she'd come.

When she arrived home more than an hour later, the three boys were sitting close together on the sofa watching television. Three sets of eyes turned to face her.

'Where'd you go?'

'I missed you, Mummy.'

'We had Oreos for dinner.'

Harry was back by then. He glanced at Samantha cautiously as she passed him in the kitchen. He never questioned why he'd come home to find three small boys home alone. She was glad he didn't. It made him complicit in her neglect.

Samantha still doesn't know who the truest version of herself was that day: the woman who walked out or the one who came home.

She expects the same can be asked of all three of them now.

When Samantha pauses to rest again she doesn't call out to the others to wait. She doesn't need them close as she once did.

She knew that the minute she saw them in the bar. So why did she agree to come away with them?

It'd be easy to blame the wine she drank that night. If she'd stuck with mineral water, maybe she wouldn't have fooled herself into thinking that past steps can, or even *should*, be retraced. Because while the place she takes those steps in now seems largely unchanged, being of rock and soil, her memories of being here are, and always will be, amorphous. And rarely do they cast her in a good light.

Lisa was gentle in her persuasion at the bar that night, not pushy or talking over the top of them like she used to. That extraordinary difference in her allowed Samantha to believe that change was possible for any one of them.

'Don't either of you have regrets?' Lisa asked.

Nicole's answer came quick and sharp. 'No. What's the point of them?'

But Samantha thought Nicole sounded like a fraud, her shrug too rehearsed.

Samantha had squirmed in her seat because she had a lot of regrets. None she wanted to share. Maybe once she would have, but not now. That's probably when she started to give too much attention to her wine glass, emptied it too quickly.

'I have regrets,' Lisa admitted. 'And I'd like to face them … face who we were.'

She was reminded again of how fearless Lisa was.

'Face who *we* were or who *you* were?' Nicole asked, finally looking at Lisa.

'All right,' Lisa acquiesced. 'Face who *I* was.'

Mollified, Nicole returned her gaze to the table.

'I don't know how else to fix it,' Lisa added, her voice uncharacteristically soft.

Nicole said nothing but nodded as though she understood.

Samantha struggles to even picture her twenty-year-old self, to give this girl shape or form, let alone face who she was. Maybe in coming back here, she too will find the courage she needs to find that girl again. Maybe even learn to like her once more.

'Do either of you even remember why we decided to go out there in the first place?' Lisa had asked them.

This Samantha had been willing to answer. 'To grow up.'

For her, it was an opportunity to stamp a footprint on her independence. She wanted to prove that she could be self-sufficient and make her own choices, away from the familiarity and security of her parents and her family home. Back then it was about the doing, not the journey – the victory air punch at the end and the shouts of *I did it!* Except there were no air punches. No victory cries. No sense of achievement.

'And how did that work out for you?' Nicole scoffed into her whisky, neat, no ice.

True, not well, but Samantha didn't say so. Instead, she took another sip from her glass.

She supposes it was a naïve belief to hold anyway, that a girl can walk herself into womanly confidence. Still, she admires this idealism of her younger self to even try. She figures in some ways she *did* grow up, because the girl who entered the trailhead all those years before wasn't the same one who left it days later. But it wasn't greater confidence that delineated the girl who started the hike from the one who finished it. It was a loss of innocence.

The ascent isn't so much steep as unending. Lisa is slowly increasing the gap between them but Samantha can still see the metronome swing of her blonde ponytail. And Nicole is a good distance further ahead again. She has short, grey-flecked hair now, so there's no hiding the way her neck muscles strain, the way she leads with her head.

Samantha's happy to accept her place as the tail-end drifter, just as she had been at school. There, she hadn't been the one who decided where the group sat for breaks or the pecking order in which they gathered around a table. Her stories weren't the ones others wanted to hear and neither was her opinion ever sought. She was the dull fragment at the end of a blazing comet pulled along by the pheromones and chutzpah of the girl leading it.

Samantha wonders if much ever changes in the hierarchy of school friendships. Somehow she doubts it. She expects many are still maintained by the unchallenged belief that the one calling the shots is the one who should. Being the loudest or the bossiest and, in the case of a bunch of thirteen-year-olds, the prettiest or the most physically developed assures that.

The assumed leader of the group she'd been desperate to join was a tall, attractive girl whose breasts had developed well before anyone else's – anyone except Samantha's that is, but even they hadn't been currency enough to make her popular. This girl had Brooke Shields hair, which she claimed to spend an hour each morning blow-drying into alluring flicked-back waves. She was a girl who got noticed – by other parents, by teachers, and by boys. And she noticed that she was noticed; a feedback loop of positive reinforcement.

Samantha couldn't help herself. She wanted some of this girl's confident self-awareness. She tried to hang out with her group, hoped it would rub off on her. She lasted a couple of weeks. Her relegation to the outer started with a few harmless enough pokes to her rubbery sides, but then the barbed comments soon followed: *Chips for lunch again? Maybe you should eat more apples?*

When she looks back on her thirteen-year-old self, Samantha can see what those girls saw when they looked at her: someone with thick thighs, full buttocks and strong arms; someone whose kneecaps and elbows and collarbones weren't delicate, defined lines and angles. She was a girl sheathed in softness when all around her was preferred, perfect thinness.

When she was eventually shown a circle of backs at break time, she had no option but to turn away and show them hers. And while she can recall her departure from the group with indifference now, at the time it had cut deeply at her confidence.

It was then that Samantha noticed Lisa, sitting alone on the steps behind the tuckshop of their school. She didn't really know her but even then Samantha had been able to tell that the strawberry-blonde with freckles had a hair-trigger for anger. She'd seen Lisa lash out at a boy in class who thought he'd help himself to the half-eaten Mars Bar on her desk.

'Don't! Dickhead!' Lisa snapped, and brought her hand down in a savage karate chop on the boy's forearm so that the pen he held flew across the room. The boy had laughed for the benefit of his mates but Samantha saw how he rubbed at the spot on his arm under his desk afterwards.

Lisa had just taken a pot shot at the rubbish bin with an apple core on the day Samantha first noticed her. The bin was two metres away and the apple core landed wide. Lisa shrugged and rested her elbows back on the step behind her, stretching her long legs out and crossing them at the ankles so that her black school shoes flopped out sideways to resemble a fish's tail. She held her freckled face up to the sun, her long blonde hair brushing the step, her flat chest pushed to the sky. When Samantha thinks back on this image now, she thinks of a selkie with sass.

'That'd give the prefects something to pick a fight over,' Samantha said.

Lisa looked from Samantha to the apple core and shrugged. 'They can *try* and pick a fight with me,' she said. 'But they won't win.' She turned her face back to the sun and smiled.

Samantha sensed she was welcome and sat down.

'You'll give yourself more freckles,' she said as she stretched out like Lisa.

'D'you reckon they'll all join up one day and I'll look really tanned?'

'Nah. Don't like your chances.'

For a slim girl, Lisa laughed big. Samantha was a big girl and knew she laughed small.

She turned to look at Samantha through one eye; the other squinted against the sun. 'I've seen you round,' she said. 'You've got big bones.'

'Yeah? So?' Samantha decided she must have sensed her welcome wrongly, so made to get up from the step, but not before she added what she hoped was an equal insult. 'And you've got no boobs, so we've both got something other girls don't want.'

Lisa grabbed Samantha's arm and kept hold of it as she laughed that big laugh again. 'Wish I was more like your stuck-up friends?' She nodded in the direction of the group of girls Samantha had been expelled from.

'They're not my friends,' she mumbled and looked away.

Lisa let go of Samantha's arm and nudged her thigh playfully.

'They were never gonna be, ya dag.'

Even all these years later, Samantha knows she didn't imagine the warm affection in Lisa's voice. She walks on now, allowing the past to walk alongside her, but grateful that this memory from it has been generous.

The track is marked by the prints of many walkers. An assortment of small rhomboids, triangles and argyle patterns are pressed into the sandy soil, each a signature of the person who has passed before. Samantha wonders at the stories these feet might carry, what hardships they've borne.

Previously they had set out on a mostly virgin trail, the paw prints of wallabies, bush rats and wombats the only signs of life. It confirmed their isolation, though they didn't speak of it. That was one of their errors, not speaking enough, not being honest enough. Samantha suspects little has changed about them in this regard.

She looks up at the backs of Lisa and Nicole now. She recalls how when they set out that first day they walked like they were already buggered, head and shoulders down. Nothing piqued their interest. They passed the landscape without remark. What happened in the car park had killed some of the joy of their anticipated adventure.

Samantha remembers how, in wanting to lift their mood, she had called out to those beaten backs. 'We can just ignore him if we see him.'

Lisa had stopped abruptly and swung round to face her. Nicole hadn't looked at either of them. Instead, she gazed off into the bush, eyes lifted high above the canopy.

'Very wise,' Lisa snapped. 'Typically, very rollover safe.' She'd turned then, pushed past Nicole and walked on, thin legs working hard. Lisa didn't look beaten after that, she looked angry; something that propelled her for the remainder of the hike.

It's easy to pinpoint all the comments and actions that if retracted, could have made a difference, Samantha's suggestion that they ignore someone's behaviour being just one of them. None of which is possible now of course.

So what is *now's* job? Samantha wonders. What is there to gain, after all this time, in facing their past actions as Lisa said she wanted to do?

Samantha had gained Harry's attention. That much she knows.

His embrace when she left had been awkward. He had his work cap on, the one with their company's name and logo embroidered on the front – *Titus Plumbing* – and the hard ridge of its peak had blocked his face and knocked against her head when she leaned in. She had to reach up and remove it in the end, just so she could kiss his cheek.

Samantha got into her car and wound down the window to say goodbye. He rested his hands on the car's roof and this giant of a man had to dip his knees so he could see in. For the second time that week, she could tell he was really looking at her.

She can't deny the thrill she got at becoming more visible as she prepared for the hike. She'd thought she was after peace or understanding or forgiveness in coming back here.

But maybe all she wants is to have her presence noted by its absence?

Harry had looked bemused as the equipment accumulated.

'What's it for?' he asked again.

'I told you. A hike.'

'A hike?'

'Uh-huh.'

'What kind of hike?'

'A bushwalking kind of hike.'

He scanned the gear laid out on the bed in the spare bedroom.

'Do you hike?' he asked eventually.

Samantha didn't answer because she knew he was asking himself this question, not her.

She watched him as he picked up a walking pole and inspected the mechanism of it before he put it back on the bed. He moved to a packet of freeze-dried food, brought it close to his face and studied the label.

'Beef stroganoff,' he read and shook the contents of the packet.

Next he picked up a resealable plastic bag with first aid gear inside, something she'd been tasked to carry.

You always had the strongest stomach, Lisa had said to her, *so you should be in charge of it*.

But Lisa's memory was wrong. Samantha had the weakest stomach.

Harry studied the contents through one side of the clear plastic – blister plasters, strapping tape, triangular bandage, safety pins – then turned it over and looked at the contents through the other side. He bounced it in his hand a few times, perhaps testing the weight of it, before he placed it back on the bed.

'How many days are you going for again?'

'It's a five-day circuit.' A loop, a circle, the end coming back round to the beginning again, except for them it only ever marked the end.

'Five? And you say you haven't seen these women for what … over twenty years?'

She shrugged. Tried to make light of the fact. 'We were close.' She didn't add *once*.

He ran a finger up the pile of folded clothes, across the T-shirts, trousers, a fleece, wet weather gear. As drab and unflattering as these items were, Samantha imagined them like a high-vis vest to Harry's normal order of things.

Then for the first time since his inspection of her gear started, he really looked at her. 'Should you be doing this?' he asked.

She imagined him looking for ways in as he studied her face, trying to connect with her usual sense of reason, looking for the calm, acquiescing woman he was used to. She recognised in that moment that if she allowed him to tap into these soft, safe places she risked losing her newly found courage. This gatekeeper would absorb any of the self-determination and spontaneity she'd recently developed. She felt an insurgent rush then. She stopped herself from saying what she was really thinking, which was *Probably not*.

'Yes,' she said. 'I should.' And the conviction in her voice had surprised her.

Samantha thinks familiarity has been their enemy. They live their lives with insufficient surprises.

She supposes she's to blame for this as much as him. She gave up on taking risks when she gave up on her friendship with Lisa and Nicole. Which probably explains her quick acceptance of safe monogamy as soon as it was offered.

She had woken that first morning to this bear of a man – the man who would become her husband – taking up more than half of her double bed. For a moment she couldn't recall how he came to be there. Then she remembered the smoky nightclub, too many tequila shooters and the loud disco beats from the night before.

He slept on his back, one arm slung above his head and he breathed softly – a bonus, she remembers thinking. As she watched him sleep, she recalled the thrill of running her nails through his thick chest hair – hair their future sons would be relieved they didn't inherit. And she liked the dark regrowth across his jaw. There would be a period during their marriage when it would become a thick and full beard. She'd had few lovers – and one she couldn't even call that – but when she looked at this one, she thought of those others as boys. This time she'd brought home a man.

He was surprisingly shy when he woke. He kept the sheet across his naked torso as he scrabbled about for his clothes on the floor beside the bed. He sat on the edge of the mattress to pull on his underpants, so all she saw was the brief flash of his pale muscular buttocks.

As she watched his self-conscious dressing she wondered if he'd liked to have been able to *un*-choose the outcome of the evening before.

He asked for her number before he left though, and he rang her that night. Her hangover was gone but the memory of him lingered.

'Can we try that again,' he asked. 'But sober?'

'What? The sex?' she teased.

'No. The meeting one another.'

She'd felt young and foolish then. But she also felt flattered. 'I'd like that,' she said and meant it.

She wonders now what happens to the fire and pluck of love's first vigour? Where does it go? Is it completely extinguished by the burden of parenting, working, providing?

She wishes all the texture of their early relationship could be returned to them – the crushing passion, the fear of absence, the urgency with which they seized love in order to not risk losing it. As it is, they might still have one another, but mostly they are lost in the same home.

When Samantha reaches the top of the next rise, the other two are already making their way down the other side. She doesn't mind. She takes the opportunity to catch her breath.

She lowers herself onto a boulder. Her bottom lands with a *thud* in the last few inches. To have the weight of her pack now resting on granite and not her shoulders is bliss.

She looks about. The area seems familiar, which she suspects is more from expectation than any actual memory of it. In coming back she knew she'd see eucalypts and bracken, banksia and she-oak. She knew there would be mountains and gullies and that each would require rigour to negotiate. She knew there would be rocky headlands, their granite faces slapped by a turbulent sea. All of this has proved accurate. But for her to say she has seen *that* tree before, or *this* boulder, is impossible.

What she can identify with clarity though is the *feeling* that comes with being here. This sensation is more reliably familiar than anything her eyes might be able to land upon. She feels it in the band that slipped round her stomach the moment she drove into the trailhead car park, and which hasn't eased off since. She feels it in the fluttering panic that keeps visiting her heart. These things she can point a finger to and say, *I know you, we've been acquainted before.*

Samantha gathers together an assortment of small flat stones from beside her. She places the largest of them – no broader than a blood plum – on the rock where she sits and builds up from there. It takes some balancing but eventually she has a small cairn, five stones high, the last no bigger than her thumb. It's a wonky tower, skewed off to the right. On reflection she should have used a better foundation stone. A flatter one.

She knows these patiently enduring stones won't last in the form she's given them. She expects they'll topple with the next walker who sits here or the next storm that brings along a cavalcade of twigs and branches, and they'll be arranged in a new order on the ground. Still, for now it's a pleasing little thing to look at. It's evidence that she's been here.

Samantha stands and adjusts the waist belt of her pack so that it sits on her hips again but the weight of it still pulls down on her shoulders. She looks to the descent ahead and feels a mixture of relief at the ease of going downhill and trepidation at the loose gravel she's to negotiate on the steep slope. Walking on this stuff is like walking on rice in new leather-soled shoes.

If Harry were here, she pictures him going confidently down the trail ahead of her. But he wouldn't think to hold his hand out to her. Wouldn't think to look back to see how she was going. He wasn't always like this. There is a layer to him that is missing now. It's the one she fell in love with.

What's gone is the man who had a quiet way of letting her know that he had her back. The man who used to hold her hand when he led her through a crowd, his body twisted just enough to place her behind him. The man who walked kerbside on a footpath. The man who quietly insisted *That's enough*, to a lewd, drunken mate. Samantha thought these acts would be there forever. But she was wrong. And now that they've gone it raises the question: is he less threatened or is she less valuable?

She scans the ground before she takes the next step, looks for the safest spot to place her foot, the most reliable. It's exhausting, this cautious progress. The fear that every step might be the one that takes her feet out from under her. She knows with a pack on her back that she's a heavy load to drop from standing.

Nicole is out of sight. Samantha imagines her at the bottom of the descent by now, probably even negotiating the next rise. Lisa is a good way ahead. She could easily keep up with Nicole. Samantha knows she's going slowly on purpose, but she wishes she wouldn't. If she falls she doesn't want any witnesses. Samantha slows and is relieved when Lisa disappears behind a bend in the trail.

The fall when it does come is sudden and surprisingly graceful. One second she's standing, the next she's flat on her back. After the initial shock passes, her first thought is if she feels any pain. The exquisite kind. The type that sets off alarm bells of a tear or a fracture. Thankfully, she feels nothing beyond the general aches she's felt all day. She doesn't have the energy or strength in her legs to push herself up, so she lies there for a while, like a turtle stranded on its back, and takes in her new sky view. She feels the depth of her exhaustion acutely. It's a fatigue she recognises, one that runs deep to the bone. The kind she'd felt as a mother with a sleepless newborn, then another and another, till she had three under four, and she'd blink asleep, sometimes standing up.

It's only mid-afternoon but from her low spot on the ground the sun is out of sight behind the tree line along the mountain ridge. White pillows of cloud amble along overhead. She imagines one of them soft under her body. A wagtail peers down at her from a gnarly old banksia branch. It pivots its head left and right a couple of times, then flits off with a quickness that her eye almost misses. She thinks about how light and ably equipped it is for the environment. Then there's her, a large and awkward thing. A blight on the landscape.

Samantha feels the hopelessness of her situation and thinks she might be about to cry. What she's doing is too hard. She wants to go home where the floors are soft and safe and she can walk across them in bare feet. Where there is air conditioning in every room and flyscreens on every window and where cold running water comes straight from a little spout in the fridge door. She wants to stop this false bravado and go back to the predictability of her life. Go back to the routine and sheer mundaneness of her days where a fall such as this is inconceivable.

She considers turning around and going back. It's too late in the day to do that now of course. But she could do it in the morning. There's nothing to stop her. She'll wave Lisa and Nicole on their way – they don't owe each other anything after all – and she'll walk back to her car. Drive home. Return to all the things she knows so well.

And this thought makes her move. It makes her roll off her back and onto her side. It makes her get onto all fours. It makes her push up with her arms and legs till she stands again, facing the way she's come and not the way she was going. And with as much care as she can muster, she turns and looks downhill again. And because she knows only too well what is at home and not enough about the woman who lives there, she looks once more for the best spot to place her foot. And tomorrow she'll do the same. And the day after that.

MIND AND BODY WERE IN TURMOIL when Lisa was here last time. There was no rhythm to her steps. No synchronicity. No connection to the land whatsoever. All she'd connected with was her rage. It was that crystalline, that *pure*, that the significance of everything else evaporated around her.

Now though, it's like she's seeing – feeling – this place for the first time. She can smell the dust that puffs and rises with each footfall. Hear the *hush* sound the breeze makes as it passes through the trees. Taste the oil the eucalypts exhale. Lisa feels as though nature has bubble-wrapped her thoughts, tempered them to something quiet and relaxed so that the landscape might present itself afresh. But she expects the feeling will be short-lived. It usually is.

For now she enjoys just being on this trail. She likes the way it's been carved to mostly go round the trees and not the trees forced to give ground for it. The eucalypts here are mostly messmate stringybarks – *Eucalyptus obliqua* – plus narrow-leaf peppermint and manna gums – *Eucalyptus radiata* and *Eucalyptus viminalis*. She'd checked the botanical names of the plants to expect before she left home. She wanted to know something of the place with certainty this time.

The flora here bears no resemblance to that of Lisa's small

suburban garden. It's not been shaped or tamed, not been made to conform. She can see where the growth has been thwarted in places by the natural elements – wind, fire – but not secateurs.

Lisa keeps her secateurs sharp, just as a surgeon's scalpel. The cuts she makes to her camellias – the pink *japonica* with its double flower and dark, glossy leaves is her favourite – are quick and precise. The plants repay her with masses of large velvety blooms. As do the Iceberg rose topiaries she's planted alongside the short path from mailbox to front door. She's even coaxed the often-woody lavender and rosemary into pleasing forms.

She came to gardening late, and only then when a man she thought she could love piqued her interest in all things botanical. But circumstance or self-sabotage – would she ever really know which made her drive him away? – has forced her to love this activity alone.

Soil, root, branch – each provides her with a welcome disconnect from the human world; they feel kinder, more generous, and the demands they make upon her are of her own design, unlike the demands other people make. In this way gardening soothes her, allows her to let her guard down, to be someone else.

'Finally put yourself into therapy,' her daughter Hannah quipped when Lisa admitted this to her.

She hadn't had the courage to ask Hannah to elaborate, to list the reasons why she'd make such a remark, but deep down she knew anyway. Hannah's witnessed enough destructive behaviour in her nineteen years upon which to base any number of opinions about her mother.

Lisa looks over her shoulder to see how far back Samantha is, but she's out of sight. Guilt bites once again and she slows her pace.

Samantha was never a slim girl, not even when they were young, so Lisa imagines she feels the weight of those few extra kilograms she carries round her waist now. They've experienced enough hardship on this trail – much of it at Lisa's hand – and here she is again, responsible for causing more. She tries to shake off the guilt though, because the one thing that hasn't changed about her is her determination to finish what they set out to do all those years ago, but this time without scars.

Nicole is ahead of her, powering down the trail like a bloody mountain goat. She looks to have barely raised a sweat. Didn't last time either as Lisa recalls.

Still so cool. So controlled.

And still so bloody *right*. Nicole takes none of the shortcuts that have been cut between switchbacks as Lisa and Samantha do. Instead, she follows the trail exactly as it's intended, as ordered in this task as in every other. And as she's increased the distance between them, Lisa can't help but think Nicole's pushing for some kind of dislocation, as though walking well ahead exempts her in some way from their collective past.

The terrain seems more challenging than previously, but Lisa knows the contours of the land have nothing to do with it. She's changed, not the place she walks through. A young woman negotiating rugged ground is one thing. But doing it again now in her forties, after years of bending and carrying, is something else. Now, her muscles and lungs burn sooner. The sun bites hotter. Thirst comes quicker. But worst of all is recognising all of these things. It only adds to the list of things that have pissed her off since they arrived, Nicole forging ahead being another one of them.

Lisa looks behind again. Samantha comes into view round a bend about fifty metres back. There is dust on the knees of her hiking trousers and her face is one of deep concentration. Every step looks to be a study in caution, even though the terrain has levelled off now and the going is easier.

Lisa calls to Nicole for her to stop, mainly because she suspects Samantha won't. 'Let's rest for a bit,' she says.

Nicole turns to face her. 'Again?' She doesn't hide her frown but stops anyway.

When Lisa reaches Nicole, she moves past her and rests the base of her pack on a stump. The stump is rotting from the centre out. It's funny to think it might have been a thriving tree when they were here last and now is on its way back to the soil. Samantha reaches them and leans her weight onto her walking poles. Nicole stands, feet wide, thumbs hooked into the hip belt of her pack. She sways slightly from side to side, as though reluctant to cease movement.

'Remind me why we're here again?' Samantha breathes.

'For answers.' That's why Lisa's here anyway.

'Answers?' Nicole scoffs.

Lisa presses back the flinty rise of her anger. It's one of the things she wants to soften about herself, wants to prove to Hannah that she can.

'I thought you'd be looking for forgiveness?'

Lisa looks hard at Nicole. She hopes to shame her. But she never flinched under such scrutiny in the past, and neither does she now. Lisa pushes down her anger again, bites back the words that almost spill. Because she knows Nicole's calling her out right now. Trying to make her say *Yep, all my fault*, so she can have a clear conscience. But Lisa can't bring herself to say it. She lifts her chin and holds Nicole's gaze. She won't give her the submission she wants.

'Why did I ever think you'd change?' Nicole's pack knocks against Lisa as she pushes past on the narrow trail.

'None of us is innocent, you know,' Lisa calls. 'No matter how much you want to tell yourself otherwise.'

Nicole ignores her. Lisa curses her no-good self for not having the same restraint. She feels guilt again too, because they relinquished the right to speak to one another like that years ago.

'I'm sorry,' she calls after Nicole. 'That was out of line.'

Nicole lifts one arm in acknowledgement and walks on without looking back.

'C'mon,' Samantha says and she raises herself tall again.

'You go first.' Lisa stands and moves to one side. 'You can set the pace.'

'And break old habits?'

Which is exactly what Lisa wishes they'd do.

Samantha waves Lisa on with her walking pole. 'You go. My pace will only frustrate you as much as it did last time.'

'It didn't frustrate me last time,' Lisa says, and she knows they both hear the lie.

Lisa moves off, recognising that patience is something else she needs to work on.

She resolves to follow the trail exactly as it's intended. No shortcuts. It's as good a place as any for her to start following the rules.

Lisa's anger has always been curious about its capabilities. As a girl, she tested it regularly – on other girls, boys, her parents. When she thinks back on her early anger now, she thinks of it as something that existed inside her but was outside of her control. A force with its own free will. She'd like to think that she has control over it more than she used to, that she commands it more than it commands her.

She remembers a day when she was fourteen or fifteen. She was on her way to the back of the tuckshop to meet Samantha and Nicole for their morning break. As she got closer she heard the chant, *Catfight!* coming from the back of the building.

Lisa's first thought was *Why is anybody settling a score here? This is our spot.*

Then she had a second thought: *What if the score being settled is with Nicole or Samantha?*

This was the thought that made pinpricks of light flash before her eyes and a band of muscle tighten round her head. She's known these responses many times since. She recognises them as the body's way of sharpening her senses. There have been times when she's welcomed the acuity.

She'd broken into a sprint along with several other curious

students who'd heard the combat cry. By the time she reached the back of the tuckshop there was a large circle of boys and girls. In the middle was Samantha, doing her level best to hold her own against the school's indestructible girl-thug.

Samantha was on her back on the ground and the girl sat astride her, legs in a vice-like grip around her soft sides. Both girls' school dresses were hoicked up so that their knickers were on show – Sam's pastel floral, the other girl's cream-coloured and lacy.

'C'mon chubs,' the bully taunted, slapping Sam around the head as gaps opened up in the shield she'd made with her arms. 'You can do better than that.'

Nicole was in the fray too, trying to pull the girl off by her school jumper. But she wasn't having much success; the knitted fabric stretched and pulled away from the girl's long frame but the weight of her remained.

Looking back, Lisa knows she gave no thought to her actions. Certainly no thought to how much smaller she was compared to this girl. Before she knew it, she'd launched herself at the girl from a running start with a cry of her own. Nicole later told her she sounded and looked like something from a *Mad Max* movie.

She smashed into the girl's side so that she tumbled from Samantha to the ground. The roles were reversed then – the bully on her back and Lisa astride her. But where the girl had used an open hand on Samantha, Lisa made hard little fists of hers. She brandished them in a flurry upon the girl wherever she could find an opening – face, chest, arms. The girl couldn't defend herself against Lisa's assault no matter how much she flourished her arms about. Before long the girl was a blubbering wreck, bleeding from nose and mouth, begging Lisa to get off.

Lisa was reluctant to give up on her quarry though. She still remembers the thrill she felt at the girl's submission, her triumph at being able to overpower her. And there was something else too. At the time she might have called it courage. But she knows now, having the words, having more experience, that it was something much more. It was a state of mind that overlooked risks and consequences. It cared nothing for dignity or honour or reputation. What she'd felt then, and has felt since, was a wildly primal compulsion to protect at all cost.

'At least no one will fuck with *my* friends again,' she'd said to Samantha and Nicole after they'd finally hauled her off the girl.

Sam, despite still being red-cheeked, had beamed at her. Lisa feels a trickle of pride come down the years and touch her once more.

In contrast, Nicole had looked pale and worried. At the time Lisa thought it was the stress of the incident. Now, she thinks she misread her. It was fear that she'd seen on Nicole's face that day. Not fear of the wilful violence of the school bully, but fear at the force of Lisa's retaliation to it.

She'd been right though. That was the first and last time any one of them was picked on by a girl at school.

On the summit of a headland, Lisa suggests they stop for a snack.

Samantha looks at her relieved. Nicole shrugs. 'If we have to.'

'*I* have to.' Samantha unbuckles the waist belt of her pack and lets it slide down her rump till it drops to the ground with a thud. She lowers herself onto a large, flat slab of granite, drags her pack towards her and starts rifling through a side pouch.

'Want some?' Samantha asks, holding out a bag of dried apricots to Lisa.

Lisa takes one before slipping one arm free from the shoulder strap of her pack, swings it round to her front and lowers it to the ground with both hands. The sudden weightlessness feels good. She feels as though she could blow away if there were a breeze. She sits beside Samantha – not close as they once would have – and stretches her legs out in front of her. She takes a muesli bar from her pack and rips open the packaging.

She watches Nicole ease off her pack and lower it to the ground with one strong, tanned arm. She stands with her back to them and looks out across the ocean.

'Beautiful view,' Lisa calls to her.

Nicole doesn't respond. She continues to stare out.

Lisa follows her gaze. The air is so clear that everything before her is preserved in crisp, precise lines. The blue ocean stretches out till it joins an even bluer sky to form a perfect seam on the horizon.

And the rocky headland and sword-sedge in the foreground is in such sharp relief to it that it makes Lisa think of a child's paper cut-out held up against this larger backdrop of blue.

Eventually Nicole shrugs a reply. 'It's okay.'

'Better visibility this time,' Samantha says.

This time. Last time, Lisa thinks. And so much time in between – twenty-four years – in which to screw up a life, or two.

Lisa had one shot at raising a child who loves her and sometimes she thinks she blew it.

She and Hannah are self-conscious when they embrace. They never whisper heartfelt or giggly secrets across a table. The territory of their conversations is mostly censored. But Lisa supposes that's better than no conversation at all, which she sometimes worries is only one poorly considered remark away.

Except for that time when it wasn't censored at all, and Lisa still doesn't know why.

She was waiting for a service call for her dishwasher that day.

'When's that bloody repairman getting here?' Lisa looked at her watch again. Four-forty. 'They said between twelve and five. A person could die waiting.' She slapped the fabric swatches she was looking through onto the kitchen bench. They slid off and loudly hit the floor. She left them where they landed.

'You can stop the fight now you know. You're divorced.' Hannah can't have been more than fifteen at the time. She was at the kitchen table in her school uniform as Lisa recalls. She'd been living between two houses for close to six years.

'I'm not fighting.'

Hannah looked at Lisa like she was the child, the one trying to get away with a lie. 'Yes you are. You're fighting right now,' she said. 'And the person isn't even here. Sometimes I think you do it because you enjoy it.'

It's a harsh judgement, especially to have made against her by her child. But it made Lisa wonder, and she doesn't think she's stopped wondering since: does she take pleasure from her anger?

She's always had strong opinions, always stood up for herself, stood up for others – and she's been proud of that, sees it as a strength. While it has caused a few fights it's also something she thought people admired in her – that she's strong, that she isn't afraid. Besides, what's the alternative? Risk being complicit in your own victimhood?

'There's nothing for you to prove anymore,' Hannah continued.

Lisa thought of the time she'd struck her now ex-husband. Slapped him hard across the face. It was close to the end of their marriage. Any civility they might have still had was gone. Matt had intentionally broken something they both loved – an antique vase – so that neither of them could own it. It was a petty and spiteful act. Lisa snapped.

She remembers how there was a satisfying heat in her hand afterwards. The skin tingled and prickled in a way that told her it was awake, not asleep, as she'd expect with such a sensation. She flexed her fingers a few times. They felt charged, alive. But she also recalls how enlivened Matt looked, how *pleased* he seemed, despite the red imprints of her fingers on his cheek. She thinks she'd finally proved to him that he was the better person.

'There's always something to prove,' Lisa said to Hannah.

'Not to me. And not to Dad anymore. So prove *what*? To *who*?'

And she'd got her there. Because who – what – was she fighting against really?

Nicole turns away from the ocean and sits on a rock across from them. Lisa looks over to her. She wants to catch her eye, draw a smile from her. But Nicole is yet to hold much eye contact with either one of them.

Once Lisa had made a game of counting the distinctive brown flecks in Nicole's hazel eyes, likened them to counting her own freckles. Now she doesn't even know if Nicole wears glasses.

A water dragon pops its thorny head over the far end of the rock where Lisa and Samantha sit. It hauls its body further onto the flat surface with its claws. Its scaly skin is striped in brown and lichen-coloured green. On the ground it could easily pass for a branch.

The reptile comes fully onto the flat stone. It pauses, its Zorro-banded head lifted to reveal a pale, aged-leather underbelly. It seems more inquisitive about their presence than frightened by it. Lisa breaks off a piece of her muesli bar and throws it towards the water dragon. It scurries in and snatches up the offering.

Before long a second, smaller water dragon comes onto the rock and a territorial claim ensues. The larger one dashes towards the smaller one, an intimidation that seems based on size and speed as much as anything else, because no contact is made. The smaller one acquiesces and retreats over the edge of the rock again. The larger one strikes a prehistoric pose, thorny crown held high.

'You shouldn't feed them.'

Lisa turns to face Nicole but she's not looking at her. She watches the water dragon.

'They're not made to eat our crappy processed food,' she adds and takes a bite from her apple.

Lisa shrugs. 'Neither are we, I suppose. Doesn't stop us though.'

'At least we have the choice not to. *It* doesn't.' Nicole nods at the water dragon. 'It's opportunistic, and you're presenting it with an opportunity.'

'Does that make me a food facilitator?' Lisa aims for playfulness. She hopes Nicole gets it.

'No,' Nicole says, and she looks directly at Lisa now. 'It makes you careless.'

Lisa hears Samantha sigh, a deep, here-we-go-again exhalation of air, just as she used to do when they were younger.

It takes willpower, but Lisa holds back the snipe she wants to make and tries instead for contrition. 'Fair enough. I promise not to feed any more of the wildlife.'

Nicole looks doubtful for a moment but eventually nods. 'Good.'

Lisa watches Nicole as she watches the water dragon, and tries to remember the girl she used to know from their school days. Nicole was kinder than this back then, warmer too. And she was funny in a dry, quick-witted way. Still self-righteous and a rule follower of course, but Lisa had got used to those things about her, came to like the dependability of them. Looking at Nicole now though, she can't reconcile her old school friend with this woman who shows none of the humour she once did. Someone who looks to walk as penance more than anything else. Did it change her so much what happened out here, Lisa wonders, or is the woman before her now the one Nicole was always going to grow into?

The water dragon remains as motionless as if it were a moulded garden figure. Lisa tries to see herself as the reptile sees her – a large imposing shape of unknown capabilities. Does it see itself as the one at risk, the one that's in danger? She doesn't think this creature is frightened of her so much as wary. But it has an advantage – its speed. Lisa wonders if it recognises this.

The water dragon makes a dash for the other side of the rock, comes close to Lisa's hand as it hurtles past. The sudden movement startles her enough to make her cry out. She feels stupid, juvenile. She'd been watching it after all, knew the speed and unpredictability with which it could move. But she supposes fear works like this – it dulls logic and reason.

'Did you think it was coming for you?' Nicole asks, voice still lacking warmth.

Coming for you.

Lisa doesn't like Nicole's choice of words and what they suggest: that her position is known; that she's being watched; opportunities are being sought.

Just thinking about it makes her arms goose flesh, despite the heat in the day.

Lisa looks at Nicole. 'I don't know what I thought.'

Nicole holds her gaze this time, and in that moment Lisa sees that her eyes are the same hazel colour they used to be.

From where they sit, Lisa can see all around the peninsula. Craggy headlands push into the sea from north to south and granite-strewn mountains fold away to the west. And the ocean, that enormous piece of rumpled silk, rolls in from the east.

It is an ancient land, fixed in time and place, but it is also damaged and damaging in turn. Bushfires have left scorched brown patches amongst the green, probably from lightning strikes. And she has seen where boulders, loosened by floods and mudslides, have gouged trails down mountainsides, as dangerous and unstoppable as an avalanche. She's witnessed the work of the ocean. Sea water runs gently between the fingers but it can also thrash against headlands in a fury, take fragments of granite back out with it where they're washed up on beaches far away.

Lisa sees the impact of these forces on the landscape but what she can't know is how much this landscape has damaged her. Damaged them. How much of what happened here has been carried with them into the everyday, washed up in their lives like those fragments of stone.

If she could remove just one experience from her life, it would be the one that happened in the car park at the start of their hike last time. She would choose to get rid of it above her divorce. Above the wariness she sees in her daughter's face when she's with her. Because Lisa suspects these things are in part legacies of this other event anyway.

She accepts now that she drove her old Datsun too fast into the unsealed car park that day. But she was g'd-up by Nirvana's 'Smells Like Teen Spirit' blasting from the radio.

It was a hot day and they had the car windows down, so a thick cloud of dust poured inside the car. She can still remember the feel of that gritty dust on her arms; the velvet film it left over the car's dash; the way it made the interior smell like drought.

The brown plume also drifted out and covered the only other car parked in the car park that day – a red Ford Falcon – along with a guy standing at the car's boot.

'You've really pissed him off,' Nicole said.

Lisa looked across to the tall, thin man standing at the open boot of the Falcon. He held a large khaki backpack upright between his legs. He looked to be in his late-twenties, so a few years older than them.

He mouthed something as he flapped his hands in front of his face. She couldn't hear what he said, but it was clear he was angry.

'He'll get over it,' she said, and cut the engine.

Samantha opened her car door and got out. 'Sorry,' she called to the man over the Datsun's roof. 'We didn't realise it was so dusty.'

The man held his hands out wide. 'Fuckin' look around you,' he said. 'It's a dirt car park.'

'Yeah ... well ... like I said, we're sorry.' Samantha ducked her head back inside the car.

'That's why you never apologise,' Lisa said, shaking her head at the man. 'Nobody ever appreciates it.'

'Unbelievable,' Nicole muttered.

Lisa nodded. 'I know.'

'I don't mean *him*. I mean *you*.'

'What'd *I* do?'

'Drove like a maniac.'

'All I did was drive into a car park. It's not my fault it's not sealed.' Lisa opened her door with enough force for it to bounce back off its hinges and almost close again. 'Must be gang-up on Lisa day,' she said as she got out of the car. 'Great start.'

Lisa heard Samantha say to Nicole, 'Just let it go. Okay?' before she slammed the door closed behind her.

The man wasn't about to let it go though. He came up to Lisa as she fumbled with her keys at the Datsun's boot.

She remembers how she stood as tall as she could as she turned to face him, chin lifted, but was still a good head and a half shorter than him. 'How many apologies do you want?' she asked.

It's funny now to think of the things she noticed about him. It had been his eyes and the long dark lashes that framed them. She remembers thinking how on a better structured face – one where the chin hadn't been forgotten, where the overbite wasn't so pronounced – that they'd be striking.

He didn't answer. He just stared at her for a time.

She grew increasingly discomfited by his gaze because those handsome eyes showed no humour, no compassion, and neither did his mouth. It was set in a thin, cruel line.

He bent down, easily as she recalls, despite the bulky pack on his back by then, and scooped up a handful of dirt.

She remembers how she watched him do this and yet didn't think about what might come next. Not even as he pulled his arm back like a pitcher and pelted the dirt into her face.

She brought her arms up to deflect it, but too late. Small stones had already stung her skin, knocked against her teeth.

The dust was already in her eyes, her mouth, coated her tongue. Later she would dig it out of her ears with a fingernail, blow it from her nose onto a tissue as dark snot.

Lisa thinks it was Nicole who got to her first, but she can't be sure because she couldn't see. But it was Nicole's voice she heard shout beside her, 'What the hell do you think you're doing?'

Sometimes their friendship was fragile if threatened by internal forces, but threaten it by external ones and it was indestructible. Lisa was grateful for the loyalty Nicole and Samantha offered that day. She felt it in their arms, the way they kept them round her as she spat and coughed and tried to wipe the grit from her eyes.

When she finally cleared them enough to see the man, he was in front of them still, calmly wiping his hands down the front of his trousers. She remembers how he grinned at her before he turned away. She's never forgotten the smugness in that victory smile.

Her body shook for a time after that, but not with fear. It was a familiar tremor, one she'd experienced before, and since. It was the tremor of rage. Her heart set up a rapid tattoo against her ribs. The blood roared into her head. Visions of punching his self-satisfied face flashed before her eyes. Her hands flexed for action.

Lisa shook Nicole and Samantha off, bent down and scooped dirt into each hand. She ran a few paces towards the man and threw it at him as he walked away. It hit his backpack with a dull, unsatisfying patter. It did little more than put dust over the small spade and binocular case strapped to the outside of it.

He stopped though, and turned to face her again. She remembers how calm and controlled he looked, how much he seemed to be enjoying himself. This, she realised later, should have unnerved her more than anything else; warned her of his potential.

He held both hands out towards her, palms up, beckoned

her closer with his fingers. Daring her. *C'mon*, he mouthed. *C'mon*.

Sam reached her first, wrapped her strong arms around her. Held her firm. Lisa supposes she can't blame Samantha for not trusting her to refuse the man's challenge. She doesn't recall having refused too many in the past.

'Crazy bitches,' he said and laughed.

He held up the middle finger of each hand and pumped the air with them before turning away again.

'Fucking prick!' Lisa shouted.

'Leave it, Lisa,' Samantha said softly. 'He's dangerous.'

But Lisa didn't give a shit about danger. She was too angry.

'Think you're a big man, do you?'

'Let it go.' Samantha was pleading by then.

'Where's your chin you ugly bastard?'

Lisa felt Samantha's arms tighten their grip, but she wrenched herself free. She walked in crazed, impotent little circles. She kicked at the ground. Puffs of dust rose up and covered her boots and bare shins.

She thought about running after him, fist-sized rocks in her hands, continuing the tit for tat till blood was drawn. But something held her back. A restraint she would later lose.

Instead, she hurled puny take-that taunts at the man, belittled his physical failings. 'People like you should be locked up, you scrawny dickhead!'

He never once looked back. Never once feared them.

Lisa only stopped shouting insults once he entered the trailhead and his backpack bobbed out of sight. She watched the empty trail for a time, breathing hard. She worked her fists, felt the gritty dust on her palms and between her fingers.

Eventually she stopped looking at the spot where he'd disappeared. She tried to find calm or purpose, she's not sure which. She put her head between her knees and raked the dirt from her hair with her fingers. To a passer-by she must have looked like some crazy woman by the way she ripped and tugged at the snags in her hair.

'You all right?' Nicole asked.

'No, I'm not all right. I'm fucking pissed off.'

Lisa stood upright again and with purity of purpose walked over to the man's car.

'Lisa? What are you doing?'

She ignored Nicole. She went round to the passenger's side, gripped the metal aerial in both hands and tried to wrench it from the panel. She wanted it to come away rubber seal, wires and all, to leave it dangling down the side of the car like entrails. But not even her anger gave her the strength she needed to dislodge it. Frustrated, she bent the metal rod backwards and forwards till it finally snapped off.

Lisa remembers it as a small and disappointing trophy in her hands. So she dragged the jagged end down the side of his car.

This memory still makes Lisa breathe hard. Still makes her heart race. She tries to steady both with the breathing mantra she's taught herself – *In, two, three. Out, two, three.*

Samantha turns to look at her. 'You all right?'

'Yeah. I'm fine.'

Lisa looks out to sea again, but she feels Samantha looking at her still and she doesn't like it. She doesn't want either of them to slip into their old roles – Lisa needing to be assessed for risk. Samantha countering it.

Lisa stands. 'Let's go.'

'Still calling the shots?' Nicole says, but gets up anyway.

Lisa keeps count as she sets out on the trail behind Nicole – *In, two, three. Out, two, three* – until calm is restored. But her anger is never far beneath it.

When they reach the cove where they're to camp for the night, Lisa sees that it has changed a great deal. There is less vegetation than she remembers. More space cleared now for hikers' tents. Only serious walkers ventured this deep onto the promontory previously, which was part of the attraction to their younger selves. All part of their pursuit of independence.

Back then they'd camped where they could find a clear enough space for their tent, which often meant flattening bracken first. They buried their rubbish along the way. Their shit too. Now there is a designated camping area, with *No Camping* signs outside of it. And a self-composting long-drop toilet. There's a gravity-fed black polypropylene pipe. It provides a water source directly to the campsite now where previously they'd had to tramp up the creek a little way to collect free-running water that was less tannin-stained, the water taking its colour from the vegetation along the stream – coastal tea-tree and swamp paperbark mostly – *Leptospermum laevigatum, Melaleuca ericifolia*. The water still has to be treated but at least one step in the process of collection has been removed.

Lisa feels a sense of smugness at having known this place at its purer, less trammelled best. She thinks today's hikers are deluded in thinking they are the rare witnesses of a wilderness. As she looks around her now, she knows she's seeing a landscape that has been tamed somewhat, that it has been forced by the will of the people wanting to walk it to give a little in order to accommodate them.

'Where do you want to pitch our tents?' Lisa asks Nicole.

Last time they'd all slept in a three-man tent. This time they have individual tents.

Nicole, hands on hips, scans from left to right.

Previously, they were the only people camped at this site. Now, there are two other tents already set up. Couples sit on logs in front of each. They watch pots boil on their camp stoves.

'I'm going over there.' Nicole indicates an area beyond the other hikers. It's a spot suitable for only one tent.

'Won't you set up with us?' Samantha calls after her.

'Not tonight.' Nicole walks on to the place she's chosen.

For the first time since Lisa has brought them back together, she feels her confidence in the decision falter. Has she banked too much on the success of it?

She hides what she feels from Samantha though. 'She'll

come round,' she says, then turns away and starts to unpack gear from her pack.

Lisa looks across to Nicole's site from time to time as she fumbles with her own unfamiliar equipment. But Nicole erected her tent quickly, stowed all her gear inside and headed off into the bush.

Lisa sits alongside Samantha on a large boulder that gently slopes down to the sea. They don't sit so close that they touch. There are years between them now.

Both are bare-footed. Lisa's feet are tender from the long day in walking boots. The granite feels rough under her soles. Thankfully there were no blisters when she took off her socks. She notices a red weal on Samantha's right heel though, a little cushion of fluid at the centre of it.

Samantha stacks small stones, one on top of the other, to construct one of her towers. This one keeps falling down. Lisa admires the persistence of her attempts to make it stand tall. She needs to use flatter stones, but Lisa doesn't tell her. Instead, she watches the gloaming sky. The colours on the horizon have shifted from shades of pink to bruised-purple now. The cove is quiet and tranquil. Sound is suspended in the calm.

The cove is a small, pretty one. Prettier even than she remembers, which only confirms how mood realigns perceptions. It is protected from the ocean swell by a narrow opening between two steep headlands. The sea laps soundlessly at the beach. The water is so clear she can see tide ripples on the sandy bottom all the way out till it meets a dark line of sea grass about twenty metres offshore.

Nicole comes out of the bush at the other end of the short beach. Lisa doesn't recall seeing a track exit from there when she walked the length of the beach earlier, so she's surprised to see her come out from where she has.

Samantha looks up from her stone stacking. 'She's been gone for ages. I wonder where she's been?'

Lisa shrugs. 'Who knows. Will you call her over? She's more likely to come if you ask her.'

They both wave when she gets closer.

'Come and join us,' Samantha calls. 'It's a great spot for watching the sunset.'

Nicole pauses then changes course to head towards them. She takes off her boots and socks and puts them side by side above the water line, then walks through the ankle deep water to get to the rock they're on. She steps from boulder to boulder with ease to reach them.

'Haven't walked far enough today?' Samantha asks.

Nicole sits further down the rock from them. 'I guess not,' she says.

'God, I have,' Samantha says.

Nicole draws up her knees, feet wide, and dangles her hands between them. Her shoulders look soft and relaxed. Lisa's still feel tense from carrying her pack. Nicole looks the most at ease with where they are, what they're doing. She didn't hesitate to seek out solitude in the campsite. Explores the area outside the perimeter of it on her own. Steps easily just now over the coarse granite in bare feet, despite the many kilometres they've already walked today. It's like she's at home here, like she owns it. Lisa envies her.

The moon is up but pale in the carmine sky. It is coming off full. As a child Lisa pretended that a full moon was a snow dome. She'd tell her parents that the grey patterns across its surface were the outline of the people who lived inside. She'd hold her small hand up to that big, creamy orb; shut one eye till it looked like she'd gripped it between thumb and fingers. She'd pretend to shake it then and tell her parents to look at how she'd rearranged those living inside.

'Imagine not having that big old thing to look forward to each month?' Lisa indicates towards the moon.

'Beats a period,' Nicole quips.

That's her, Lisa thinks. There she is.

Samantha laughs. 'You always cracked me up.'

'Always?'

'Pretty much.'

'I think I'd disappoint you now.'

Lisa looks to the darkening sky and brightening moon and doesn't say anything. After a time though, she turns to Nicole and says, 'I don't think we know one another well enough anymore to know whether we'd disappoint each other or not.'

Nicole seems to think about this then nods. 'You're probably right.'

'We should play our game,' Samantha says, and she sounds young again. 'Remember? The one where we had to work out if we were lying or not.'

Lisa remembers. And so must Nicole because she dips her head, the slightest of nods.

It was a game they played at school. Each would take a turn to make a statement, either about themselves or somebody else, and the other two had to decide if it was true or not. They started playing it to make a game of gossiping about other people mostly. *Amy cheated off Bec in the Maths test* or *Trev wears his father's Y-fronts*. That sort of thing. Then it became confessional.

'Okay. Why not?' Lisa says.

Nicole doesn't commit.

'I'll go first … since I suggested it.' Samantha pauses briefly then says, 'I thought about turning back today.'

'True,' Lisa answers, 'because I expect we all thought about it.'

Samantha nods.

A silence follows and Lisa knows it's hers to fill. 'I'm on a twelve month good behaviour bond for driving offences.'

'True,' Nicole says without hesitation.

'No. False. I've got one point left. If I lose that, then I will be.'

Lisa expects there to be a long silence while they wait for Nicole to make a statement, if at all, but she's wrong.

'I've never received a demerit point on my driver's licence.'

'That can't be true?' But when Lisa looks at Nicole she knows it is. 'Is that one of the perks of running a licensing centre?'

'No. I obey the road rules.'

Samantha pauses before she starts the next round. 'I was already pregnant when Harry and I got married.'

Lisa weighs this statement. She sees no reason for Samantha to lie about such a thing. 'I expect it's true,' she says. 'Hardly a big deal though.'

'Not like it's the fifties anymore,' Nicole says and for the first time today she smiles.

It's Lisa's turn again, and before she can censure herself she says, 'I hit my ex once.'

'Did he deserve it?' Samantha asks.

'Does anyone deserve it?' Nicole looks away. Lisa thinks she's embarrassed.

The silence stretches out. Nicole seems unwilling to take a turn.

Samantha fills the silence in a rush. 'I drink a bottle of wine a day.'

Lisa recognises the quick honesty in this statement but she won't cast the first stone, so doesn't answer.

Nicole does though, and her voice is gentle. 'I think it's a lie,' she says. 'Because I bet there's some days when you *don't* finish the bottle.'

After a while Samantha says, 'You know … you're right. Sometimes I don't.'

Nicole nods, satisfied.

'My daughter is frightened of me,' Lisa says and the pain of this fact sits like a sharp stone under her ribcage.

'Why would she be frightened of you?' Samantha asks, disbelief right there, in the folds of her forehead. 'You're her mother?'

'Frightened *of* you or *for* you?' Nicole asks but doesn't face Lisa.

'That's not the game,' Lisa says.

But neither of them answers one way or the other, and Lisa's surprised by how relieved it makes her feel.

'My father wishes my mother would die,' Nicole says.

'I expect it's true from what you've said,' Samantha answers.

Nicole nods but doesn't say anything more.

None of them speaks for a time and Lisa is pleased. She doesn't want to play anymore.

But then Samantha breaks the silence. 'Harry and I haven't had sex for two and a half years.' She flushes pink when she says this.

'You've made that up,' Lisa says.

Samantha blushes further and Lisa knows she hasn't.

'Do you miss it?' Nicole asks quietly.

'Yes. It's like a small death.'

The game stalls again, then Nicole says, 'I don't.'

Too many truths. And Lisa can tell it hurts each of them to admit it.

NICOLE DOESN'T LIKE THE SLOW, STEADY rhythm of walking. She prefers to run. For brief moments she's airborne, both feet off the ground, weightless. Not so with walking. It demands at least one foot always on the ground, planted, bound to the earth.

Here her feet feel as though they're hitting the trail with more force than they ever do the footpaths around her home – no levitational lightness, no weightlessness. Because she's angry. A rare thing for her. Anger was always Lisa's bag. Which is one of the reasons Nicole's upset now. It used to be so easy to read Lisa. She was always the stroppy one, the loose cannon, the firebrand. The one of little control or restraint. But at least she was predictable in this. Not anymore. Which is why her reasonableness to date is unsettling Nicole so much, messing with her sense of certainty.

She won't deny that when Lisa admitted in the bar that she had regrets and wanted to face who she was back then, it had made Nicole think about what might also be possible for her. Because who wouldn't want a more innocent time returned to them? But now it just feels like Lisa's brought them on some kind of pilgrimage. It's as if in offering them back to the landscape that took things from them – from *Nicole* – that she believes they'll have what they lost returned to them. Fat chance of that. All they'll get is fatigue and blisters. And as for all that *looking for answers* bullshit Lisa mentioned earlier. Answers to what? There aren't any. Shit happens. People move on. That's the answer.

Nicole reckons what Lisa's really after is absolution but won't admit it, not to Nicole and Samantha, and especially not to herself. While she's prepared to go along with it until Lisa's ready, it doesn't mean she has to smile and joke her way through the whole process.

As for Samantha, why did she even agree to do this? Watching the way she struggles only adds another layer of worry to the whole thing. Nicole's been alone for too long so she's not sure she's up to the dependency, not anymore.

She still feels a fondness for Samantha though. She was always the integral third wheel in their friendship. In her absence, Nicole and Lisa often stalled, brought to a standstill by their mutual stubbornness. Sam was the one who drew them in till their foreheads touched with her harmless gossip and unifying pacts that set their trio aside from others.

But time doesn't look to have done Samantha any favours. Nicole doesn't think this unkindly. Sam was never someone she could feel anything but charity towards. When she watched her walk into the bar that night, she looked weighed down by more than a couple of extra kilograms. Maybe it was the prospect of them seeing one another again. Nicole knows she was anxious. Or maybe what she saw was the person Sam is now, a woman made heavy by cares and responsibilities. Once she'd have felt she could ask her – maybe even guessed at it – but not anymore. Time and circumstance have taken away not just the insight, but also the right to ask the question.

By the time they left the bar that night, after Lisa had conned them into agreeing to this (for surely that's what it was, a con?), Samantha looked lighter for the decision when she walked away. Nicole doesn't think it was the alcohol she'd drunk that made her stand taller. And as she watched her hail a taxi, her arm was out more forthright and determined than she'd ever remembered it being in the past. And part of Nicole, the part that still cares, was pleased that Lisa had been able to do that, to bring about this sense of purpose in Samantha. Because it had hurt to see any of Sam's easy-going, younger self diminished.

Mostly when Nicole glances over her shoulder to the other two, they are a good way back. Sometimes they have disappeared from her view altogether, lost around a bend or over a rise. They aren't walking as friends might – in a close and chatty group – and Nicole knows that in great part she's to blame. She pushes ahead as if she's walking alone, keeps the distance between them and the past they share. Maybe she thinks if she moves quickly enough she can outpace her thoughts, leave them and her memories behind. She can't say that it's working so far.

What are they to each other now anyway, Nicole wonders, friend or enemy? Is that one of the questions Lisa wants answered? Is that part of the reason why she's brought them together again, to find out? Maybe she's afraid of what they might one day do to each other with their collective history, their shared knowledge. Or is that what still obviously binds them, the past, in inexplicable but necessary ways, like an oath, a pledge, a blood-sharing pact? Maybe Lisa recognises – perhaps aptly – that it's time to check the facts.

The rhythm of Nicole's feet, the lift-plant-push of one then the other, pulses on, as does the memory loop. Thoughts fill the minutes, the miles, recycle a history she thought – she'd *hoped* – she'd forgotten. Anger often comes from fear, she knows that, but if that's the case, what is it she's afraid of? He's not on the trail anymore, so it can't be him. Maybe it's her younger self she fears.

No matter how much Nicole wishes she could distance herself from the others, there's no denying that the two of them claimed her once and she still feels the pull of that friendship.

Nicole blames her parents for this.

She'd come along twelve years after her brother, and she imagines her arrival was something of a shock to her teetotalling, say-Grace-before-meals parents. A change of life baby. A flagrant declaration to the neighbours that they still had sex. She reckons that's how her brother saw it anyway. He described her to his mates as that *embarrassing little sprog*.

Her brother escaped the family home by the time she was seven and she doesn't recall him coming back too often afterwards. Which left her the sole beneficiary of her parents' attention in their time-rich retirement, and to this task they applied consummate diligence. Strict study rules were put in place. ABC television only. Friends were vetted and rationed.

When they sold up their business Nicole became their new work project. She was home-schooled to thirteen because they didn't trust anyone else to the task. When she failed to measure up (and their measure of failure was anything less than an A) they expressed their disappointment with a weary shake of the head and comments of *Try harder*.

So she tried as hard as she could, but genetics and neural connectivity were only ever going to allow her to achieve an A-minus. Her parents had set the bar too high; placed their ambition over her ability. And no matter how diligent they were, no matter how many times they shook their heads or told her to lift her game, she could never be as successful as their pre-Internet newsagency.

The legacy of this upbringing was that she started her school-based education (and only then because her parents had coached her so well in persuasive arguing) a self-reliant child. But one who had never seen an episode of *Neighbours* or *Hey Hey It's Saturday* and neither had she ever had a friend over to stay for the night.

Nicole entered the large Assembly Hall of her new school and was assaulted by the noise inside. At home, learning was associated with the soft ticking of the kitchen clock and the ABC World Service News at lunchtime. But at high school the shrillness of the girls' voices, and the other, even shriller ones, which she later recognised to be the unbroken voices of the boys, reminded her of a gibbon enclosure at feeding time. This, along with the ineffectual shouts from teachers asking everyone to *All take a seat, please! Now!* (her parents never shouted, they never needed to), put her in auditory overload and in the front row of the hall. She questioned the merit of winning this particular argument with her parents as she sat there (an argument based on the belief that she was missing out on something), while she tried to shut out the sea of chattering children behind her. Fortunately, she was calmed somewhat by the Headmaster's orientation talk, which included the rules and expectations of the school. She could draw similarities to those expected at home.

Nicole wasn't a girl who knew how to find a companion. She'd always relied upon a companion finding *her*, and then hoped that her parents would allow her to be kept.

None did find her that first day of school or for several weeks after it. She spent her breaks wandering mostly. She made laps of Main Block, the Home Ec and Science buildings, the tuckshop, Sports Hall and playing fields. Occasionally she'd hang around the fringes of a group of girls, mostly unnoticed, but if she was ever given a *What d'you want?* look, she'd set off on her rambling journey once more. On wet days she went to the library where she put her A-minus brain to work on Donaldson's *The Chronicles of Thomas Covenant*.

So no one claimed her. Her wandering didn't allow them to.

It took the miscalculation of the steps at the back of the tuckshop, a tumble and a badly grazed knee to finally do that, when her wandering landed her at the feet of a largish girl who wore her brown hair pulled forward over her chest and a skinny, long-haired blonde who seemed to wear a perpetual frown. The larger girl helped her up. The skinny one frowned deeply at Nicole's knee and told her to sit down on the step so she could clean her up.

'Am I going to live?' Nicole kidded to hold back the tears from the stinging pain.

'If you're lucky,' the blonde girl said as she gently dabbed at Nicole's wound with a tissue.

'I hope so. I haven't even seen *Return of the Jedi* yet.'

Nicole figured their kindness meant she'd been found, so her wandering ceased.

But ultimately their friendship had fallen apart and for Nicole the fracture had felt first like a necessity, then before long a habit. She'd wanted to carry what they experienced out here on her own, till she could forget it. That way the truth could be whatever she wanted it to be. But then Lisa digs it all up again, and with the three of them together once more, the truth can only be itself and Nicole is reminded that she can't have buried everything. And maybe this is what she is afraid of.

'Do you ever wonder what sort of people we'd be now if things had ended differently?' Lisa had asked them in the bar.

'Or *started* differently,' Nicole reminded her.

'Yes, that too.' Lisa looked calmly at Nicole when she said this and there was surprisingly no accusation in her voice.

Nicole felt her confusion grow. The past started to take on a new landscape, one she'd not negotiated before: that Lisa could have regrets.

'I feel like I've lost so much,' Lisa said.

Nicole's temper flared. This, she thought, was typical of Lisa, so selfish. 'You didn't lose anything,' she snapped, and the conversation stopped for a while after that.

And then Samantha took the tension from the air, just as she used to do. 'We lost each other,' she offered.

Nicole calmed again, because she couldn't argue with that.

Their friendship has been the yardstick for her friendships since. None have measured up. It's as though their union all those years before embedded itself into her psyche and refuses to be given up or allow others in.

So here she is, back in a place she never wanted to see

again, surrounded by a bushland she only remembers as hostile. And all the while she's trying not to notice just how hard Lisa is trying to make everything right again.

Nicole has sharp vision. It works with safety in mind. She saw a snake's tail yesterday as it slithered off the trail and into the undergrowth. It was a brown one, not too thick, but thick enough to have a bite that could be lethal. She imagines there have been others, ones she hasn't seen, too camouflaged or hidden even for her eyes.

All her senses are heightened when she's out running. Sometimes when she runs she feels like she's being pursued and not like she's the one pursing something – fitness, endurance, release. The truth is, she's often afraid. She imagines hands reaching for her from behind walls or trees or the corners of buildings. Fingers ready to pluck her from the footpath with too-quick ease. She can't surrender fully to this favoured exercise because of the fear that another person's agenda will be written over it.

Men have gone out of their way to harass her when she runs. Men as old as her father. Others young enough to be her son. Some wear business shirts; others are shirtless or in high-vis. They drive round roundabouts a second time to take the exit to the street she's run down. Do illegal U-turns at traffic lights to get onto her side of the road. Some have driven past so close that she's felt the air sucked from around her by the movement of their car. One guy jumped the median strip in his four-by-four once so he could crawl along the kerb beside her and asked if she'd blow him instead of all that hot air. They've called *Nice arse!* more times than she can count, whistled, made kissing noises, blasted horns right alongside her, banged their hands on the sides of their car doors. She's been startled enough by these sudden, close sounds to stumble. Once she fell. They laugh as they drive away.

She still runs.

People ask her why she risks it. *Go to a gym*, they say.

She tells them gyms are no different. The creeps just have bigger mirrors.

But she's not an idiot; she runs at the high tide of caution. She runs where it's well lit. Never near warehouses with their dark-mouthed doors or through parks with their pillars of trees. She faces oncoming traffic so she can see what is coming towards her. She wears a black cap. Never white. White shines like a virtuous beacon begging to be sullied. Under black she can hide.

Nicole can't stop this activity. She knows if she does, that her fears will have leaked into every aspect of her life and she'll no longer resemble anything of the girl she used to be.

So she pretends she's somebody else when she runs. Someone more like Lisa. As she pushes herself out hard and the endorphins build, she sees a strong woman with muscles as tough as granite. This woman has a stony, don't-mess-with-me stare. She chants *fuck off* in her head when she hears catcalls or horns trumpeting. She is alert and agile and fast. She can outrun anyone. For a time she is reborn. She's high on the body's natural drugs. She's a junkie. Free of the reality that she's not invincible.

Nicole had been sure he was out there that first night. Close but out of sight. None of them spoke of it, but neither did they need to. Their silence on the topic was admission enough. A convenient if-we-don't-talk-about-it mindset, then it can't be true. Instead, they acted like the independent young women they believed they were when they first set out.

They cleared a site of stones and branches and set up their three-man tent with home-practised skill. They changed into their swimmers then and raced each other into the sea. Nicole remembers how the tightness she'd held in her muscles for most of that day was gradually released by the cool sea water.

Together, they collected fresh water from upstream and cooked a meal of Continental ready-made pasta before it grew too dark. Once the sun had dropped out of sight and a waxing half-moon took its place in the night sky, Lisa rigged up her torch so that it hung from the centre of their tent. It provided weak, but adequate light. They sat up in their sleeping bags, huddled beneath it.

Nicole rummaged through her pack till she found the bottle of *Southern Comfort* she'd brought along as a surprise. 'Ta-da!' she declared, holding it up.

'Another reason to love you!' Sam cheered.

Nicole poured a measure into each of their cups.

'To day one!' they chorused and chinked plastic.

'I can't believe we're actually here,' Sam said, taking a sip.

Nicole found it hard to believe too. They'd talked about doing this hike for so long but had never put that talk into action. Now here they were.

'Yep. A shaky start, but we did it. Close to twenty Ks with a kick-arse pack.' Lisa pushed Sam playfully, so that she toppled backwards, giggling, her cup held safely aloft.

It was the only reference any one of them made that night about the incident in the car park. And as their cheeks took on a glow from the warming alcohol, Nicole started to believe they could put it behind them. Reduce it to an unpleasant encounter, one they need not allow spoil their fun.

As the alcohol lubricated laughter and jokes about near falls and moments of despair throughout the day – each made as insignificant as the man had become in their minds by then – Nicole had felt like she could conquer anything.

She needed to go to the toilet before she went to sleep that night. She pushed the sleeping bag off her legs and crawled out of the tent. She moved a short way into the scrub, just beyond the perimeter of the tent light. She could still hear the others chatting and giggling,

The hand-held torch she took with her was inadequate. Its dull beam barely lit the ground in front of her. In daylight, the brain and eyes work to interpret simultaneously. During the day, big noises were the ones she noticed: reptiles and mammals scurrying amongst the bracken, birds calling, laughing, taking flight. But in the dark, not even her sharp vision was much use to her. Darkness takes orientation without regret or apology. Interpretation becomes subject to the imagination.

The alcohol might have made her irrational, but she imagined she could hear all manner of industry in the earth beneath her bare arse, only centimetres above the bristly undergrowth. It was as though night held a microphone to sound and amplified it. Small, unseen creatures – wood slaters, beetles and centipedes – suddenly seemed large and forbidding as she imagined them working their way through bark and soil. So when she heard a genuinely loud *crack* like a twig breaking a few metres behind her, it sounded like a tree had been felled.

Her urine flow stopped of its own accord. She held the squat as though made of stone. She no longer noticed the burn in her tired thighs. She thinks she also held her breath, or slowed it at least to a barely detectable shift of air.

Whatever caused that siren crack must have paused in wary paralysis too, because everything went silent for a time. Nicole imagined the aperture of its pupils opening and closing as they adjusted to her white arse in the dark. She imagined its nose lifted to check the air, catching the acidic scent of her urine. And the sonar cups of its ears twitched as they funnelled the smallest sounds into them. She'd felt ill equipped in comparison. Incapable of determining the location or movement of whatever was out there. She was the intruder, the one without the necessary wiring to navigate a nocturnal terrain.

Then there was another *crack*. Louder. Closer. Or had her imagination drawn the sound in?

She could still feel the press of urine in her bladder. She willed the flow to start again, but it wouldn't come. Briefly she wished she could urinate standing up, like a man. So little of them exposed. So little of them vulnerable. They could still run if they had to. But not women. Not her. She was brought to the ground, ankles hobbled by clothes, forced to expose the most private parts of her body just to excrete its wastes.

Another *crack* fired off. This time to her left.

Was it circling her?

Nicole had a strong sense of being watched. That whatever was out there knew her location. Sensed her vulnerability. She cast the limited torch beam round but it fell short.

She tensed the muscles round her bladder and finally the flow began again. She pushed the urine out in a hard, steaming gush. It sprayed back against her ankles as it hit the ground. She didn't care. Finishing, she pulled up her pants and shorts too soon. The last dribble of urine wet the crotch of each.

She turned back towards the tent but stumbled on the rough terrain in her haste. As she righted herself, she thought she heard a soft laugh coming from somewhere in the bush behind her.

Get a grip, she scolded.

But she lost hold of her courage after that, rushing back towards the tent light and leaving the darkness to what or who occupied it.

That's why yesterday, after she'd set up her tent – still annoyed at Lisa for pretending she could be someone else – she'd set off to give tangible evidence to her imagination from that night. She needed to know where he'd been. The same way people need to know the details of a death or an accident. And it had felt good to be the hunter.

She had followed the creek, working on the assumption that he, like them, would have needed water, and would have made camp not far from it. It was easy going initially, but as the terrain became steeper and the scrub more dense, she struggled to cut a path alongside the creek. Trees had fallen in places. She had to climb over or around them.

Twenty minutes in, about when she was thinking the terrain had got the better of her, the rise suddenly plateaued and the creek widened again into a sizeable pool fed by a small waterfall upstream. Behind it, the contour of the land rose sharply again. There was a patch of flattish land to one side of the pool, large enough for a tent. She set her mind to work, tried to see his tent erected there. The image came easily.

She had stayed there for a while. Sat on the ground with her knees drawn up and her arms wrapped round them; an innocent and childlike pose to strike while she tried to imagine the thoughts of a man determined to terrorise them.

Nicole has placed a filter over many of her memories of having been here previously. They are more pixelated monochrome than sharp colour – the edges of them are ill-defined; their brightness dulled; their form incomplete. But the deeply embedded *feeling* of the things that happened here, they still weigh heavily, still try to pull her under.

She had left the area gasping for air.

There have been moments since they started out yesterday, when she's wondered if all that they experienced wasn't the fanciful thinking of young minds determined to insert drama into their lives. She feels nothing of the isolation and wilderness that she'd felt back then. They pass other hikers on the track now. And there were four other tents set up beyond theirs by nightfall last night. Last time, their yellow three-man tent was the only one on the barely cleared space. The dark sandy soil of the campsite is now so well trodden that it is packed down hard and the roots of the remaining tea-tree are exposed like the blood vessels on the back of a hand. The bracken that she'd once had to push through to go to the toilet previously is all but gone and excretion now occurs in the privacy of an elevated wooden structure.

She recognises it as the same promontory of land. But it is also nothing like it was. It's had to give in many ways to satisfy the demands of walkers. The bridge she's on now is such an example. Previously, they had to leave the cove early on the second morning because they needed to cross a tidal creek. Their departure time was dictated by low tide. They left their socks and boots off, tied the laces of them together and hung them round their necks to wade through the water. She is shorter than the other two, so the cold, brown water had come above her knees, soaked the hem of her hiking shorts. The rocks were slippery underfoot. She remembers the care she took to keep her balance. She didn't want to risk falling and wetting her gear. Once across, they sat on a large, flat rock to dry their feet and put their socks and boots on. The rock is still there, just as she remembers it, but the timber bridge constructed over the waterway, like the long-drop toilet, is a new addition to the landscape.

The bridge annoys her. It's a cheat. It takes away the need to think or plan. It also takes away the challenge. But worst of all, the slick convenience of it dumbs down the extremes of their previous experience. She recalls with ease the fear she'd felt back then. The nagging sense that their activities were being secretly observed. Trivialising anything about that offends her. She stamps across the bridge now and makes its boards rattle.

They walk in the same order as yesterday, in the same order that they crossed the waterway years before: Nicole in the lead, then Lisa, and Samantha several paces behind.

It's a shorter day today, but more difficult as she remembers it. She hopes Samantha copes.

She has decided to walk slower today, so Samantha doesn't feel she has to rush. But equally, Nicole wants to hold the ground beneath her feet for longer. Maybe then she'll find the courage to hold her thoughts for longer too. Try and make sense of them. Make sense of why she's here.

They have to climb up a steep and rocky headland to get out of the cove. But first they have to pass the spot that confirmed for her all those years before that it wasn't the paranoid imagination of a young woman that made her believe they were being watched that first night.

They start what is initially a gentle climb, but the track soon becomes steeper and they have to step up onto increasingly larger rocks. Even though they walk closely together, they mostly walk in silence.

Nicole imagines all three of them are having the same memory. The cube-shaped clusters of wombat scat they pass must be a reminder for each of them. And just as she recognised the rock they sat on to dry their feet, Nicole recognises the rock where they discovered another kind of scat. This one wasn't cube-shaped. It was long and brown and fell in the shape of a child's back-to-front six. It was unmistakably human.

She remembers how she stopped so abruptly when she saw it that Lisa ran into the back of her.

'What's the matter?' Lisa asked and peered round her. 'Bloody hell. What animal did *that*?'

'No animal,' Nicole said. 'Not a furry one anyway.'

'How do you know?'

'Animals don't use toilet paper.' She pointed to a few squares of brown-smeared tissue paper discarded in a bush.

'It's his, isn't it?' Samantha said once she reached them.

'It might be someone else's?' Lisa offered.

'Then that means there's two sickos out here,' Nicole said.

Lisa's eyes shone bright with anger as she looked around. 'Bastard.' She drew the word out softly.

Samantha brought her hands up to cover her mouth.

Nicole expects the others remember something of her expression too. Maybe she paled. Maybe her shoulders dropped, defeated. Because that's how she felt when they found that talisman, that filthy thing that confirmed his presence.

'It's not worth it,' Nicole said. 'I think we should call the whole thing off. Turn around and go back.'

'Go back?' Lisa snapped. 'Because of that creep? No way.'

There was a new and dangerous edge to Lisa's anger. Nicole felt weak in the face of it.

'You know *why* he's left his fucking shit on a rock, don't you?' Lisa stabbed her finger towards the brown, tapered stool.

'Because he's gutless, that's why. BECAUSE HE DOESN'T HAVE ANY FUCKING BALLS!' She shouted this, hands cupped round her mouth. Her words echoed round the cove.

'Shh,' Samantha hissed. 'He'll hear you.'

'Good.'

'It's not good,' Nicole said. 'Nothing about this is good.'

'He's playing games with us. Childish games he thinks make him look like a tough guy. But it makes him look STUPID!'

Samantha looked around, fearful. 'You'll only make things worse.'

'It's a *turd*, Sam,' Lisa snapped. 'He probably still lights his farts as well. Seriously ... three of us against *that*? Where's the challenge?'

Nicole remembers how fierce Lisa looked. Her face dared them to do just that, to challenge her.

Nicole tried to, but her effort seems lame now. 'But we don't know what else he's capable of.'

'I know what *I'm* capable of.' Lisa had stood tall despite the weight of her pack. 'And that's not to let him fuck with *my* head the way you're letting him fuck with *yours*.'

They were harsh words. Hurtful. And they shamed Nicole, because Lisa was right, she *had* let him fuck with her head.

'We could come back another time,' Samantha offered. But there was no conviction in her statement.

Lisa pounced on it. 'Oh sure we will. Just like we'll do that trip to Bali we're always talking about ... or we'll learn how to ski ... or scuba dive. We're always *going* to do something, but we never do anything other than the same old safe shit we've always done. And now here we are, actually doing something different and you two want to quit.' Lisa barged past Nicole then, disturbed the flies that had settled on the shit as she stepped over it, and pushed on up the rise. '*I'm* going to finish what we started,' she called over her shoulder. 'You two can do what you like.'

Which of course was for Nicole and Samantha to follow her.

Today, none of them mentions this episode from years before. No one admits that this was the point at which they could have altered the course of things by turning back.

Nicole steps over the bare space on the rock and walks on, just as she did previously.

SAMANTHA HAS TO CLAMBER UP AND over great blocks of stone as they head out of the cove. Several are taller than her and she struggles to find a foothold. And when she does she doesn't then always have the strength to lift her weight, along with the weight of her pack. A couple of times she has to take her backpack off and push it up onto the boulder ahead of her. It's a slow and demoralising activity. One neither Nicole nor Lisa need do. So each time she has to she feels another chip knocked from her confidence. Another reminder that she's not fit enough. Not agile enough. The others say nothing of the fact that she has to do this, not even a critical side-glance. It's a reminder that they were close once. And it's this thought that helps Samantha face this next boulder now without groaning.

Lisa waits at the top to help take her pack.

'Sorry,' Samantha says as she clambers onto the rocky plateau, breathing hard.

'Enough with the sorry. I don't mind.'

Intrinsically Samantha knows that she doesn't. They had that kind of friendship once. They were tight. Inseparable. Individual slights led to collective umbrage. Heart scars were shared. It's hard, even after all this time, to unlearn the quality of it.

Samantha thinks friendship and love have much in common. In the early days each is ferociously intense but in the dying ones, achingly painful. She still feels the loss of what they had. She registers it as an irretrievable absence inside her. Some days this void takes up more space than others, hollows her out, but never so much that she can't go on. She just lives with sadness for a time. She imagines this is how people feel when they grieve. They live in emotional flux. Some days, life just feels less kind.

How much those heart scars were shared was proved when a group of them went camping one weekend. They'd finished school about six months earlier. Lisa brought her new boyfriend along – a guy she claimed to be super keen on – and a friend of his, who Samantha had only met once before. The guy Samantha had been going out with for three months had just dumped her, so her confidence was bruised.

The boys brought a bag of marijuana with them. Before long a thick joint was passed around. She'd smoked pot a couple of times before, but this was stronger than she was used to. By the time a second joint made a circuit, her confidence was restored. She no longer cared what others saw when they looked at her. She stopped thinking about holding her stomach in. She stopped laughing small. She pushed her hair off her chest so that it no longer hid her full breasts. She relaxed back and felt beautiful and equal.

After a while Lisa and her boyfriend moved off to their tent, giggling and pawing at one another as they went.

The other boy got up from his camping chair and walked over to where Samantha and Nicole sat on a picnic rug. He mimicked a truck reversing as he pushed his butt backwards to sit between them. *Bip. Bip. Bip.* Nicole's laugh was controlled. Samantha fell about giggling, which escalated when he landed with an unsteady *thud* and fell backwards.

'Whoops-a-daisy,' he said, which made her giggle more.

Samantha and Nicole each took one of his arms and hauled him back up again. He sat between them then, Samantha under his right arm, Nicole under his left.

'My girls,' he said and squeezed them closer.

His breath smelt of beer, his clothes and hair of wood smoke. Samantha thinks he was trying for the hippy look in his baggy, colourful cotton trousers and dashiki shirt, his long hair pushed up under a beanie. The beanie was beige though, so the look was more home-knitted dag than Rasta.

She liked that he called her his girl. She also liked that he kept his arm round her. She doesn't think Nicole did though. She wriggled out from under it and put some space between them on the rug.

'It's getting late, Sam,' Nicole said, her voice sober and lucid. 'We should go to bed.'

Samantha was to share a tent with Nicole.

'Soon.' Samantha still liked the sensation of floating under his arm.

'Well, I'm going,' Nicole said. 'Why don't you come too?'

'All three of us?' the boy asked and Samantha giggled along with him.

Nicole got up from the rug. She paused a moment and looked at Samantha. 'You sure?'

'Aw, come on beautiful,' he said and patted the rug beside him.

Samantha stayed where she was, even though he didn't call her beautiful. Even when he said, 'I always scare the pretty ones off,' as Nicole walked to the tent.

He pulled her tighter against him. She decided he smelt more like sandalwood than wood smoke. And his daggy beanie had slipped to the side when he toppled, releasing his long sandy-coloured hair. It was surprisingly soft where she expected greasy cords.

In her stoned and trippy state, she became attuned to the bush around her. She believed she could hear the zigzag movement of lizards' spines as they scuttled through the undergrowth. The gnawing jaws of white ants as they worked through wood. The nudging nub of sightless worms as they pushed through soil. But before long her drug-induced confidence gave way to doubt again and she saw herself as grotesquely large compared to these delicate creatures. An ungainly blot on an otherwise perfectly integrated landscape.

She looked up and saw a possum staring down at her from a branch above. This she remembers as real. Its eyes were spookily red. Its tail was thick and twitched left and right, left and right, like the pendulum of a grandfather clock. Then, irrationally, she believed she could read the possum's mind. *Last choice*, it was thinking. *Leftovers*. She remembers hoping the boy couldn't read its mind as well.

She also hoped when he kissed her that it was because he desired her. That she had been chosen.

The sex was rough and selfish. The ground hard against her tailbone. Her stoned brain worried for the worms under her back. Worried that their burrows would collapse under the weight of her and the poor blind things would be crushed.

Then, as the marijuana fug started to clear, she saw what was happening for what it was: an opportunistic fuck for someone who neither knew nor cared for her.

'No. I don't want to.' She tried to scramble out from under him.

'Bit late for no.' He took each of her hands in his and pinned them to the ground above her head.

She turned her head away, unable to look at that heaving, breathing face above her. His long hair hit against her skin like rain.

She asked herself: *Is this rape? Am I being raped?*

'No. No. No,' she chanted in time to his thrusts. She wanted to believe that she was experiencing the consequences of a bad choice. She compared it to choosing a new flavoured ice cream – an exotic one – that disappointed. But then this silly stoner thought made her laugh.

He pounded her tailbone harder into the ground.

He eventually came with a grunt and a shudder and immediately rolled off her.

'You're crazy,' he said as he pulled up his hippy trousers.

Samantha pulled her skirt down, fumbled round till she found her knickers. She clambered out of the tent and felt his cum run down her thighs.

She went to the tent she was to share with Nicole and unzipped the front closure. She was crying by then and Nicole immediately sat up.

Samantha told her what happened and Nicole put her arms round her till she felt safe.

She lay awake for the rest of the night, sullied and ashamed. She worried about how she was going to show herself in a different light the next morning. Someone who wasn't an easy, leftover slut. She decided she couldn't. So at dawn she woke Nicole and told her she wanted to leave.

Lisa left too, of course. Their friendship was impossible to splinter back then. She hoped her departure looked like a statement of disgust to the too-late-to-say-no guy. But in truth she knew she was a coward. She ran away from her shame and he probably didn't even care that she'd gone.

Samantha imagined him retelling the story to Lisa's boyfriend. Probably called her a tease. Said the fat ones should be grateful, like he'd done her a favour. She imagined he laughed about having taken one for the team.

Lisa split with her boyfriend two days later. She told him nobody treated her friends like that, and she wouldn't go out with anyone who hung out with a fucked-up creep who did.

Samantha expects it was this solidarity between them that made her and Nicole step over the man's shit that day and follow Lisa. Even though her stomach twisted with worry, and the weight of her pack suddenly seemed to double, like it wanted to drag her down, make her buckle under it so she couldn't go on.

And then it was too late for any one of them to make a

different choice. Too late to say no. Because soon enough they reached the point on the circuit where it was as far for them to go back as it was to continue on.

They also reached the point where they lost orientation of where he might be. Was he near or far? Ahead or behind? Above or below? But by then he seemed to be everywhere anyway, so what did it matter?

The heat takes hold of Samantha as tightly as humiliation. It is all-encompassing, refuses to let go. There's no relief even from the gentle breeze that came up earlier. The wind puffs its cheeks but the air it blows is hot and dry. Her T-shirt is soaked through once more. A constant trickle of sweat runs down the sides of her face, between her breasts, the crack of her arse. She itches with the tickle of it. She expects she smells like a horse.

The natural padding across her shoulders and hips has some advantages though. This morning she noticed red marks across Lisa's collarbones, saw the way she grimaced when she hoisted her pack on. No such complaints from Samantha. Her complaints are reserved for muscles alone. And what they tell her mostly is that they've had enough, that they want to take her home. She tries not to give much attention to the ache and burn in them. Instead, she marches her legs on – one step, two step, three step, four – like an automaton.

She focuses on the landscape to take her mind off the pain. She notices the way the mountains become bluer as they push upward, how the outline of the eucalypts that rise with them lack clarity; their edges blurred by the fumes of their own breath. How the gum flowers – perfect circles of cream-coloured filaments – spill across the ground. They make her think of the fallen skirts of May Gibbs's gumnut babies. A childish thought, one born of a mother of three once small boys, but it's a soothing image, and one that distracts.

And she notices the birds. The creaking-hinge call of bold yellow-tailed cockatoos and the more elusive wattlebirds, whose song sounds more like a warning to *be careful*. There are dainty-legged fantails and wagtails and restless red-throated mistletoe birds. Those that don't flee as she approaches skitter and flit from branch to branch, brave in their swift agility. As are the small brown lizards that scuttle across the trail in front of her. Samantha feels cumbrous compared to these delicate creatures.

But mostly she notices the silence. There is the low thrum of flies, like cars on a distant motorway. The earth and rocks and wood tick as they draw heat into them. And there's the dull thud of her boots as they hit the ground, felt more than heard. These sounds are almost mute in their soft constancy. And yet the bigger sounds, particularly the voices of other hikers, don't carry far at all, not when she passes them going in the opposite direction or when those who walk more quickly come upon her from behind. These people seem to come out of nowhere, unannounced. She doesn't recall that this happened last time, probably because they'd barely encountered anyone else on the trail. And the one person they knew was out there navigated the silence with intentional stealth.

Silence is uncommon at home. She lives with four men, all of them tumbleweeds of activity, so silence rarely has a chance to catch up with her there.

Lately though, she's not the only female in the house. Her eldest son has a girlfriend and she stays over some nights.

A pair of shoes marked her arrival into their home. Black leather and gold-studded gladiator-styled footwear, giddily high, left at the front door. Samantha paused to study those carelessly toppled shoes that first morning. She tried to form a picture of their owner. Was she a reckless girl or a trusting one? Slutty or sexually confident? Was she stirring in her son's bed with regret or contentment? Did her son pursue her or did she pursue him?

Oddly, the shoes had brought Lisa to mind – a brief flash to the past before this full-on return she's brought them on. Lisa would've had the courage to kick her shoes off at the door of a boy she'd only just met too.

'He could have told us,' Samantha said to Harry. 'It would've been embarrassing if one of us had walked in on him this morning.'

'Maybe that's why they're there. To let us know we can't do that anymore.'

'Odd way of telling us.'

'He's just letting us know he's a man now, Sam. Not a boy.'

'Having sex doesn't make you a man.'

Harry's pride was palpable. He looked at Samantha with a smile fuller than any she'd seen for their son's other achievements. 'They could have been loafers,' he said.

'So that's why you're so pleased?'

'I won't deny it.'

Samantha's first son was born with a concern for others that she thought normal until the other two came along. Then she realised this quality was unique to him. He never had an interest for the violent Xbox games that the other two liked to play. And while all three were talented schoolboy athletes, he never had the swagger of his brothers. Never had their coarse mouths or rough and tumble forthrightness. Never had their certainty.

Harry works in a man's world. He works with men who sweat and swear and wolf whistle at women. He's worked on sites where Fridays are celebrated with cases of beer and a stripper. He works with male pipes. He works with female pipes. They are a natural fit, one into the other.

'At least I can stop worrying now.'

Samantha worries about one-punch drunks and brain tumours and car accidents. He worries about whom his child chooses to love?

She wanted to burst his self-satisfied bubble. Burst his stupid notion that a bad diagnosis had just been exchanged for a good one. Remind him that a pair of heels at the front door might only indicate a confused young man trying to conform.

'Maybe he's still trying to work it out,' she said. 'Maybe next time it will be loafers. What'll you do then?'

Harry looked down at those black strappy heels for some time. They represented everything easy and known and ordered to him. They took away the need for him to reconfigure his thinking. They allowed him to be the same man he's always been. Eventually he sighed long and deep, which made Samantha think she'd achieved that rupture.

'What I've always done,' he said. 'Love him.' He stepped over the girl's shoes then and walked out the door.

He's stepped over other shoes of hers since – different heels, ballet pumps, scuffed sneakers. Samantha knows their presence is like a shrine at their front door. They bring Harry peace. She still expects to see loafers.

Samantha looks ahead to Lisa. She's far enough in front not to look like she's holding herself back to wait for her, but close enough that she can still keep an eye on her progress. She probably thinks Samantha doesn't notice what she's doing. All those casual stops she makes to look off into the scrub as though she's spotted something of interest.

But it's not just the pauses. Samantha knows Lisa could walk much faster too if she wanted to. She was always a lean and sporty girl; ribs on show more often than not like corrugations on a road. From what Samantha can tell, not much has changed. And despite the passage of time and the lines that come with age, the loss of tone and shine to skin and hair, she thinks Lisa will take her good looks into middle age with ease.

Samantha's often thought about the opportunities that being thin and pretty brings to a girl, especially as she becomes aware of her body, notices the way it's read by others – by boys, men, other women. She recognised early on that thinness awarded girls a confidence that larger girls didn't or couldn't always possess; a way of being amongst others that the non-thin had little experience of or understanding for. Growing up,

Lisa was pretty but unaware. Still is it seems. That she never attempted to exploit her good fortune is something Samantha always admired about her.

She remembers a time when the three of them were in Lisa's bedroom getting ready for a school disco. They dressed under the poster gaze of Madonna, Cyndi Lauper and Annie Lennox, their faces carefully pulled from *Smash Hits* magazines and stuck to Lisa's walls with Blu-Tack.

They were at Lisa's because she had more make-up than Samantha and Nicole combined. And Lisa's mother wouldn't tell them to take off their too liberally applied blue eye shadow and candy pink blusher before they left the house as Samantha's or Nicole's mothers would. And regardless of what they wore, Lisa's mother always told them they looked lovely.

Samantha's mother was more honest. Mostly though, Samantha sensed her mother's opinion of what she wore more than her actually expressing it. She had an arch eyebrow and stern look that conveyed a thousand words worth of criticism.

She had hauled Samantha off to a specialist lingerie store when she was eleven. There, a stranger scooped and cupped and levered her already wholesome breasts into a sturdy and supportive underwire bra. Samantha's trim but buxom mother looked on, that eyebrow arched to indicate this was serious business. *They're a liability, not an asset*, she told her until she finally believed it.

And Samantha learned just how much of a liability when the boys at school with their tit-sensing radars sneaked up behind her and ran a finger down her spine and over the bra's fastener. *Yep!* They called to their mates.

Samantha always thought Lisa was better equipped to manage the liability of breasts like hers. She'd have kept all sides of her clear when she walked between classes. Left plenty of space to swing her fists.

Samantha put on her usual loose-fitting top to wear to the disco this day. The type her mother encouraged. It fell like a tent from her boobs. It was buttercup yellow. She thought it looked good with her long nutmeg-coloured hair. It was sequined round the neckline, which Samantha hoped would catch the disco lights. She wore it loose over black stirrup pants and sparkly court shoes.

Lisa wore an electric blue jumpsuit with shoulders big enough to be cast in *Dynasty*. She came up to Samantha once she was dressed and fiddled with the hem of her long, loose top. She gathered it together at one hip, held it there with one hand. She leaned back to appraise the effect.

'What d'you think?' she asked Nicole.

Nicole nodded. 'Better.'

Lisa dropped the hem of Samantha's top and went over to her dressing table. She rummaged through one of its drawers till she found what she was after. She came back with a round diamante-studded T-shirt clip in her hand. She held it between her lips as she made a tail of the hem of Samantha's top again, then took the clip from her mouth and threaded the fabric through it so that it was nipped in across Samantha's waist and hips.

'Doesn't it make them look bigger?' The look went against her mother's longstanding advice: *Don't draw attention to them. Don't give people cause to stare.* By *people* she came to expect her mother meant *boys*.

'It makes you look in proportion,' Nicole said. 'Curvy.' And she shimmied her own lithe body.

Nicole never looked out of proportion, not then in her short denim skirt and pedal pushers. Not in track pants or flannelette pyjamas or baggy jumpers. Samantha took comfort – confidence – from her friend's appraisal. She made the simple tethering of her top sound scientific.

'You look great!' Lisa said and she ran her hands down Samantha's sides, moved her own body in sync to Samantha's curves.

Samantha went and stood in front of the long mirror on Lisa's wardrobe door. She stared at her reflection for a good while, turned from one side to the other. Nicole was right. To accentuate her waist, neat compared to her hips and bust, gave her form. She *did* look curvy and in proportion, and not oversized. She looked up at them, reflected in the mirror behind her and nodded. 'Better,' she agreed. 'Maybe not as gorgeous as you two, but definitely better.'

Lisa frowned. 'I hate that word,' she said. 'The way girls say *Oh you look gorgeous in that*.' She drew the word *gorgeous* out in a high voice as Samantha had heard girls do when they praised one another.

'But you can just tell what they *really* wished was that the other girl looked like shit,' Lisa continued.

'They're mint Aero bars,' Nicole nodded. 'Chocolate sweet on the outside. *Green* on the inside.'

Lisa laughed. 'Exactly! And I don't ever want *us* to be *Aero* bars.'

Even at fourteen, Lisa was so certain of herself.

Samantha quite liked a compliment if she could get one, so she was a bit disappointed that it looked as though they were about to come to an end.

But then Lisa said, 'I'll *always* think you two are gorgeous whether I say it or not.'

The conviction in Lisa's voice made Samantha believe it was true. But she also felt that her words were meant just for her. That she was saying it didn't matter what Samantha looked like, it didn't matter what she wore or how her clothes wore her, she would always be good enough. Lisa allowed Samantha to believe that she was beautiful too. But then their friendship had unravelled and Samantha doesn't think she's felt good about herself since.

So is that why she's agreed to do something she doesn't have the fitness for, to put herself at risk, just to be with the people who once made her feel beautiful? It's a shallow thought and she doesn't want to believe it of herself.

Besides, this morning she'd felt anything but beautiful when she crawled out of her tent. In the crisp, early morning light she saw all about her things of natural beauty, not manufactured. She saw the way individual parts complemented one another. How the sea made the otherwise dull, grey granite glisten as it washed over it. How the melaleucas shed their paperbark like onion skins to reveal a soft sunrise of colours beneath. The way the red throats of Mistletoe birds shone like cherries in the trees.

Samantha stood alongside her yellow tent in purple and white spotted pyjamas (packed because they weighed practically nothing, but in that moment they seemed ridiculous), and had felt unnatural and garish in comparison. A bastard hybrid of the animal kingdom trying to insinuate itself on the real thing. She clambered back inside her tent. When she came out again a few minutes later in charcoal trousers and a black T-shirt, she still didn't feel like she belonged but at least she blended in.

At home, she doesn't dress to blend in. She dresses to be noticed. She's like a solitary rainbow lorikeet fluttering its plumage in her colourful tops and dresses, always worn nipped at the waist now. Harry used to notice, proved her mother wrong in fact. She knew by the way he used to nuzzle and cup her breasts that he thought them her greatest asset. In fact, he used to navigate all the contours of her body with care and attention. They were hands she trusted.

Then his touches became perfunctory. His hands traversed her body by rote. They often rushed. Darted from one previously tested spot to the next.

Here's always worked, his fingers suggested. *Or here*.

She expects he believed they gave enough. But they were like the recruits of enforced charity.

And now they've stopped altogether.

She spent her earlier years wary of boys who might want to grope at her, and here she is now with a man at her fingertips who no longer chooses to touch her. She never thought when she opted for marriage that she'd co-opt into her own eventual sexual irrelevance.

Which is why her hands take their time, to disprove this. She runs them over the contours of her body with curiosity as much as desire. *Here I am*, her body says beneath them, *the physical sum of me, laid bare*.

It's a body that's changed over the years. It has a hardy worn-inness to it now. Her breasts fall off to the sides a little when she lies on her back, so that they rest gently on her upper arms. Her nipples have matured to a pliable, well-oiled leatheriness. Her abdomen is a sea of soft undulations. There is a silky, silvered caesarean scar, a legacy from her third, stuck son, still numb after seventeen years. Her pubic hair has coarsened. A soft, fatty pillow cushions the bone beneath.

But the centre of her sex, that place which has been numbed, scoured and electrified with fingers, tongues and cocks, remains unchanged. And with spit-moistened fingers, she has come to know herself. Her fingers remain committed and present.

It seems ironic that at home she wants the full image of her femininity noticed. Celebrated. Revered even. But out here she wants to blend in with nature's palette. She expects it's because this place once made her feel like an intruder. That it was somewhere she shouldn't be.

Back then she wanted to pass unchecked beneath the shadows of trees. She didn't want to be seen coming from behind boulders or over crests or around corners. She didn't want to leave her footprints on the beaches or leave the grass flattened where she slept. She wanted to slip through unnoticed. Undetected. And it seems part of her still does.

So where is it that she truly belongs if not here, but not at home either?

She walks on now in her muted, sweat-stained tones, grateful for the reprieve of not having to see that the man she still loves no longer celebrates her womanhood. Who for reasons she doesn't fully understand is as disconnected from her as she is from this place in her silly spotted pyjamas.

***

There is some relief from the heat as the trail finally leads them out of the rocky cove and into an area of thick bush. They must cross a saddle of land before they head down to the next cove. Ubiquitous eucalypts shade the track. These trees huddle together like kin. Their crowns touch to hold back the light from their feet so the moisture is kept there. The understorey is a thin and scruffy mix of saplings and low scrub. The humus on the forest floor doesn't smell of decay so much as a place moist and rich with life. The track is carpeted in crescent-shaped gum leaves. They make the ground soft.

Oddly, Samantha doesn't recall this part of the trail. That's how disconnected *she* was.

What a Harry, she thinks and smiles to herself.

Except it was no joking matter back then. Not when her attention was always drawn to what could lie ahead instead of what beauty was around her. She'd thought nothing of nature's trophies offered along the way. She never noticed the tree hollows, let alone took time to consider the years in their making or what might live in them. She never once saw a bark-blended nightjar, head pulled into its neck as it dozed on a branch. So far she's seen three. And last time she only noticed the toadstool caps, like those that still push up through the litter on the forest floor, if they were recently crushed or broken. She is surprised now by the great variety of colours in these fungi. It's like looking at the various shells of eggs from home-reared hens, with some as bright as their yolks.

Back then she searched for things mostly unrelated to the land – aberrations and anomalies to an otherwise harmonised terrain. She looked only for signs of the man – discarded food wrappers or a flash of uncharacteristic colour amongst the trees or scrub. Recently snapped branches. More human waste.

She was given a clue to his whereabouts when they swam at one of the beaches along the way. It was a clue she neither heeded nor shared with the others.

To have the heat drawn from her feet by the cold, crystalline sea water had been a heavenly thing after hours of walking in thick woollen socks and leather boots. This time she wears thin Climalite socks and her boots are made of breathable Gore-Tex. She's still footsore, so the times she's bathed them have felt just as good as it had before.

She swam warily last time. She stripped down to her underwear quickly and sprinted down the beach. She wanted to get her body under the water as soon as possible. Not so she could hide it from Lisa or Nicole, or even from other hikers (there were none on the beaches back then), but to hide it from a creepy, spying guy who she imagined would sneer when he looked at her body. The same guy who thought it reasonable to throw dirt in a girl's face, to leave his shit on a rock.

Samantha felt his presence the whole time after she stepped over his filthy turd. She tried not to think about him being out there, tried to adopt some of Lisa's insouciance. But she'd never been able to ignore the agendas of others, not the way Lisa could.

Samantha imagined his eyes on her when she came out of the water that day and towelled herself off. She wondered what he thought as he glimpsed the dark triangle of hair at her crotch through her wet knickers, her flabby waist. The way her thighs chafed and how her cold nipples pushed out hard against her DD-cup.

Fat slut.

If it hadn't been so hot, if the cleansing of her body had not felt so good, she probably wouldn't have risked the exposure at all.

And when she spotted that double flash of light amongst the trees on the hill above the beach, like sun hitting glass, she told herself that she'd imagined it. When she caught the glint for a second time, she hastily dressed.

WHEN LISA THINKS BACK TO THE girl she was all those years before, she sees the smooth, unblemished face of her daughter walking this trail. The Hannah of now is not much younger than the Lisa of then. She sees her slim shoulders pressed down by the load she carries, her long legs propelling her forward.

Is it possible that a similar history could repeat itself in her daughter? Could – *does* – Hannah have the same reckless disregard for danger in her urban terrain as Lisa had in this wild one? Somehow she doubts it. Hannah is far more cautious. Always has been.

Lisa had watched her daughter through the front windscreen of her car one day as she walked through the school gates. She recognised her easily amongst all the other students. It could have been Lisa at the same age: no breast buds or waist, her torso a straight conduit punctuated top and bottom by bony shoulders and hips. A gangly girl with disproportionately long feet and fingers. But in contrast, Hannah's jaw has always had a soft, doll-like curve. This is where physical mimicry between mother and daughter diverge. Lisa knows her jaw has kept all of its hard angles and that her face leads with it.

She noticed how Hannah's school dress was rucked

halfway up her long thigh by the heavy bag she carried across one shoulder. She knew the bag would contain neatly written and detailed class notes. She noticed also the still perfectly bowed navy ribbon at the end of her long blonde plait which she wore pulled forward across one shoulder, yet strands of hair had pulled free from it and they fell untidily around her face. She saw the neat turndowns of her still-white school socks, but the way she dragged the heels of her scuffed brown school shoes, which wore them down prematurely. Hannah was an adolescent emblematic as much of order as disorder. Would she eventually grow into one over the other? Lisa wondered. Did she even have a choice?

Lisa was still watching Hannah's progress when a group of boys came gambolling up behind her daughter. They represented disorder in every way – uniform, gait, grooming. The group split like water to pass either side of Hannah, and merged again in front of her. They all walked on except for one tall boy. He turned and walked backwards to face her.

Hannah stopped walking and so did the boy. She moved to the left to slip around him but he followed, arms out wide as though herding an animal. She moved to the right, he did the same.

Lisa felt the familiar tightening in her hard-angled jaw, the sharpening of her vision that allowed her to scan widely, to take in and assess the actions – the *danger* – of all the boys in the group, not just the one badgering her daughter. Fleetingly, she wondered what caused this acute attention, was it memory or motherhood?

From what she could tell Hannah didn't say anything to the boy. She didn't even look into his face. She gripped the strap of her school bag with both hands and tried to manoeuvre round his outstretched arms again, shifted quickly left, then right. But the boy matched her pace. After one more attempt, Hannah stopped and stood motionless, gaze fixed on the ground.

Was she crying? God, Lisa hoped not. Where would that

get her? She watched Hannah blush, that awkward rush of colour she still gets. It starts somewhere below her neckline and travels all the way to her ears. The boy must have liked this response because he threw his head back and laughed.

The fighter in Lisa slipped off her heels and reached for the handle of the car door, but she pushed down her protective instinct. She restrained it with another – one that told her not to embarrass her adolescent daughter in front of her peers.

When the boy moved in to stand only centimetres from Hannah and coiled her long plait round his hand to force her to look up at him, Lisa responded on autopilot.

Her pencil skirt was tight but she still managed to cross the ground quickly from car to school gate in bare feet. She gripped the boy's shoulder in her hand when she reached him, dug her nails in as she turned him to face her. She still remembers the thrill of feeling the hard press of bone beneath them.

'What the fuck?'

'What d'you think you're doing?'

The boy flushed crimson. 'I'm not doin' nothin'.'

Lisa wished she could have kept her nails hooked under the edge of his collarbone for longer, but it wasn't to be. He wrenched his shoulder free and skulked off, muttered something that sounded like *mad bitch*.

'What did you say?' she called after him.

But he walked on without answering, hands pushed deep into the front pockets of his school trousers.

'I know your face now,' she said.

His mates laughed hard. His ears were as red as Hannah's by the time he caught them up. 'Pussy,' one goaded, which set off another round of laughter.

Hannah wouldn't walk alongside her back to the car. Lisa made the barefoot journey alone.

'Why did you let him intimidate you like that?' she asked, once they were in the car.

'I *wasn't* intimidated.'

'You looked it. You should have thumped him one. I would have.'

'I'm not you though! I never want to be you!'

Lisa turned to face this soon-to-be young woman, with her soft, sweet chin and her big trusting eyes, and she realised that Hannah was right, her daughter wasn't like her. That she'd *never* be like her. Hannah would never be a fighter.

She'd got it wrong. It wasn't order or disorder Hannah would grow into. It was a version of herself that was as far removed as possible from that of her mother. Lisa hadn't known whether to feel proud, disappointed or terrified for her.

The bush thins again as the track takes them back towards the coast. It also means more boulders. Lisa waits to help Samantha up another of the many they've had to negotiate that day.

'I've got this one,' Samantha says.

Lisa steps back. Gives her space. She resists the urge to grab the strap on the top of Samantha's pack and help haul her up by it.

'Hopefully that's the last one,' she says to Samantha as she steadies herself.

'I can do it, you know.'

'I know you can.'

Lisa also knows that she doesn't want her to wait for her, so walks on, leaving Samantha to take sips from the tube that connects to her CamelBak reservoir. Nicole is ahead and out of sight. For a time Lisa has a sense of being alone.

The sun is still off high, but already warm. There is a gentle breeze that helps cool her, only a little but it's better than nothing. The air around the eucalypts is stained mauve. She can taste their breath when she takes her own. The trail meanders through an area of thick, untidy scrub, punctuated with stringybarks and native grass trees resplendent with their up-do of long needle-like leaves. *Xanthorrhoea australis* they'd be labelled in a plant nursery in the city, with a price tag of several hundred dollars apiece. Here Lisa enjoys them for free.

A pair of swamp wallabies stare at her from atop an area of flat granite amongst the scrub about thirty metres in from the trail. They rest, pear-shaped, on their haunches, poised in perfect stillness, black noses lifted. Their ears twitch as they cup the sound of her approach. A laughing kookaburra starts up a racket. The wallabies don't even flinch. She's the interloper. As she gets closer, they bound off, rumps working hard.

That was one thing the three of them didn't have to work hard at: escaping their friendship. It was easier than she'd ever have thought possible. Memory might try and serve it differently, that one person instigated the split more than another, but in truth they were all complicit in the rupture. Nicole didn't return calls. Lisa stopped making them. Samantha didn't insist they must. It only took two weeks to undo eight years. Maybe it was better like that.

Back then Lisa believed it reflected the weakness of their bond, reduced it to the equivalent of a passing schoolgirl crush. But the truth is they weren't old enough, hadn't lived enough, to understand the subtext of it. Now she knows they weren't running from each other. They were running from themselves. She thinks she probably still is.

Unlike Hannah, Lisa chose not to be like her parents for the wrong reasons. Because the traits she disowned in them were probably the ones she should have adopted. Her parents lived their lives on a plateau of calm even-mindedness. Not once had she known either of them to take themselves to the edge of their personality to see what might exist beyond their bountiful decency.

She remembers when she learned about the principles of Newton's first law in physics at school, the one that declared an object exists in a state of rest or of uniform motion, and she thought: *That's it! That's my parents!* Once she also learned that external forces could unbalance this state, she looked for opportunities to become that force.

She vacillated between being a perfect teenager and a horrid one. All the usual things. Room tidy one minute, a tip the next. She gave them backchat or sulked or was smugly secretive. She might do her homework diligently one term, then the next her parents would receive calls from her teachers. Once she declared herself vegetarian, only to resume eating meat after her mother had replanned their entire menu and adjusted her food shopping accordingly.

But it was an experiment that failed. Lisa got nothing. Not an angry word. Not a sigh or sideways glance. No hint of frustration at all. It infuriated her. She was an only child. Weren't her parents *meant* to try and control her life?

Sometimes she fantasised that the restraint her parents exercised at home was a façade for people capable of much worse out of it, like shoplifting or acts of road rage. But they were both relaxed drivers and it was Lisa who took up shoplifting.

It started when she was about twelve, and for no other reason she expects now than she wanted to be noticed. She stole cosmetics or sweets mostly. Stuff she had the pocket money to buy but the desire to own only by theft. She ate the sweets but used little of the other items. She didn't even try to hide from her parents what she took. She arranged the growing number of lipsticks and bottles of nail varnish on a shelf in her bathroom, almost like a dare for them to challenge her over their origins. But the steadily accumulating items remained ignored.

When her mother received a call from a shopping centre security manager, requesting she come and discuss the circumstances of Lisa being in his office, her languid mother arrived as if collecting a parcel from the post office.

She listened serenely to what the manager had to say, that Lisa had been caught slipping an eye shadow into her school bag. The security manager said he wouldn't report the incident to the police. Said he'd give Lisa the benefit of the doubt that it was a one-off, so long as her mother saw to it that it never happened again.

And it didn't. Not because Lisa's mother shouted at her or grounded her or raised a hand to her. She didn't do any of those things. Lisa stopped because she was embarrassed by how her mother failed to rage at her in front of the security manager, or to even look ashamed.

Later, when she made the transition from adolescence to adulthood, Lisa questioned what it was her parents tried to achieve by raising her in this way. She struggled to come up with an answer beyond the possibility that they genuinely didn't care what she did. But as she matured and started to look beyond her own self-importance, she wondered if her parents were doing their level best to prevent her living a life that was entirely of their making.

Then, when Lisa had a child of her own, she realised just how *difficult* it must have been for them to maintain such calmness, such restraint, when faced with the trials of her adolescence. And how much she *hated* the sound of her own shrewish voice when Hannah tested her as a teenager.

Now when Lisa thinks of her parents, she thinks what extraordinary people they were for their time. And she wishes she'd chosen to be more like them.

They stop to rest on a rocky outcrop at the top of a rise. The view is more spectacular than Lisa remembers.

There are no tall trees on this exposed point. What grows here is tortured and stunted. The air is almost still now, but the vegetation suggests this isn't always the case. Gnarled coastal trees tilt inland. Their trunks curved like the spines of the elderly. Spiky sword-sedge and shrubs of bottlebrush and kunzea – *Callistemon pallidus* and *Kunzea ambigua* – clutch to the hungry soil between granite boulders. Lisa likes the resilience of this vegetation. She likes the way it's yielded to its environment but not surrendered. She likes the way it holds on.

She holds on to very little. Lets little hold on to her.

She thinks of the lovers she's had since Matt. Relationships she's tried to build from the ground up but which always seem to be set out on the bedrock of what could go wrong. She's built few walls from what could go right. The effort of maintaining civility defeats her she thinks, that and not trusting herself to do so. She imagines it's hard for a man to want to be with a woman who is quick with a putdown.

She's not attracted to men with clean, clipped nails and smooth, flawless skin anymore. She likes scarred, calloused hands, ones with a bruise under a fingernail, evidence that here is a man who's taken risks.

She came close to spending more than a few months with a landscape gardener once. She liked that he smelt of sweat, peaty compost and the limey bite of fertiliser. She also liked that he spoke about his work in Latin – *Phlox subulata*, *Felicia amelloides*, *Dianthus barbatus*. Matt, a pharmacist, spoke of inhibitors, suppressants and antagonists, drugs that were anti-this and anti-that.

This man's hands were stained and imperfect, gentle and commanding in turn. He could haul rocks about to build a retaining wall then kneel down to tickle the delicate root ball of the perennials he'd plant behind it. But in the end his hardworking hands were probably too gentle. Too often put off by the force of her.

'I'm not the enemy you know,' he said.

She expects she'd rebuffed him in some way. He sought to put an arm too firmly round her waist. She didn't like the feel of the ownership.

'There's the potential for an enemy in everybody,' she told him.

He shrugged. 'I suppose if you keep looking for one, then that's what you'll eventually find.'

She left him in the end, before she did more damage than

he deserved. He left her with an enduring interest in botanical names. She often practises their pronunciation, as with those plants about her now, *Banksia marginata*, *Correa reflexa*: silver banksia, native fuchsia. She does this to exercise her memory as much as her memories of him. She also likes the decisiveness of a plant's real name.

Lisa thought of Hannah earlier when she passed through an area charred by fire. Saplings filled the space where the understorey had been destroyed. Lithe, like Hannah, they strove without pause. Their shape was defined by their habitat. Steal their sunlight and they pushed in new directions, found a new way.

Hannah hasn't always been shown a sunny life.

Yet at just nineteen she is so sure of herself, so sure of who she's not and never will be. Lisa thinks her daughter is too young to have a live-in boyfriend. She tactfully suggested as much.

'You're not even who you're going to be yet, so why give someone else a say in it.'

'Maybe I'll end up a better person for being with him.'

Lisa wanted to argue this point, tell her daughter that she alone was best placed to build her own character. But then she decided against it, because what did Lisa know about building anything?

But the other thing that silenced her is that Hannah's boyfriend is a nice boy. It's a bland word *nice*. It suggests ordinariness. Someone staid. Boring.

He looked Lisa in the eye when they first met. His handshake was firm. He called her *Lisa* without asking if he could. She took it as a sign of his commitment, not disrespect. And Hannah makes no attempt to talk him up. There is nothing about him she tries to manipulate or massage.

They have cute nicknames for one another. They are inseparable. When Hannah speaks to him, he pauses in whatever he's doing. If he doesn't agree with her he says *I'm sorry, but* before he explains why. She does the same with him.

Lisa's never seen him sulk or get angry. She's never heard him raise his voice. But neither has she seen him laugh himself to tears.

Maybe the word she should use to describe him is *good*. He is a *good* man.

Matt doesn't like him. He told Hannah so.

Not man enough, he said. *No spine*.

Hannah told Matt to keep his opinions to himself and didn't ring him for a month. Good girl. Maybe there's something of her mother in her yet.

Sometimes though, Lisa worries that this boy is too steady for Hannah. That she'll give him her best years only to discover that she feels the lack of a challenge. He demands nothing of her, beyond her presence. Lisa thinks this is the rub. Their reliance on one another gives neither the opportunity to be more when necessary.

Hannah silenced her on this too.

'Maybe I'm all I need to be.'

'Which is?'

Hannah hadn't answered her and neither did she need to.

Because they both know what she isn't. She is not her mother. And neither is she her father. She doesn't need to best, to win, to triumph. That was the sport of her parents.

Lisa holds her tongue now. Because who is she to think she can guide this certain but gentle girl on how to be her best self? What would she know?

A patchwork of clouds cast dark shadows over the ocean. Where the sun shines through gaps, a beam of ethereal light reaches down and touches the water. Her eye would have the ocean ending on the eastern horizon, but she knows it's a trick, the deception of a vanishing point. Lisa pictures how it continues to curve round the full belly of the earth, barely interrupted by land for thousands of kilometres.

Nicole also looks east across the ocean. 'We're nothing compared to that,' she says.

Lisa doesn't answer. Instead, she turns her mind's eye away from this expanse of water and observes them as though her body has been borne up by one of the silver gulls that drift overhead. She sees them as tiny specks with this new world view. She decides she doesn't like this reductive image though, which only seems to diminish them, so returns her gaze to Nicole, sitting on a boulder across from her.

What she prefers is the clear and defined detail of Nicole, the complex matrix of skin and muscle and bone and tendon. Lisa knows a heart beats in her chest; that her lungs fill and empty; that a network of nerves transmit an endless current of important messages from her brain right throughout her body. She feels. She hurts. She expects she loves and hates. She *is* real. *They* are real. None of them is an inconsequential speck.

'You're right,' Lisa says. 'We can't compare with something like that.' She indicates towards the ocean. 'But I don't think we're nothing. Not then. Not now. We're something. We're important. We always were.'

When Nicole turns to look at her, Lisa glimpses some of the fear and vulnerability from last time.

She thinks about how guarded Nicole has been since they met up again, how distant and closed off she is from her and Samantha. In a cowardly way, Lisa wishes Nicole had remained behind that barrier just now. She could keep up the pretence then, just as she knows Nicole is, that they've put their experiences from the past behind them.

'Our mistake,' Lisa continues, 'was allowing him to treat us like we were nothing.'

Nicole looks at her a while longer. It becomes an unfriendly stare again, her vulnerability pushed back to the place where she holds it tight inside her.

'I thought the mistake was *you* not realising he had the capacity to do that right from the start.'

Lisa forces silence. Looks away. She tries to be more like her daughter. Certain of who she doesn't want to be.

It is late afternoon when they step off the track and onto the fine white sand of the beach. Like last time, the grains squeak like mice under Lisa's boots.

That second day, when they reached this beach, they stripped down to their underwear and raced into the sea. Lisa floated on her back, arms and legs out like Vitruvian man, small breasts pushed to the sky. She remembers how the shrill whir of the cicadas that she'd heard on and off that day was extinguished by the briny water as it filled her ears.

'Should we have a swim, then set up camp?' Lisa asks the others now.

'I'm going to set up first,' Nicole says and walks off.

Lisa watches Nicole as she heads up the beach to a path that cuts through the narrow band of coastal dunes and on to the camping area in the bush just behind. Her strong tanned runner's legs and the black gaiters that cover her shins are about the only thing she can see of Nicole's body between the ground and the sky; her large backpack obscures the rest. Before long even they march out of sight over the grass-bristled dune. Lisa's left to stare at the footprints she's left behind.

Samantha takes a step forward as though to follow, then stops.

Lisa wrestles with indecision too. Should she give Nicole the space she thinks she wants or fill it with the company Lisa knows she needs? She can't force her though. She has to be patient. Restrained. Things that don't come easily to her.

'Should we follow her?' Samantha asks.

'No. Let her go.' Lisa lowers her pack onto the sand. 'I don't think we should crowd her.'

Samantha looks uncertain then eventually agrees. 'You're probably right.' She frees one arm from her pack and swings it round so that it lands, then topples, on the sand in front of her. 'What a relief,' she says and rolls her shoulders. 'I feel like I could float away.'

'Light as a feather?'

'Yeah. A featherweight.'

Lisa wants to tell Samantha that she's proud of her. That she knows what they're doing isn't easy. That she thinks she's tough and dogged and brave. But her words would feel like too much too late to make a difference.

Instead, she says, 'None of us is as fit as we were.'

'Was I *ever* fit?'

'Yes.' And she means it. 'You just never gave yourself credit for it.'

Samantha looks down. Lisa thinks she's pleased.

'Come on,' Lisa says. 'We stink.'

They don't strip to their underwear as they did last time. Instead, they find a spot behind some boulders at one end of the short beach and with their backs to one another they change into their swimming costumes – a black bikini for Lisa and turquoise one-piece with deep sides and a supportive bra for Samantha.

The temperature of the sea water is a shock initially. Lisa's feet are hot and feel swollen from being in socks and boots all day. Once underwater though, the skin pales and pickle-wrinkles. Her abdomen retracts from the cold as she walks out. Then as she dips down to cover her shoulders, her temperature soon normalises with the sea and the cold becomes a salve for overworked muscles.

Samantha, in comparison, walks a short way out into the water then dives straight under. She swims out and away from Lisa, her strong freestyle arms windmilling as gracefully as she remembers them from their school days. Once out in the deep, Samantha stops and treads water. Lisa watches as the gentle swell lifts her then lowers her again like a sigh. Still weightless, she thinks. Still lighter and fitter than she allows herself to believe.

Lisa stretches out and floats on her back. The water washes over her body and fills her ears till the only sound she can hear is the pulse of blood going into her head. She closes her eyes and enjoys her own weightlessness after the burden of carrying a pack. She's bruised in places from the bite of it – collarbones, hips, tailbone. The water soothes these sore places. Soothes her mind. The sensation reminds her of Hannah.

She was a nervy baby. Startled easily to most sounds, soft or loud. She rarely out-and-out bawled. It was more of a needy mewl she had. Lisa learned that the best way to settle her was to fill the bath and hop in with her. It was a tricky business to get two wet and slippery bodies out and dried off again later, but it was worth it to see Hannah's fretful little body stilled. Lisa would lay her against her chest and lap the warm water across her downy back. Eventually she'd quieten but rarely did she go to sleep. She imagined Hannah's tiny ear pressed to her chest like a stethoscope, hypnotised into calmness by the steady *lup-dup* of her heart as her fragile body moved up and down with the bellows breath of her lungs.

Matt came home to this watery scene many times. He never offered to take their baby and wrap her in a towel with his soft, clean pharmacist hands while Lisa dried herself off.

Instead, he'd poke his head round the bathroom door and say, 'Great. Everyone looks happy here. I'm off to the gym.'

Or a cycle. Or a run. Or to play *Tetris*, headphones on.

'Hold on!'

But he never did hold on. Not to their child or for any of the other things Lisa could have used his help with.

She'd flounder and splash with Hannah in her arms to get them both safely from the bath. Hannah would startle back to her nervy, edgy state again so that she squirmed like a slick fish against her.

'Couldn't you have given me five minutes?' she'd flare later.

'For what?'

His bemusement at these requests angered Lisa more than if he'd looked at her with contempt for having asked. The way it never occurred to him that he could act differently. How a small gesture like wrapping a towel round his child could make her life easier with little hardship to his own. Not understanding the notion that they were meant to be in this together. That they were a team. Equals.

She doesn't know how many times she shouted at him. Threw things. Pushed past him to leave a room, felt the satisfying hardness of her shoulder against his. He never retaliated to these outbursts. They seemed to amuse him more than anything. A childish game that he tolerated. He never doubted his superiority. She never doubted her determination not to have a second child. Because what did *he* give up for someone to call him Daddy?

She often asked herself if his restraint during her outbursts made him the better person. Once she might have believed so. Before the taunts and name-calling started, the way he goaded her because he knew he could. *Crazy woman. Hormone fever. Want some medication for that mood?*

Later, when Hannah was too big to lie on her chest in the bath, Lisa wondered if what her daughter had really heard when her ear was pressed against her was the humming current of her anger. The same way that electricity hums as it travels along high-tension powerlines, something unseen, but alive and dangerous. And if this is what Hannah sensed, then maybe it was fear that stilled her tiny body and not the tick of her mother's heart.

Lisa hears Samantha swim towards her. She drops her feet to the bottom and stands in the chest-deep water as Samantha comes and stands alongside her. They look inland. Samantha moves her head from left to right and Lisa follows her gaze, past the dune line and the scrappy coastal tea-tree, up to the silvery-leaved eucalypts that follow the design of the mountains behind.

'I thought I saw something up there when we swam here last time.' Samantha points to a spot on their right.

Lisa looks where Samantha indicates.

'It was a double flash of light. Like when the sun reflects off glass.'

Binoculars, Lisa thinks straight away. She looks at Samantha, surprised. 'You never said anything?'

'I don't think I wanted to believe it was real.'

'That was my problem. I didn't want to believe any of it was real either.' Lisa's anger and the truth were incompatible back then, despite it being there in the facts for her to see all along.

'It still creeps me out,' Samantha says, 'to think of him spying on us.'

'We were sport to him. A game.'

Just as her rages were a sport to Matt.

'With no winners,' Samantha says.

'No. No winners.'

And they've never learned who ended up losing the most.

For the first few years of Lisa's marriage there were no winners or losers. Matt treated what he called her *wifely disobediences* with humour. He'd shake his head and smile when his underpants, socks and T-shirts were returned to him clean, but still inside out. When she pretended she could no longer start the lawnmower. When the leaves built up in the carport; the lid wouldn't close on the too-full bin under the sink.

'What am I going to do with this lazy pixie?' And he'd pinch her arse – not too hard – then kiss her neck.

She returned his smiles during these small intimate campaigns. She thought these, what still felt like, friendly challenges were how two young people started out in a marriage – a harmless clash of expectations until finally a common path upon which to tread was established.

Sex was their great unifier. He liked that she wasn't shy. Liked that she'd initiate it. Liked that she demanded variety, satisfaction. He had a deft touch, staying power. She suspects it was these things that kept them together for as long as they were. A common path found in sweaty, primal nudity.

They often had sex after an argument. Not with any redemptive gentleness. She thinks it was some perverse attempt to continue the fight, take it into the bedroom like a bar room brawl; sanctioned the use of nails and teeth and hard, deep thrusts. What was more perverse though was that she suspects they both enjoyed this sex best. There were no winners or losers with it. They both got what they wanted. They both slept soundly afterwards. It allowed them to start the next day with a clean slate.

Nicole walks over the low dune and onto the beach. She wears a brown bikini; her blue chamois towel slung over one shoulder. Nicole is perfectly proportioned, muscular and athletic. She moves further along the sand and places her towel on a rock. She strides down to the water's edge without looking in their direction, walks out till she's thigh-deep then dives straight under as Samantha had. She swims out to the deep with an equally precise stroke, only faster.

Lisa watches her power through the water. She no longer knows why Nicole drives herself so hard. In her youth it had been to meet the demands of her high-achieving parents. Now she can't be sure. But it hurts to see her push herself as she does, to watch her compete against what seems to be nothing more than her own determination. Lisa wishes she could put a restraining hand on her shoulder as Nicole used to do with her. Because it might give her the permission she won't give herself to slow down, to ease back, to enjoy these small moments where nothing and no one is making demands upon her.

She told them she has never married. No children.

Noisy pests, Nicole said as they filled in some of the gaps of their lives in the bar that night. *Like fruit bats. They don't shut up till they go to sleep.*

So what does Nicole have if not these things, Lisa wonders, beyond her public service career, a two-bedroom apartment and a detached manner?

Is her absence of love and family by chance or design? In what way has Lisa contributed to it? How much is she to blame?

But maybe Lisa is wrong and someone *is* making demands of Nicole, right now. What if she is?

And it's when Lisa has thoughts like these that she wonders why she thinks she can make anything better by bringing them back here. What gives her the authority to even try? And what if in trying, she only ends up making everything worse.

THE BEACH IS EXACTLY AS NICOLE remembers it – nestled calmly between the arms of two protective headlands. In contrast, as she walked today she could almost forget that she's been here before because the tracks are so well maintained now. The further they penetrated this land previously, the narrower and more uneven the trails became. The scrub grew right to its edges back then, and some of the tea-trees' branches formed a low roof across it in places as though trying to reclaim the territory taken from them. There were times when she had to force her way through the blade grass. It cut her naked legs and left fine lines of blood that clotted and scabbed to the colour of liver. Saw-toothed banksia leaves did the same to her bare arms, and the scrappy branches of these gnarled trees snagged her pack and jerked her backwards. She'd been more wary of snakes then too, frightened that one would be asleep exactly where she was about to place her foot on the obscured path.

There had been deep washouts in gravel sections of the trail then, which made the descents treacherously slippery in parts. In other areas the ground was a tangle of braided roots that threatened to trip her up. Branches and whole trees had fallen across the trail. In places it looked like the forest was playing a game of giant pickup-sticks. They had to clamber over or under them. At other times, when they were too large, they had to cut a path through the scrub round their broken, splintered trunks or network of roots ripped from the earth. Trees and branches still fall, but now the obstructing section is cleared by a chainsaw and she simply passes between two neatly cut ends.

Nicole's imagination ran away from her last time. Many of the places it took her mind to seem silly now. Like the way she pictured the faces of grotesque monsters on the weathered surface of the granite boulders. She conjured misshapen noses and lopsided eyes in those big Frankenstein-shaped domes. Fracture lines gave up grim mouths full of broken teeth. Patches of lichen became poxy green and orange lesions on illusionary cheeks. They were the games of a child, like looking for animal shapes in clouds. But at the time it hadn't felt like a game at all. It had felt like the reasonable manifestation of a deep and warranted fear.

Little seems to have changed about these boulders in the years since Nicole last passed them. If she wanted to she expects she could still imagine a ghoulish face, still find things to unsettle her on these eroded and stained surfaces.

And she remembers how she fretted over Samantha. Her parents' penchant for nature documentaries hadn't helped. They'd taught her about vulnerability and how this was what predators looked for in their prey. The way they sought out the weakest or slowest. The straggler. Nicole didn't worry for Lisa in the same way. Lisa was a fighter.

Nicole was, and still is, a compulsively fast walker. She was already a keen runner back then and hadn't known how to slow her body down, how to make it fall in with the slower pace of others. If she tried to, she became agitated with restlessness. A kind of madness in stasis. Her body tensed with the urge to move. She had to consciously hold herself back like a pulled bowstring, while her mind – her conscience – said that she *must* stop, that she *must* wait. The mind and the body wrestled for a time, but the body nearly always won out. Samantha would barely come into sight on the trail behind her and Nicole would be off again. She was the hare. Samantha the tortoise.

The day had been warm and her T-shirt was soaked with sweat beneath her pack when she took it off at the second campsite. It was the sweat of hard work, of putting in. The best kind.

Sections of the trail were mean today, steep descents, slippery with scree. They demanded much of the knees. Her boots threatened to slip out from under her at every step. The weight of her pack didn't help. It pulled her off balance as she slipped more than stepped downwards. She looked only to the ground, always searching for the best place to next put her foot. Attention limited to a zone little more than a metre in front of her.

Leather boots suddenly filled that zone when she was here last time. She'd let out an involuntary squeal when she saw them. She hated herself for doing it. It made her feel weak.

Nicole had looked up slowly from those brown boots, recognised them for a man's footwear. She looked up from their silver eyelets and black laces. Up khaki coloured trousers to the wide hip strap of his backpack, gripped low on his waist. Up the sweat-stained grey T-shirt that covered his lean torso. And she remembers wondering if she'd eventually reach a weak chin, a cruel mouth and dark hateful eyes. Nicole expects this search from boots to face took only seconds, but at the time it felt like those seconds moved through tar.

'Sorry, love. Did I frighten you?'

His face was tanned and creased in kind lines. His smile was easy and full. He was an older man with grey at the sides of closely cropped hair. It seems odd to think that he was probably only ten or fifteen years older than Nicole is now.

She wonders if he's still fit enough to hike. If so, does he continue to come here, loving the region still, as he told her he did back then. Maybe he was even amongst the group of older hikers she'd passed earlier that day. It's unnerving to think that she might share this place now with someone she'd met here previously. Because if that kind-looking man was here, then why not the other, hateful one? Is it even a possibility?

Nicole recalls how she blushed and mumbled something about being easily startled, despite the fact that she wasn't, not normally.

They chatted briefly about the terrain and distances and water supply.

'You're not on your own are you?' he asked. He sounded concerned, fatherly.

'No. There're two girls behind me.'

'An all-girl adventure,' he said, and nodded his approval.

'Something like that. Have you passed anyone else?'

In retrospect she knows she asked this too quickly, too keenly.

'No. You're the first person today. Not such a busy area. That's why I love it here. Get away from the city nutters. Our little secret, eh?' And he tapped the side of his nose just as her father would have done.

'Don't forget there's two after me,' Nicole called as the man moved off. 'They'll probably scream too.'

'I'll whistle then.' He started up a tune she recognised as 'It's a Long Way to Tipperary'. It was a tune her father liked to whistle.

They'd passed so few hikers till then that her isolation had felt all encompassing and absolute. But she remembers how after this encounter she felt strangely calm for a time. She stopped seeing rock monsters. Stopped jumping at shadows and fearing concealed bends and sudden movements in the bush. She stopped listening for sardonic laughter and imagining boulders being levered down upon her. Meeting this time-seasoned man had made her think of her father. A sensible and practical man. Someone who would never allow an irrational imagination to spook him. And Nicole knew her father would have laughed at her for having allowed hers to.

She rarely hears her father laugh now. Much of the joy has been taken from his life by her mother's Alzheimer's.

Nicole thinks her father takes a guilty pleasure from her singleness. She's the child who left home but who always comes back. No one else makes demands on her time, so he can and does. She imagines he now considers his unexpected late-in-life baby a great boon. She's always good for a late night call when her mother wakes confused between night and day.

'Where's Dad?' Nicole asks her.

'Oh, just having a lie down. I should probably wake him. I expect he'll want his tea soon.'

Her mother hasn't been able to cook for years.

'Look out the window, Mum. What can you see?'

Nicole hears her mother's shuffling feet, her wet breath.

'Pretty stars,' she says. There is always the sound of youthful optimism in her mother's voice.

Nicole doesn't mind these calls. It's a bonus that she remembers enough at these times to recognise Nicole's name on speed dial. She often stays on the line with her and they chat for a while. Sometimes she gets a glimpse of the wise teacher her mother once was, the woman who knew the difference between a clause and a phrase, made the rules of algebra seem easy. Someone with an understanding of the changes that come with the seasons or the effects of an illness.

The crepe myrtle's early this year, she might say, or *Your father seems tired. I expect he worries about me.*

They've never asked Nicole why she hasn't married. Not that she'd have been able to answer them if they had. There's an abstraction to the reasons, which she's never been able to put form to. All she knows is that she followed the rules but then the rules proved liquid. Maybe she decided she couldn't put her faith in something whose contours might shift.

She doesn't like to think about who will orientate her to the world should she need it, by telling her to look out her window.

***

For a couple of hours after her encounter with the older hiker that day, Nicole heard her father's encouragement amongst the bush sounds and not the malevolent laughter of the man from the car park.

Pull yourself together, she imagined her father saying. *You're meant to be enjoying yourself.*

So Nicole did pull herself together for a time. She stopped listening to the childish follies of her mind and channelled her father's robust home-school teachings instead. Particularly the one that said if she wanted to achieve a task then all she need do was apply herself to it.

So she decided to make this rarely visited and special landscape hers, just as her father would have wanted her to. *She'd* own it. Not the car park whacko. Not the *city nutters*.

She was reminded of why she chose to hike out here – to prove to herself that she could do it; so she could grow, not shrink – to feel untouchable for a while. Capable. But it was a short-lived confidence. Because then she lost her way and in doing so learned that her father didn't know everything.

There was little signage on the track back then. There was a faded map locked inside a scratched Perspex-fronted noticeboard at the trailhead. It seems primitive compared to the covered structure that's there now, with its extensive information boards about flora and fauna, safety and rescue. And the map of the area at the trailhead is large now. The *You Are Here* printed on it is almost worn away by the many fingers that have touched it. Nicole carried a copy of the original map with her previously, but the detail was limited and often proved inadequate.

There had been the occasional timber sign with a directional arrow along the trail, mostly where geographical variations might cause confusion for hikers. Now there are many.

She was ahead of the other two when she reached the narrow gorge last time. She could still hear bits of their chatter, so assumed they weren't far behind.

The trail till then had followed the shoulder of a mountain. It took them gently upwards and inland for a few kilometres. The further they moved from the coast, the hotter it became. And the breeze she'd felt earlier dropped off altogether once they moved inland.

A breeze like the soft one that blew today makes branches creak, leaves quiver, grasses rustle. In the previous stifling and still closeness, sounds were mostly the scratch, buzz and whir of insects and the tinnitus thrum of cicadas.

The track had narrowed the further inland they went, and became rocky underfoot as it wended round increasingly larger outcrops of granite. Nicole's father would have called it a goat track. It was hard going underfoot and she had to lean away from some boulders to get around them. When she held her hand to them she felt the heat stored there. And the vegetation – mostly prickly tea-tree and she-oaks – looked parched.

Nicole suspects now that the gorge she wrongly mistook for the trail was a dry watercourse. It probably only flowed after heavy rainfall. It looked the wider of the two options when she came to the unmarked bifurcation. The trail to her left seemed to peter out a few metres on. Later, she would learn that a large overhang of rock obscured where it continued round.

At the time, the gorge had looked the obvious way. She veered to the right and continued on over increasingly boulder-strewn ground. The map indicated only that the trail travelled inland for a good way, then veered right to take them back down to the coast. She assumed this was where they were to veer right.

When she thinks back on this day, she thinks of her stupidity at not waiting for the others. She sees a careless young woman, someone who was more like Lisa. But back then she'd felt so *certain*, so *sure* of herself under the spell of her father's insistence for confidence. And she could still hear the other two at that point – Lisa's voice had a loud confidence to it, so Nicole heard it cut through the stillness, bounce off rock walls. She hadn't considered herself alone so much as a short distance ahead of her friends.

Within a few hundred metres, she had to weave her way round ever-larger boulders. They rose up tall to form walls either side of her. Lisa's and Samantha's voices disappeared altogether as the gorge narrowed. The mad whirring of cicadas took over instead.

She stopped and waited. One of those rare times she'd been able to still her tautness to move. Small, black flies heckled her face and tickled the backs of her bare legs, and the larger docile March flies tried to sting her. Being slow and lazy feeders, she slapped and killed several while she waited. They released a honey scent into the air.

A slash of blue sky separated the opposing grey cliffs. The sun was directly overhead. It drilled down mercilessly through the space. The rocks ticked with heat and her body dripped with perspiration. But it was the absolute stillness that unsettled her the most. Tomblike, she remembers thinking. She imagined her father calling her to task for her melodrama.

Then the stillness was shattered.

A single stone the size of a teacup dropped from above. It hit the rocky ground with an amplified crash in the narrow gorge. It landed not far behind her. She startled badly. Lost her balance on the rocky terrain, almost rolled her ankle.

A heart doesn't go gently into fright. It stampedes. The cicadas were silenced by the *whoosh* of blood that raced up her neck and into her head.

More rocks followed. A cascade of various sized stones. All had the potential to do serious harm. She was paralysed to act for a few seconds. By fear. Confusion. It was time enough for her to wonder what it was disturbing the cliff top. A kangaroo? Echidna? Goanna?

But then she had another thought. What if it's *him*? What if *he's* causing this dangerous avalanche of rocks?

This thought finally set her in motion. All she could think about then was getting back to the others. Returning to safety in numbers. But it meant going back the way she'd just come. Past where a rock the size of a football had just crashed down.

She scrambled towards the rock face from where the rocks were … what? Falling? Being thrown? She took shelter beneath the cantilever, hoped she was out of sight from who or what was above her.

She got down on all fours, like an animal. She no longer cared about the safe placement of hands or feet. She only cared about getting out of there. She stayed close to the cliff face, moving quickly over the rocky ground. She didn't look back. She didn't look up. She concentrated only on moving forward as quickly as she could. And her pack – a burden of weight all of that day – had felt light and inconsequential as she scurried beneath its load.

She was breathing hard by the time she felt able to fully stand again and the gorge widened once more. The rocks underfoot became smaller, more manageable. It was only then that she noticed the bloodied scratches on her palms and shins.

In stark contrast to the terror she felt as she escaped the gorge, was the easy stance of Lisa and Samantha when they came into view.

'*There* she is,' Samantha called on seeing her.

'You ever heard of waiting?' Lisa scolded. 'We've been standing here for ages wondering which way you went.'

Then the two of them must have seen her wide-eyed fear and heard her heaving breath, because they closed in round her. They made her feel safe while she explained what happened.

In the retelling though, she wondered whether or not she'd spectacularly panicked at what was a normal shift in the topography, something Lisa must have thought as well. 'Rocks probably fall round here all the time,' Lisa said, pointing to the cliff tops. There was little vegetation along their upper reaches to hold them firm.

Nicole laughed then in a way she hoped conveyed that she was nothing more than a silly, irrational girl. 'I guess we're just not normally standing underneath them,' she said. 'I must have looked like Wile E. Coyote trying to get away from the Road Runner.'

'Beep. Beep,' Samantha said, and they all laughed.

They studied the bifurcation in the track after that. Noticed what looked like a collapsed cairn of stones. Buried beneath this rubble was a piece of rotting timber with a black arrow carved into it that indicated left. The tufty grass under the stones looked newly flattened.

Nicole still doesn't know if it was the landscape against her that day or humanity.

Nicole regrets now not going for a swim with the others before she set up camp. Because when she gets back from the beach after Lisa and Samantha, they have squeezed their tents alongside hers on the site she thought small enough to avoid this.

She pauses when she sees them pushing their tent pegs into the sandy soil with the heels of their boots, and thinks about how she can tactfully pack up and move elsewhere. But then Samantha turns and waves at her with that needy look she still has, and she can't bring herself to do it. She'd feel like a bitch.

'How was the swim?' Lisa calls brightly.

Still too jolly. Still trying too hard. Why can't she be the two-fingers-to-the-world girl she used to be? At least she knew where she stood with her. This new Lisa, the one who gives a shit, creeps her out.

'Cold,' Nicole replies and crawls into her tent to change out of her wet swimming costume.

She stays in her tent for a while after she's changed. Lies on her back on her sleeping mat and wonders if she can reasonably stay there till morning, wile away the next twelve hours cocooned inside.

She puts her hands beneath her head, not bothered by the confined space, the way the nylon mesh is close to her face or the way her elbows push against the tent's thin walls. She needs to collect her thoughts before she goes out, un-jumble them enough for her to be in a group.

She thinks company is overrated. A condition forced upon people at birth till they don't know how to be alone anymore. It's something she unlearned to need a long time ago. And here she is now, forced to relearn it once again.

It makes her think of the few times she's tried to accommodate men in her life. Mostly she remembers how she felt her apartment contract around her as they took up more and more space, more and more often. She reached a point where her home felt smaller than this tent feels to her now.

Maybe it was about ownership. Not wanting to relinquish any part of what she'd worked hard for. But maybe it was more than this, reasons that only a three-hundred-dollar-an-hour shrink could extract about trust or control.

Still, she feels the lack in her now at not being able to relearn the simple act of companionship with these two once-close friends. But they are separated from her now by much more than thin nylon. There are more than two decades between them as well. And yet, even now, she expects they know her better than anyone else.

She listens to them as they discuss what they're going to have for their dinner.

'I think I'll try the nasi goreng,' Samantha says.

'Curried beef for me.'

'Have you noticed how all the meat in these packets is cut exactly the same size and shape?'

'I know. They look like dog treats.'

Nicole smiles at this. The two of them seem to have taken up easily from where they left off. She feels a pang of regret at not being able to do the same. The fracture though had to come. The alternative was unbearable. If they'd remained friends their experiences out here would always be magnified threefold. The memory of it kept large between them so that she could never look away and forget. To shrink it, to reduce it to the size of a small bitter pill was only possible if she was on her own. She misses them though. Sometimes.

You filthy cunt, Nicole hears him say again.

She says the word softly now, as she sometimes does. 'Cunt.' She tries to reduce the sound of it to something as harmless as the sound of *hat* or *bean*. But the single syllable leaves her mouth like a dry and jagged stone.

She says it again. 'Cunt.'

She still hates that he owned this word, that it was his stone to spit and not hers.

And because she doesn't want to think about him anymore, she unzips the opening of her tent and crawls out to join the others.

The moon isn't the big, bright bauble it was last time. It doesn't silver the leaves of the surrounding trees or cast shadows as it had back then. It's not the moon she remembers cupping in her hand and closing one eye to so that it looked to rest as an almost perfect orb in the nest of her palm. She holds her cupped hand up now and briefly cradles tonight's half empty moon in it. The stars are a vast decoration around it. She picks one – a bright one. Perhaps it's Jupiter or Venus, and not a star at all. She lines it up with the dark silhouette of a tree branch, stretched out like a finger, and waits.

'Last time we were here,' Samantha says, 'I hoped the moon would stay bright the whole time.'

Each of them has turned off their headlamps and they sit around Nicole's camp light. It looks like a saucer-sized spaceship with its ring of tiny LED lights positioned like portholes around the perimeter of it. It is efficient though, far better than the handheld torch she had last time; it had failed to illuminate much of anything at all. The spaceship light hides enough though that she can't clearly see the expressions on the faces of the others to know how Samantha's recollection is affecting them.

'So we could see more?' Lisa asks.

'Uh-huh.'

None of them speaks for a while. Nicole looks back to the branch and sees that the bright star has shifted position in relation to it. Only a little, but it's enough to remind her that they exist on something that's moving; that they're mere tenants of something grander.

'I wished it'd go away.' Nicole supposes she's spoken because she thinks they can't see much of her face either.

'Did you? Why?' Samantha asks.

'So we could see less.'

None of them claimed to have slept well or for long the last time they were here. They'd blamed the discomfort of their cramped, shared tent or aching muscles, the restlessness of one or the other. But Nicole knew for her there was more at play than a too-close sleeping companion. She'd stirred from her sleep after what felt like only ten minutes into it. Her sleeping bag had twisted uncomfortably round her legs and she sat up to untangle it.

Fatigue must have caught up with Samantha as she lay motionless, her breath coming in regular little puffs. Lisa was restless. She kicked her legs about and her breath was uneven, periodically coming in rushed pants. Nicole wondered who or what it was she fought against.

Nicole lay down again, but sleep felt a long way off.

The night sounds took over.

In retrospect, she should have burrowed her head inside her sleeping bag to shut out the noises, to blind her. But it was oppressive with three in the tent. And she was too alert by then to shut much of anything out.

The moon was full and bright. It illuminated the inside of their tent in sepia tones. She could easily make out the features of the other two alongside her, Samantha in the middle, then Lisa. She could also see the shapes of trees that cast their dark shadows across the fabric. A soft breeze had come in sometime through the night so their leaves flickered.

A dark blob came into view on the branch of a tree. Nicole

thought it might be a possum. Its shape rocked from side to side as it shifted along the branch. She watched its slow progress for a while then it suddenly took off and disappeared into the canopy.

A new shape came into view.

She tried to blink and squint this vertical shadow into the silhouette of a kangaroo – she'd seen plenty of them in the bush each day. She's not sure if it was her imagination that made the shadow's head too large and its shoulders too broad for it to be this marsupial. And neither did she have the chance to find out. The shape disappeared as a cloud passed across the moon and all went dark for a time.

Senses alert though, she sat up once more. Her imagination was left to fill in what she could no longer see and it had no problem giving the silhouette the shape of a man. Before long her ears started in on the act as well.

She heard kissing noises. Soft. Wet. Close.

Her body froze around a galloping heart. Did she even breathe? At the time it didn't feel like it.

It's a possum, she reasoned.

But her imagination was having none of that. It could only be the taunting, smacking lips of a weak chinned man.

Lisa suddenly sat up too and Nicole stifled a cry.

She expects Lisa was woken by her dream, the one that made her toss about like she was running.

'What's wrong?' Lisa whispered.

'I thought I saw something. A shadow. Outside the tent,' Nicole said quietly. She hoped Samantha wouldn't wake too. She didn't want to panic her.

Lisa remained still. Nicole expects she listened, watched, just as she was. They stayed like that for several minutes. But there was nothing more to see or hear. The moon came out from behind clouds but only trees took shape through the tent's fabric.

'You probably imagined it,' Lisa said and she lay down again.

Everything about that night became a discordant mess after that, like musicians tuning their instruments before an orchestra plays. Nicole lay down again too, but she held her body tense as she listened to the susurrations of the bush. Each sound amplified and distorted and reimagined. Every one of them became the result of a single, dark shape. Her imagination placed him only centimetres from her head. It gave him a log to smash it in. A knife to slash through the thin fabric of their tent. Through her skin.

She eventually became inured to the sounds, or was too exhausted to be kept awake by them. She woke when the sky was transitioning from night grey to dawn pink and things couldn't hide so easily in shadows.

But reality was so altered for her by the time she crawled out of the tent on that third morning, puffy-eyed and groggy with fatigue, that she thought her memory couldn't be trusted anymore either.

She wanted to go for a swim. Wake herself up. She looked to the place where she'd hung her bikini to dry from the day before. It wasn't there. In her mind, she retraced her steps of the previous day, pictured herself drape it over a low branch.

The loss of her favourite bikini hadn't disturbed her as much as the thought of the person who had taken it. She imagined him doing unspeakable things with it, and only hours after it had touched her skin. It would still have carried her scent.

Later, when they packed up the tent, they discovered that one of the tension ropes from the tent's fly had been taken.

Darkness, Nicole decided, might give free rein to the imagination, but that doesn't mean it lies.

SAMANTHA NOTICES A SHIFT THE NEXT morning. The shift is in Nicole. She doesn't forge ahead as usual; chin out, neck muscles straining to pull away from them. This morning she walks only a few paces in front. She says little still, but Samantha doesn't mind. Just to have her close is enough.

It's easy to forget that they'd been children for the greater part of their lives when they were here last time. Now here they are again, and the opposite is true.

Lisa and Nicole were the steady hands that guided Samantha through the insecurities of her adolescence. They held her up when others sought to push her down.

Girls can be vicious. They chip away mercilessly, insidiously, at the confidence of others in order to bolster their own. Some girls frozen out by silence and cold stares. Others attacked from all sides with cruel words. No one was safe.

Didn't you wear those knickers yesterday?

Nice shade of slut you're wearing.

I heard she let him finger her behind the sports shed.

Secrets confided at morning tea were currency against the confessor by lunchtime. Backs were stabbed. Alliances shifted and morphed from one day to the next.

But Samantha knows it's not just girls who can be unkind. Boys can be too.

Her middle son has an accusation of thoughtless unkindness that hangs over him. Or is it a crime?

He told Samantha the unkindness grew from a dare. So somebody else's fault? The actions of a boy too unsure of himself to refuse. An honest boy but not a smart one. Led, not a leader.

This is when Samantha feels unfit to mother sons. Love is too powerful. It masks blame. Negates possibilities of guilt. And there are so many dialects to the language of it – those for her son, those for the sons of others – which erode any common language.

The accusation involved a mobile phone under a desk. Photos. The spread-wide legs of a girl who ... what? Wasn't told, like Samantha, to keep them together? Who liked the attention she got when she didn't? Who just didn't think or care or notice that she hadn't? A naïve girl? A defiant one?

Samantha's sons live in a sharing world. But not the age-old exchange of labour or goods. They share for *Likes*. They share for re-shares.

A lot of people *liked* the image of the girl's floral knickers. A lot of people *shared* it. Girls as well as boys. This astounded Samantha almost as much as her son's actions. That others, especially girls, could look and click in a heartbeat, before the blood from it had even reached their brains and made them think about whether they should or not.

The school was involved. The Headmaster. A suspension. Threats of the police. Threats of a lawyer.

'Family's tryin' to ruin the kid,' Harry blustered in private. *Should have kept her legs together*, friends said.

Never had a photo taken of her on the beach in a bikini? I hear she liked the attention.

Harry nodded at these remarks, but he didn't protest in public.

Samantha didn't acknowledge or rebuke these scapegoat

comments either. She stuck to the script. The one her mother began for her when she was a child. The one that says blood is thicker than water. The one she bought into wholesale when her first son was born. She still feels ashamed.

The girl got a tidy sum deposited into her bank account. A nest egg. A bribe. A little something to take the sting from her humiliation.

Samantha's son got high-fives.

Even if there had been such a thing as this callous, disconnected sharing of information when she was at school, Samantha knows the three of them would never have succumbed to the disloyalty of it. They were united. Impenetrable. Their fealty sworn by their pacts and actions, through their repertoire of gestures that sought to warn or protect one another. Without this unity, Samantha would have lived her school years on the knife-edge of someone else's favour.

As a girl, she imagined there was an invisible string that held their friendship together. It gave a little, but not much. She liked that it didn't. If there was an absence of one, or some ill feeling between them, she felt that string strain. She saw it as her job to pull on it, to reel them back in, keep them close. But then she stopped even trying and that string snapped. The frayed end of it has trailed after her ever since.

Samantha adjusts her backpack, settles the belt lower onto her hips, frustrated by its weight as much as by her thoughts.

Despite the hardship of what she's doing, she bears the burden of both pack and path without complaint. Just as she bears the blister on her right heel, the size and colour of a sugarplum when she checked it this morning. Just as she bears the itchy sweat rash under her breasts, the stinging chafe between her thighs, the deep ache in her lower back.

She's managed to separate mind from body. Ignores its pleas to *Stop!* Each footfall is just another beat to the drum that sings her onwards. Because to stop, to give in, to give up, will only leave that tattered string trailing in the dust behind her forever. This is her one opportunity to make amends. And she can't waste it.

There was a shift when they left this campsite last time too. After Nicole's bikini and the tent rope were taken, and she told Samantha something about the shape she'd seen through the tent during the night, the kissing noises, a sense of unease entered their group like a fourth person. It was someone who talked too much, joked too much, laughed too quickly and with a shrill and unnatural pitch.

'Maybe a koala's wearing it now.' Samantha pulled a low eucalypt branch in front of her face as she said this, pretended to eat the leaves while she batted her eyelashes at Nicole. She also remembers that she giggled like a child.

Nicole forced a laugh. 'It'll probably fit his skinny arse better than it fitted mine anyway,' she said and dismissed her bikini with a flick of her hand.

And the two of them laughed a bit more.

But Samantha knows now it was the hysterical laughter of girls who recognised they were out of their depth.

The shift in Lisa was different. She didn't laugh. Instead, her anger steadily built throughout that third day. It began with a declaration.

'We need to arm ourselves.'

Samantha and Nicole were sobered by her remark. They remained silent as Lisa marched off into the bush. She came back a minute later brandishing a smooth-barked branch, half as tall again as her. At its thickest it was the size of an axe handle. She measured the stick against Nicole, eyed it from top to bottom then laid the narrower end across her knee. She grimaced with the effort as she snapped through the red bark and into the blond fibrous timber. The splintering *crack* confirmed the wood's hardness. Lisa pushed her weight down on it to test its strength. Satisfied, she handed the stick to Nicole who reluctantly took it. She headed back into the bush then and returned soon after with two more. She measured, broke to length and tested the strength of each without saying a word.

Lisa took the lead that day, her staff an unyielding iron-like rod beside her.

Samantha doesn't recall having felt any braver for holding a length of timber, no matter how hard the wood.

Last time when they crossed the wetland the track had taken them round the fringe of coastal lagoon, the safe-looking tufted peaks of swamp-mat and brookweed proved an illusion of high, dry ground though. More often than not they collapsed under Samantha's weight and her boots sunk into the mud. They ended up caked in the stuff. Several times the peat-rich mire was reluctant to give up her boot again. When it did, it was with sucking, kissing sounds.

She remembers how the murky water released a symphony of plops and splashes. Water skaters left hovercraft wakes across its surface. The air vibrated with the manic whir of cicadas and there was a steady drone of petrol-coloured dragonflies. Stealthy sandflies left red welts on bare skin. Mosquitoes whined round her head. Her slaps rang out like the crack of dry timber. The air smelt of wet dog.

Once again, the body of water is as busy as a city with insect life. But now Samantha's boots clatter across a timber boardwalk that's been erected over the swamp. She's high and dry. Protected. Safe. It's a reprieve from the steep climbs of yesterday.

Change isn't always as obvious as these new planks of wood though. Sometimes it comes about in small imperceptible shifts, till one day, you think: *Hold on, how did that happen?*

The changes to her marriage have occurred like this. Slowly. Insidiously. Small shifts and adjustments unknowingly made till they're normalised.

She recalls a day when Harry rested his hand on the back of her chair in her home office. The fabric is badly worn from the years he's done this. Sometimes she thinks about how she'd have one shoulder lower than the other if he rested it there instead. But he doesn't.

'You haven't billed the right work to the McGovern job,' he said, and pointed to the computer screen.

'Haven't I?'

'Looks like you've mixed it up with the Miller job. Here, let me find it.' He bent forward, gripped the mouse and scrolled down.

He'd just got out of the shower. He smelt of Dove soap and his hair was still damp. Samantha felt the coolness of it alongside her face. He was so close that she turned and kissed him, soft as a breath on his cheek.

He didn't react or pause in what he was doing. 'Miller. Miller. It's gotta be here somewhere.'

She kissed him again, but this time she left her lips on his cheek for a moment. His skin was warm and freshly shaved smooth. It smelt faintly of Gillette shaving cream. It is a scent so familiar that she instinctively finds it calming.

He continued to scroll down. 'Ah, here it is,' he said.

She took his chin in her hand and turned his face towards hers. 'And here *I* am.'

He looked at her for a moment, this shape in the room. She saw his confusion at what he should do or say.

'So you are,' he said and stood tall again. He returned his hand to the back of her chair. She felt it sink a little under the weight of it.

'No need to do anything with it tonight,' he said. 'It can wait till the morning.'

He is good to his employees. Patient. Generous with time off if needed. They – she – work hard for him.

'Everything else looks good.' He patted the back of Samantha's chair twice. Job done.

She remembers how an image of a bee had come to her, the way they bump up against a window when trapped inside. Like the bee, all she needed – wanted – was right before her, but it was unattainable. Some days she fantasises about changing the view.

'Thanks boss,' she saluted.

Harry paused at the door, then turned to face her. 'I know you're here,' he said, 'and I'm glad of it.' He tapped the doorframe twice before he left the room.

Samantha focuses on her pain. It's the one thing that's true and loyal to the past.

She can tell there's a blister on her left heel now as well. The blister on the right one macerated and split yesterday. She's covered each with a blister plaster but she still walks tenderly. And her left knee clicks and creaks. Sometimes it's so loud she wonders why the other two don't remark upon it. The three of them walk with their bodies leaning forward, chins pushed out. They're a study in counterweight and balance. Samantha imagines a musician could play a tune on the thick cords of her neck muscles.

There's a dull, nagging ache in her lower back. It reminds her of the back pain she had when she was in labour. No amount of repositioning or massage or pain relief helped with it then either. The only remedy was to expel the source of the pain, and once she did, the relief had been almost instantaneous. Somehow, unlike delivering a baby, an excruciating act that ultimately brings joy, Samantha doesn't expect any instantaneous relief or moments of joy from her current labours. Not even once she takes her backpack off for good at the end of it. She might eventually lose the muscle memory of having carried it, but not so the memory of when she was last here. It's woven a durable thread in the fabric of her life.

Her memories threaten to pull her under sometimes, like this muddy swamp had tried to do previously. She has also been pulled under by – felt drowned by at times – the responsibility of raising good men. She's been up against it time and again, the narrative of respect she wants to instil in them countered by an alternative one.

Samantha has worked around men a great deal, being the wife of a plumber. She has delivered parts to Harry on site, dropped off forgotten lunches in the early days when money was tight and the budget didn't extend to buying it. She contributes to their business from home mostly now, it being successful enough that Harry employs enough lads who can run the errands and he buys his lunch three days out of five. But she still remembers the times she's had to pick her way round concrete wash and sheets of reinforcing mesh to drop things off to him.

Once she had to deliver a special order to him. She pulled up in front of the site in her car and looked for Harry amongst the men there but couldn't see him anywhere. Her eldest son was with her, off sick from school, and the other two, too young for school, were asleep in their booster seats in the back. It was a quick errand, so she left the younger boys in the car, took her eldest son by the hand and headed off to find Harry.

A small team of bricklayers was on site this day. Samantha felt the scrutiny of them as she carefully picked her way across the boggy ground. She felt it in the way their voices fleetingly softened, how their flurry of activity momentarily stalled.

She still couldn't find Harry so headed over to the men to find out if they knew where he was. They stopped work and stared as she approached. Experience sends her conflicted messages on how best to hold herself when she must confront a group like this, and while she might sometimes have haughty pretensions – chin lifted, shoulders pressed back – she almost always adopts the cautious pose she's been taught – shoulders rolled in, head dipped.

She spoke to an older man. Harry, he said, had ducked off to get something. Samantha thought her husband's timing lousy.

This man put his hands on his sun-spotted knees so his face

was level with her son's. 'You're a lucky boy having such a pretty mum,' he said.

Her son, a shy boy, pressed closer to Samantha's side.

The man stood tall again. 'And your dad's a very lucky boy too.' He said this to Samantha's breasts, his lascivious grin aimed right at her cleavage. One of the younger men chuckled behind him.

She expects the man thought he was being generous, that he was doing what good blokes do, complimenting a woman, acknowledging her assets. Samantha hadn't known what to say. She gave the man a half-hearted smile and hated herself for it.

She gripped her son's hand firmly as she turned away. She doesn't know if it was her imagination or years of feeling as though her body was there for the entertainment of an audience, but she had felt the eyes of those men on her arse in the silence that followed her retreat. Then before long the sound of scraping trowels and the tap of bricks resumed.

But what added to this sensation as she walked away was the filth all around her – the mud and slurry and litter, the oily puddles afloat with cigarette butts – and how out of place she was amongst it in her floral blouse and skirt. Her mother's words had come to her: *You're asking for trouble.*

'Do you know that man, Mum?' her son asked as they headed back towards the car.

'Never seen him before.'

'He likes you.' Her son sounded pleased.

She'd had to pull him along to keep him moving, so keen was he to keep turning back to feed his curiosity over this man whom he thought admired his mother as much as he did.

She wanted to tell her son that the man didn't even know if he liked her or not, that he only knew that he liked *parts* of her. She thought about how she could explain it to him by way of drawing comparisons with the lollies her son favoured in a sweet shop – red frogs preferred over green, Fantales over Jaffas. She wanted to tell him that a woman's body wasn't a confection though; that women weren't a free-for-all feast of the eyes with some bits of them looking tastier than others.

She said nothing to her son though. Instead, she hurried him on to the car.

In this she knows she failed him.

Samantha had felt she was asking for trouble when she was here last time. That the pain she experienced back then was something she deserved; that everything they experienced was something they deserved. Now she knows the real problem was that she lacked the confidence to believe she had the same right as the man to go where she pleased.

So she doesn't think of her aches and pains and chafing as a punishment now. She thinks of them as a rite of passage. She steps off the boardwalk and leaves the teeming primordial body of water behind her.

LISA STOPS AND WAITS FOR SAMANTHA. The track is wide enough here for the two of them to walk alongside one another. Lisa sees how pinched Samantha's face is as she approaches. She hasn't complained once, but Lisa can tell she's hurting, even on this easier section of the trail. When it's time to end the breaks they take along the way, Samantha grimaces even before she rises. And then when she does, she moves off with something like fear on her face. Nothing like the wide-eyed panic of last time. This is more hand wringing. A fear of failure perhaps, not of harm.

Samantha is a dogged, albeit one-geared walker, with a slow, steady pace regardless of the terrain. Yet her feet touch the ground with surprising lightness.

'You're a graceful walker,' Lisa says as her steps fall in time to Samantha's. 'I stomp.'

'Still angry?'

'I guess so.'

Samantha nods. 'Figured as much.'

'Why'd you ask then?'

'To check you did.'

How couldn't she? It's the one thing that's kept her upright. There have been periods when there's been a diamond-hard purity to it. Like on this hike all those years before. To walk with anger foremost in her mind then had allowed her to walk without fear.

'It's the one constant thing about me,' Lisa says.

'And how's that served you so far?'

Lisa's shoulders slump. It's a rare moment where she feels defeated, because she knows it's served little that's good, not for her or Hannah.

'Don't you get it?' Samantha says, 'If you *stay* angry, he wins.'

'So just act like nothing happened?'

'No. Just don't let him keep controlling how you feel about what happened.'

Samantha slows then, lets Lisa pull ahead.

There was a time in her past when Lisa let go of her anger. Exhaustion from carrying it was probably what drew her to Matt in the first place. Always being at the ready, always on the lookout for those willing to take her down. She'd become a hand-to-hand combatant in her own war on life. She thinks she was probably worn out from the fight. So when Matt offered to help her down from her high horse, she willingly took his hand, believing he was her best opportunity for change. And she was content for a while with being less.

Equally though, she'd lost the two people who were worth fighting for. She thinks that took some of the pluck out of her. Maybe if she'd still had to look out for them, then they'd have looked out for her and steered her away from a man they would have recognised as good at manipulation where Lisa hadn't.

If she were a better driver – a slower, more attentive one – two things might have been different about her life. She wouldn't have come up against the man in the car park, and all that followed. And she wouldn't have met Matt.

She'd been distracted on the day they first met, one hand scrabbling round inside her handbag on the passenger seat trying to locate a packet of gum. If she'd been paying more attention she'd have seen the traffic lights change. Seen the red Toyota Celica come to a halt in front of her. As it was, she drove her Datsun into the back of Matt's car with enough force to throw her handbag from the seat. It landed upside down in the footwell, contents spilled. When it came time to pick it all up again later, there wasn't even any gum amongst it.

He got out of his car, long legs first, broad shoulders followed, with a pugilist's glare. His neat white-collar-worker hands were in tight fists at his sides. Once he saw Lisa though – young, pretty, vulnerable – his stance softened to something more cavalier. He walked her safely to the kerb, hand at her back. Rallied passers-by to push her car off to the side. Organised the tow truck. Took the pen from her hand when it shook too much for her to write down her details. He took charge of everything and she let him.

She's surprised now by her meekness in the face of this event. Anger is a weighty thing to carry though. And hers had already caused the loss of her two greatest friends. Here was a chance to prove she could let it go. That she could be a better person.

'C'mon,' he said, when Lisa couldn't control her quavering chin or tears any longer. 'It's not that bad.'

He rested his soft pharmacist hands on her shoulders so tenderly, so soothingly, that a floodgate was opened and she wept uncontrollably. It seems stupid now, to think she allowed a simple act of kindness to leave her vulnerable. Especially when it turned out not to be an act of kindness so much as an act of control, with her submission laying the groundwork for his unending belief that she owed him something.

But she supposes she colluded with their mutual deceptions. She presented a version of herself that was neither genuine nor sustainable either.

Matt was – is – a greedy man. Always took more than his fair share. His speech booming louder than anyone else's. Always asking questions but then never listening to the answers. His elbows were pointy V'd weapons when he stood. Knees wide when he sat. Time and money was his to spend. Hers to earn.

While Lisa contributed financially, he was happy. Then she stopped work for a few years when they had Hannah. His perceived value soared. Hers plummeted. She was a poor investment. She was never enough.

The ATM's home!

Easy day by the pool, ladies?

Jokes, he said, but they stung.

She might have had a dollar value put on her, but not so the things he bought. Expensive bicycles and surfboards and gym equipment littered their garage; golf weekends filled his calendar. Ted Baker shirts and Hugo Boss jeans hung in his wardrobe. The Celica was upgraded for a Honda Prelude, the Prelude for a BMW.

'I thought things were tight this month?' she'd say.

He'd shrug.

Lisa went back to work. She had two jobs. Only one she was paid for. Barely covered after-school care. Her other job was billed to womanhood.

The real Lisa eventually returned. The fighter.

She challenged him, chin out, a toddler on her hip. She argued, shoulders squared, a pre-teen standing alongside her. She raged at night. She raged in the small hours.

She fought for relevancy. She fought for respect. She banked neither.

Hannah, not even an adolescent: 'Can't you two *ever* let it go?'

Matt laughed. Because he knew Lisa couldn't.

Their daughter chose another way at these times. She calmly laid her magazine or book on the sofa or gathered up her homework from the table, and left the room. She always closed her bedroom door quietly behind her. She never cranked up the music to drown them out. She was too certain of who she didn't want to be.

Lisa's anger broke items she loved. Risked seven years of bad luck. It gave Matt more reason to do and be less.

Eventually, reluctantly, he signed divorce papers.

And finally she had proof that she'd added value. The courts told him how much. It's the only time he fought back. He slammed her up against the doorframe when he walked out of the house for the last time. Left bruises on her hip and shoulder the size of saucers. Lisa wore those purple, green and yellow hues with pride. They were the colour of her worth.

Hannah stepped over the carnage of their separation and moved out as soon as she finished school.

Matt has a new partner now. Lisa's never met her. Hannah says she's nothing like her, that she's softer. Lisa doesn't know if Hannah means this woman doesn't have her hard-angled bones or is softer in nature. Possibly both.

'Do you like her?' she asked Hannah.

'She's nice enough.'

Enough. Adequate. Satisfactory. Hannah never speaks in extremes – love, hate, terror, ecstasy. She is an emblem of forbearance.

'She seems to make Dad happy enough.'

Enough.

'They don't argue. Not that I've heard anyway.'

Lisa tried to imagine Matt without a sparring partner. She could see only a man who looked bored.

'Is he kind to her?'

Hannah shrugged. 'From what I can tell he treats her much the same as he treated you.'

Lisa's still not sure whose behaviour was normalised the most for Hannah – Matt's or hers.

'Do you think they'll marry?'

Hannah shook her head. 'Dad said there's nothing in it for either of them to bother.'

Lisa doesn't regret her anger. Only her inability to harness it into something more eloquent. It is an isolating trait. But to

capitulate is worse. The equivalent of an apology for who –
what – she is. An apology for not being enough.

Nicole had given up her position in the lead that third day
without argument. Lisa took her place. Her stick was a
pendulum at her side. She led them with authority. She was
Boudicca. Resolute. Unflinching. Each time she brought
her right foot down she stabbed that stick into the ground
alongside it. She left a line of deep pockmarks in the earth
behind her.

The day was cooler than the previous one, the heat sucked
up by a low-pressure system building to the southwest. Dark,
broody clouds were clotted along the horizon.

The trail out of their second campsite followed the coastline
initially, first through low-lying swamp and then a sinuous,
sandy line that threaded between tortuous coastal tea-tree.
Their upper branches arched over the track in parts, met above
her head like steepled fingers. Lisa had to stoop in places to
pass. Fleshy toadstools grew in shaded areas. Some had toxic
yellow underbellies; their tops blackened and leathered like
torched skin. Others were the colour of perfectly browned
meringue.

It was easy going. The hills and gullies neither steep nor
long.

She walked quickly. In part because she no longer had
to hold herself back to wait for Samantha. Mostly though
because she was wired, tight as a spring, with fury. The only
way she knew to release the trapped energy of it was in the
rapid turnover of her legs. Her anger pushed down through
the soles of her boots. The ground witnessed the force of it.
If she hoped for some kind of purification though, she'd be
disappointed.

She put distance between herself and the other two. Not
enough to lose sight of them. Enough though, that they didn't
have to see Nicole's red bikini bottom when she came across
it. It was laid out in the centre of the trail with care. The gusset

pointed towards her. An image was drawn in the sandy soil beside it. A cock with balls. The tip of it penetrated the bikini's left leg hole.

Lisa supposes she should have grown fearful at this point. Sensed the perverted risk of the man. But she didn't. Instead, she was furious. It was the childishness of it that enraged her. The image he'd drawn reminded her of the graffitied desks and textbooks and toilet doors of her school days. If it wasn't *Foo woz here* or arrowed hearts scribbled across these surfaces, it was this silly, slit-eyed tuber. Never vulvas. Occasionally some caricature of a girl with F-cup breasts. Mostly it was this stupid image that littered these surfaces. Always majestically erect, lest she forget they existed inside boys' trousers, looking for opportunities to burst out.

Lisa glanced behind her. Nicole and Samantha were just rounding a gentle curve in the trail, their heads down.

She wouldn't be able to hide the bikini top they'd find later, but she'd been able to hide this.

She hooked her stick under the stained and stiffened garment and flicked it into the scrub where it landed out of sight behind a clump of sword-sedge. She quickly scrubbed out the crude image with her boot and walked on.

She grew wary after that. Sensate. Vigilant for acts of cunning. Attacks.

Her anger became less indignant and more vengeful throughout that day. It flared and hissed inside her, like water on hot rocks. She was no longer simply on a girls-only hike. She was on a crusade. Her long staff tapped along to the drumbeat of her marching feet.

They stop for lunch in a gully. Water from a narrow creek chatters across mossy rocks. Hardy tree ferns – *Cyathea australis* – provide shade. The open trail pushes upward either side of where they rest into full sun. They are in the cool oasis of its V.

Nicole lies on a flat rock, pack as pillow, knees drawn up.

She has pulled her peaked cap over her face. Samantha has taken her boots and socks off and cools her feet in the water.

'Why didn't you stick with selling real estate?' Nicole asks Lisa out of the blue, words muffled under her cap.

Lisa's started many things in her life. Many remain unfinished. Unfulfilled. A Bachelor of Arts. A marriage. Jobs. Selling real estate just one of them. Disillusionment derailed some plans. Anger others. Forced her in different directions. Brought about a new purpose.

'I was too honest,' she says.

Nicole lifts her cap from one eye to look at Lisa. She doesn't try to hide her disbelief.

'Buyers liked that about me.' Lisa tries not to sound defensive. 'But it made me a lousy seller.'

'How does honesty fit with what you do now?'

Lisa thinks about the work she does, fitting out properties for sale with furniture packages to enhance their appeal. She does it prettily, but often impractically.

'I provide buyers with the means to imagine. That's all.'

'So you're paid to create an illusion?'

She wants to tell Nicole that the truth isn't always what it's cracked up to be, so why not fiddle with the edges of it, make it more palatable. But she doesn't. Instead, she shrugs and agrees with her. 'I guess so.'

'Hard to believe people can't see through it,' Nicole muses. 'How they let a few baubles and cushions cinch the most expensive deal of their lives.'

Lisa doesn't argue with her. She knows what Nicole's doing. She's trying to pull her character apart. See what new faults she's cultivated over the years. Surely Lisa doesn't have any room inside her for more than those she already carries?

She wonders how much of the anger that flickers inside her comes from the chemistry of her conception, and how much from the steady drip of circumstance and experience. It's been with her for as long as she can remember, so something of it must have been planted like a seed in those first cells.

Sometimes it rumbles softly inside her like distant thunder. Other times it's close and dangerous and sparks like downed powerlines.

Hannah has always sensed it. Lisa thinks it was this that unnerved her as a baby. Made her cower as a child. Embarrassed her throughout adolescence. Then, as soon as she could she escaped it. Made a new home well away from Lisa's, and Matt's, in a share house that not even Lisa could tart up.

Lisa doesn't think either of them deserved such a gentle daughter anyway.

Samantha lifts one foot from the creek, shakes the water from it. 'At least you get to source different baubles,' she says. 'Same shit, different sewer when you keep the books for a plumber.'

Lisa smiles at this. At life.

Later, as they breach the rise of a headland and start the descent, the trees thin and through them Lisa glimpses patches of pale sand. She knows even without being able to see all of it that it's the long beach, and that it curves in a gentle arc all the way round to the next headland.

Long beaches make Lisa think of sex. Think of the way the sand moulds to the shape of the body. How grains of sand drift from pockets and cuffs and seams for weeks later.

Sex was a commodity at school. Traded and bartered for popularity, attention, kudos. Lisa wasn't interested in any of that. But she was interested in sex. How some girls knew, as if by instinct, the postural tweaks and adjustments – chin lifted, thigh turned out, just so – that bestowed them with its pervasive power. She'd watch these courtship performances but never copied. There was something needy about having to work for it.

Lisa ambushed her first lover. No pouty lips or hair flicking required. Or maybe he ambushed her?

She was on a beach holiday with her parents. There were

few other fifteen-year-olds staying at the resort, so she spent a great deal of time on her own. As an only child she was good at this.

Their resort was at one end of a long beach. Lisa would go beachcombing after the tide went out most days. She combed for shells, driftwood and sea glass. She found plenty, kept none. She lost track of time and distance on her hunts. Which was mostly the purpose of them, to take a large chunk out of the long days. She could easily make it to the end of the beach, some two kilometres long, without realising it till she looked up and saw the rocky headland that marked its end just ahead of her.

She was about halfway along the beach this day when a brown-haired boy walked out from a track between the dunes and came onto the beach. He was barefoot and wore unevenly rolled up Levis with ripped knees and an unbuttoned checked shirt that blew open so that she could see his tanned, hairless chest. She doesn't know where it was he had come from or where it was he was going to, but he fell in step with her and she slowed her pace.

He was older than her. Maybe twenty. He spoke of university share houses and seasonal fruit picking and having seen INXS and Duran Duran in concert, of Bob Hawke and Mikhail Gorbachev and the *Rainbow Warrior*. She listened mostly. She didn't talk about her family or school or any of the preoccupations adolescents have. She didn't want to show him how little she'd lived.

Lisa doesn't know if neurochemistry exists between two people, if there is something unseen that attracts one to the other, like sodium attracts chloride, hydrogen does oxygen. But that day, she felt that there was.

Their conversation came easily and naturally to sex.

'Have you?' he asked.

'No,' she said and didn't feel embarrassed to admit it.

Was she being groomed? Possibly. Did she care? No. He was the one. She wanted him.

On soft, dry sand in a dip behind the dunes, Lisa took off her sundress and laid it on the ground. He took off his shirt and laid it over her dress. She thought this chivalrous at the time, but suspects it was something more practical. He took his wallet from his back pocket and removed a condom from inside. She remembers thinking that at least one of them knew what they were doing.

It didn't hurt at all which surprised her. In fact it was the most respectful, gentle and ardent sex she's ever had. A gift. Something given with no known past or any expectation there be a future. They had just that moment. She didn't waste it being shy or self-conscious. She approached it with all the curiosity a new experience deserves. He taught her things about her body she didn't know it capable of. In some ways he spoilt it for later lovers.

Afterwards, they kissed goodbye and he walked on. She walked back. She didn't learn his name and neither did he learn hers.

This glimpse of sand Lisa spots through the trees now doesn't bring back sensuous feelings of unselfish sex. It brings back feelings of confusion, trickery and cunning.

At the time she thought the other two made too much of the man. He was a shapeshifter. And they, the people for whom his deceptions were intended, had decided the shape of him. So just as darkness makes sounds bigger than they really are, Lisa believed Samantha's and Nicole's fear had made the threat of the man greater than it need be. They'd left the door open for this bogeyman to come and go as he pleased. Lisa refused to let him in.

That's how sure of herself she was back then. How stupid.

Lisa looks down the trail to Nicole. She's not striking out for distance between them today. And she pauses to look around more often. Lisa watches as she stops now and casts her eyes up to the canopy. Is she looking for something new, she wonders, or something familiar?

'What have you spotted?' she calls to her.

Nicole looks at her briefly before she walks on without answering. Lisa pauses to scan the land too.

Rocks. Mountains. Trees. Trail. It's difficult for her memory to discern any one of these things as uniquely familiar. But collectively the contour of them forms a picture of having been seen before. She doesn't know if this is because this place is connected with an experience, or if the shape of her life since that experience has connected her with this place. Either way, she feels this land has something of her and it's not likely to ever give it back.

She wonders what the others see when they look around. Maybe the terrain represents something altogether different to each one of them. Courage. Loss. Fragility. Can any of them see just its beauty without also feeling their own pain?

And what shape does the man take in Nicole's and Samantha's minds now? Do they keep the door open to him still, through which he comes and goes? Or are they, like her, able to keep it tightly closed against him?

Lisa might have little physical memory of him now, but what she hasn't been able to shut out is the ugly geography of her own failings in the face of him.

This is the thing that haunts her. Not the man.

LAST NIGHT NICOLE SLEPT POORLY AGAIN. Her body felt sluggish when she set out this morning, older than its forty-four years. Even though the sun has slipped past its midday high, her limbs still carry this earlier lethargy. It has caused her to slow her pace, shorten the gap between her and the others. She isn't sure if this is a good or a bad thing.

It allowed her to hear all that Lisa and Samantha said earlier about anger and forgiveness though. She could have contributed something to their conversation, but didn't, for reasons of charity. She doubts she'd have been as generous to Lisa as Samantha was. Lisa's right. Her anger is the one constant thing about her. And while it lacks nothing in function and form, it's also her Achilles heel.

Despite today's trail being familiar in a distant-through-time kind of way, Nicole feels she's rerouted herself on it somehow. Taken a subversive detour into what she thought was an abandoned past, but which in truth hasn't really been abandoned at all.

When she thinks about the terrain she's crossed, she thinks about how it must hold some impression of her having been here no matter how much time has passed. She broke branches, which must have caused trees and bushes to push in different directions, cast new shadows and with it alter what grew beneath their canopy. Or the rocks she disturbed that found new ground and provided an alternative haven for creatures beneath them. They fashioned hideouts. Forged new trails. Shortcuts. Diversions. These things must have left some imprint of her story.

She thinks in part this is why she's agreed to come back, to have it proved to her that what happened here has been recorded in some way. That the landscape carries if not a memory of it, then at least a scar.

But now that she's here, she knows the truth is something else. While these trees and rocks bare witness to everything that passes before them, they hold no sentient proof of it. And any physical changes she might have brought about have long been integrated into the matrix of the land. Grown over. Supplanted. Erased. Even her mistakes. *Hopefully* her mistakes. She wishes she were a rock or a tree.

Not enough has been erased from the landscape though, or from Nicole's memory, for her not to recognise that they will reach the long beach soon.

But first she must pass the tree where he'd hung her bikini top. Maybe it's the boredom of walking that frees her mind to allow such precise recollections. They are recollections that have become sharper each day. Or maybe this memory is as sharp as it is because of the visceral punch-like response she had when she saw the scant fabric strung from a branch.

Nicole wonders if Lisa's and Samantha's memories have the same precision. She's been tempted to ask them to recall their defining feature of the man. But she expects if any one of them were asked to draw his most distinctive characteristic, then all three of them would come up with a completely different image. Each though, would provide a jigsaw piece of what they'd experienced.

Nicole's image would focus on the wide span of his

hands. The tiny forest of coarse black hairs that grew above the middle knuckle of each finger. She has always imagined these hands as part-animal, part-human. Hands caught in evolutionary confusion.

As it turns out, Nicole doesn't recognise the exact tree where they found her bikini top. It could be any one of a number of tall eucalypts alongside the trail.

The tree was a sapling back then. Now that it's aged more than twenty years, it's quite possible that it's been victim to environmental hazards – bushfires, drought, lightning strikes – which might have stunted it or obliterated it altogether. Or alternatively, it's healthy and thriving and metres taller. Unrecognisable. Like meeting a child at age two and being expected to recognise it again in its mid-twenties.

Nicole looks up into the lush canopy and for a moment she selfishly hopes that the tree has been erased from the landscape and that something purer, something without a history, has taken its place.

She can't stop herself. She pauses when she reaches the spot and looks around. What does she hope to find? Some tatty remnant of red Lycra? Maybe she thinks if she sees something of it, rotted amongst the humus on the forest floor and home to ants, or fibres of it intricately threaded into a bird's nest, then it will confirm that this landscape was marked for her all those years before.

As it is, when she looks around all she sees is nature's colours: greens, browns and greys. Nothing of her at all.

The bush is quiet but Nicole's memories of it shout. Especially those of how she'd yelled 'Leave it!' at Samantha when she reached up with her stick to lift the bikini top down from the branch that day. Her words had carried with enough force to silence the call of a magpie.

Samantha had withdrawn her stick. 'Don't you want it?' she'd asked timidly.

'No!' Nicole didn't need to see close up what he'd done with it.

It took Samantha a moment to see why. To see the brown stains.

Even if it hadn't been smeared with excrement, Nicole wouldn't have reclaimed it. To disown it somehow reduced the violation.

'At least we know he takes a dump every day,' Lisa said.

So blasé. So tough and brave and *stupid*.

Lisa and Samantha pause behind her. They also look up into the trees, tall and reaching with enough branches now to hold hundreds of bikinis.

Why do they search where there's nothing to find? Nicole wonders. Do they hope to find some scrap of their innocent younger selves?

She knows Lisa would have them walk out of here with their previous story erased. A new one written with the soles of their boots. But all stories contain the ground stock of past ones. And the roots of them are like those of trees; they run long and deep.

When no one speaks, Nicole moves on. Her feet cross the ground and the unalterable history for which it's lucky enough to hold no trace.

As Nicole pushes her feet into the squeaky grains of white sand she has a sense of unease. Is it dread? Mounting shame? Fear? She can't be sure, but imagines it's something similar to what people feel when confronted by the figure of their phobia.

There are several sets of footprints on the beach this time. Last time there had been only one. And the tide is on its way out. Just as it had been previously. There is a damp line above where the sea currently reaches. Further up the beach, beyond the high-tide line, the sand is fine, pale and dry. It is strewn with dark scraps of shrivelled kelp, sun-bleached shells and coral, the occasional slipper of parched cuttlefish.

Nicole watches the waves froth along the shore, notices how they push a little less up the beach each time.

They used the tide line previously to figure out how long

it had been since he'd crossed this beach. His footprints were pushed deep into the still-wet sand, less than a metre above the receding sea.

So did this represent half an hour? An hour?

They argued about it. As if it mattered.

Nicole sees now that the length of time each of them offered reflected the extent to which their fear controlled them. She said half an hour. Samantha estimated closer to fifteen minutes. Lisa supported neither.

'Why assume they're even his?' She stabbed the stick she'd taken up to protect herself against him into the centre of one of the footprints. The irony of this gesture still makes Nicole shake her head.

She never understood – still doesn't – why Lisa could recognise the threat of him one minute, but then deny he even existed the next. It was like one part of her fought against the reality of their situation – or refused to be controlled by it at any rate – then this other part, the one that saw the need for them to carry a weapon, presented itself like an actor on a stage. Lisa cast herself as their fearless protector. Postured with toughness. Ignored all the signs that they were being lured into a game.

Nicole never doubted the footprints were the man's. And neither could Lisa in the end. Not just because of the size of them – long, which fit with his tall, lanky frame – or that the heel of them sunk deep into the sand as they would with the large pack he carried. But because not far along they found an arrow drawn in the sand and alongside it the words: *THIS WAY SLUTS*.

He left these tokens – stole things – but mostly he was unseen, only sensed. A phantom. A masquerade for their imagination. Nicole felt the trickery of him though. He knew of the dark places that existed in a girl's mind, the deep pockets of fear they hold. And he knew the ways to evoke them.

The beach is close to two kilometres long. They must walk the length of it to pick up the trail again at the other end.

Nicole holds her hand above her eyes against the sun's glare and looks along it. There are several hikers ahead of them. Each a dark dot in the distance. Mostly they walk in pairs. A group of three form a staggered line about halfway along. The progress of all looks slow in their miniaturised form.

She held her hand to her eyes last time too. So did the others.

'Why can't we see him?' Samantha asked. 'He can't be that far ahead.'

'Maybe he's left the beach. Gone behind the dunes.' Nicole pointed towards the line of coastal dunes that were a buffer to the saltmarsh behind.

'You keep assuming it's him!'

'Who else could it be!' It was from this point on that Nicole's anger started to build. Not just with Lisa and the situation she'd put them in. She was also angry at the tenacious cunning of their stalker.

'I suppose we've got no choice but to go this way.' Samantha said this but made no effort to move off.

'Not if we want to get out of here there isn't.' Nicole struck out first along the beach.

This way sluts.

While it's unarguably the same place, it's an altogether different day. This time the air is still and the sun shines. Last time dark clouds had built up around them. The wind gusted and pushed against their chests. It carried horizontal sheets of fine dry sand with it that stung the front of Nicole's naked legs. The wind snatched at her hair, long then. Tied it in knots. Whipped it against her face. Beach spinifex tumbled past on spiny legs. The sea was whipped into meringue peaks. Silver gulls, beaks to the wind, flapped their wings but went nowhere, till they tilted away and soared downwind with no effort at all.

Nicole had walked head down, shoulders rolled in. Each

step taunted by the footprints that hers overlaid. They were a declaration. A staked claim. *Still here*, they said.

Until they weren't.

About two-thirds of the way along the beach, his footprints just disappeared. There was no right-angled turn to them that led down to the sea or up to the dunes. There was no doubling back or change of course to walk along higher ground.

They just stopped dead.

Nicole pulled up as suddenly as the footprints had. She held her arms out from her sides. 'Stay back.'

She looked either side of the last footprints, two neat imprints positioned side by side in the sand. She walked in a wide arc around them. Lisa mumbled something, which Nicole thought was *Girl Guide*.

For the first time one of them lost it then. Really lost it.

'This is sick!' Samantha cried. 'Fucking sick!' She put her head in her hands, walked a few metres in the direction they'd just come from, turned and walked several metres in an altogether different direction. It was as though she sought a way out.

Nicole watched Samantha do this not knowing what to do. Samantha eventually stopped pacing, dropped heavily to her knees and made big, hitching sobs into her hands.

Lisa took her pack off and went to Samantha then. She let her sob against her, till she'd cried herself out.

Today, only the sun bites at her legs and their long shadows reach across the sand in front of them. They walk in pace order again, Nicole in front, Samantha at the rear. Every now and then Lisa draws nearer and Nicole steps on the shadow of her head.

'Bully,' she jokes from behind.

Nicole increases her pace to lengthen the gap between them.

It's tough going on the beach. Nicole's probably the fittest of the three, but even she feels the difficulty of walking on the soft sand. The weight of her pack pushes her boots deep into it. She has to forcefully lift each foot out of the depression it makes to clear it before she can take another step. They aren't even halfway along and already her thighs burn with the effort and she can feel the gritty chafe of sand in her socks. She thinks about Samantha and how much more difficult it must be for her. And all for what? This folly of Lisa's?

Nicole looks over her shoulder. Samantha has dropped well back. It's a demoralising gap. She stops and waits for her. So does Lisa. 'You're killing her,' Nicole says.

She immediately regrets her words because Lisa looks at her as though she's been slapped.

In a flurry of decisive movements, Lisa releases the buckles securing her pack and writhes out of her load.

'I'm going to take some of her gear,' she says and walks back to Samantha.

It's Nicole's turn to feel smacked with shame. She's just been telling herself she's the fittest, but hasn't once considered lightening the load of the weakest.

They always had one another's backs once. There was no weakest or strongest. No better or worse. Theirs wasn't like other groups of girls. Groups that fluxed with shifting alliances. Girls cast out, isolated, often abruptly. Groups only able to remain intact if each of its members thought and acted the same. Not one of them chose the other along lines of beauty or athleticism or popularity. They were misfits united through their differences. They only had to be themselves. That's what made their friendship strong.

Nicole unbuckles her pack and lowers it to the sand. She watches Samantha as Lisa walks towards her. Her eyes are cast down. When Lisa reaches her, Sam lifts her head and smiles. It could be a front, but she seems to brighten with Lisa's approach. Her previously strained features soften.

The two walk side by side then. Lisa chats easily. Nicole hears her coax her on. And Samantha seems to limp less for the attention. Frowns less. They walk close together. They seem at ease with one another.

Nicole has an unrecognisable pang as she watches the two of them approach. It feels heavy like regret. Pressing like sadness. It might even be jealousy. It makes her realise just how far removed from them she's become.

Nicole makes room in her pack for some of Sam's gear. She's reluctant to give anything up to begin with, but Nicole takes it from her anyway. She doesn't notice the extra weight after a while. It soon becomes a part of her own.

ONCE AGAIN SHE'S PROPPED UP BY others who are stronger. Fitter. More capable. She was the first to cry last time. Blubbered like a baby. Left tears and snot down the front of Lisa's shirt.

But those disappearing footprints unnerved Samantha more than anything else that had happened till then. Leaving his shit on a rock was more schoolboy than psycho. Stealing someone's bikini top and using it for toilet paper was disgusting. But the evaporation of his trail, that had all the hallmarks of some kind of evil wizardry. A manipulative force more powerful than the force the three of them combined could hope to project. This was the point at which Samantha realised they were no match for him.

Nicole debunked the myth that he was magical though. As pragmatic as ever, she looked for ways to solve the puzzle of the missing footprints. She walked slowly up the beach towards the dune line. She studied the ground carefully, paused at the sea-litter strewn along the high water mark. She scaled the dune and stood on this higher ground, brown ponytail flayed about by the wind. Legs wide, she slowly scanned from left to right. She looked like an explorer. When she came back, she reported that she could see inland for quite a way. She hadn't been able to see him she said, but she found his footprints going down the other side of the dune.

'He's covered his tracks then, leading up to the dunes?' Lisa asked.

'Looks like it,' Nicole said.

And once they looked round rationally, they found some of his poorly filled in footprints in the sand. It didn't make Samantha feel any better though. It only confirmed that whatever agenda he might have started his hike with had surely shifted to something else altogether.

The beach walk is as much of a low point for Samantha this time as it was previously. To walk on soft sand is to walk through molasses. Each time one foot sinks down, the other must be forcefully pulled out. Her thigh muscles quiver and burn with the effort. She doesn't dare stop in case her legs let her down completely and she drops to the ground in a pathetic display of hopelessness. She talks to her legs. Scolds them. Calls them fat. Lazy. Useless. She encourages them. Congratulates them. But still they tremble.

Fatigue doesn't help. She's not slept well since they set off three days ago. Her thin sleeping mat doesn't cushion much against the lumps and bumps of pebbles and sticks and clods of dirt she thinks she'd adequately cleared away before she'd erected her tent. Maybe she's a princess, her mattress stippled with peas. She smiles at this delicate image of herself.

Last time they'd shared a tent. This time they have their own. Take away the fact that they've not seen each other for more than twenty years, and Samantha's not sure that she prefers the solo arrangement. She'd be happy to share her tent if it also meant sharing the night sounds. She startles awake often. Then can't remember where she is. And once she does, she must remind herself that it is now, not then. Her nerves are frayed by then though, so it's difficult to get back to sleep.

A kangaroo woke her first last night. She heard it bound through the campground. Once she recognised what it was, she listened to the force of its springy hind legs, the brief pause between landfalls. She counted its fading leaps – one, two, three, four, five – until they disappeared.

And in the quiet solitude that followed, memories pushed through. Last night, thoughts of her youngest son came to her.

For as long as she can remember he has wanted a girlfriend. Not a girl friend. A girlfriend.

'I'd hold hands with her,' he'd say to Samantha as a small boy. 'All the time. And maybe kiss her. Like this.'

And he'd gently pat her cheek with his lips to demonstrate.

'What I like best about girls is they smell like lollies.' He was still young enough to sit up on his knees on his chair at the breakfast bar.

'Is that right?'

'Uh-huh. Honey bears mostly. Some smell like musk sticks but.'

They'd smelt of sweat and blood and fear when they were here last time. Candy to the man?

'Dad? Are wives hard to find?' he asked Harry one day.

'Sure are, mate. Good ones, anyway.'

'Where'd you find Mum?'

'In a nightclub.'

He took a moment to do the maths on his fingers. 'I can't find one at a nightclub for eleven years!'

'You might find yours some place else,' Harry offered. 'Maybe at the park.'

Picked up like dropped coins. Pocketed.

'Girls have a say in it you know,' Samantha told him. 'And some girls might not want to be *found* straight away.'

'Girls *always* wanna be found, Mum. The ones at school do anyway. Especially Alice. She's the worst hider. I *always* find her first because she doesn't even *try* to hide. Then she sticks to me like a *leech* and doesn't even help while I look for the others.' He clamped his arms straight by his sides to demonstrate Alice's closeness.

Samantha stood on the other side of the breakfast bar this

day. She was peeling an apple for him, trying to do it in one long ribbon, the challenge he always gave her. 'Meeting a girl isn't the same as a game of hide and seek.'

'Sometimes it is,' Harry said and laughed. 'There'll be some girls you'll wanna hide from, mate.'

'Like Alice?'

'Your Alice sounds like she might be trouble, so maybe.'

Samantha looked up from what she was doing. The ribbon of apple skin broke and fell to the floor. 'And there are men that women need to hide from.' She stabbed the air in front of her son with the knife. 'Don't be one of them.'

'Whoa!' He reared back, nearly toppled his chair.

What kind of mother points a knife at her seven-year-old child, practically threatens him with it?

'Reckon we need to hide from Mum,' he said to Harry and giggled behind his hand.

'She's armed and dangerous, all right.'

Her son's laugh was young, squeaky. Harry's was deep and old enough to know better.

Her youngest son is seventeen now. He no longer expresses an interest in finding a wife. And Samantha expects he's kissed more than a girl's cheek. She hopes he treats them well.

Her younger self probably reached the end of the beach walk in worse shape than the older version of her does now. Samantha had looked up to the next boulder-strewn headland they were to climb. It was no higher than the many others they'd had to walk over, but in that moment it seemed insurmountable.

She had thrown her stick onto the sand, unbuckled her pack and let it thump down at her feet. She then slumped onto a rock, rested her forearms across her thighs and lowered her head onto them. She was spent. Done in. She just wanted to sleep, the deep, deep sleep of a child. To go home.

'Come on, Sam,' Lisa coaxed. 'You can do it.'

Lisa nudged Samantha's leg gently with her stick. Samantha still recalls how this action sent a rush of heat from somewhere deep in her belly all the way up into her head. She snapped her head up and glared at Lisa. Her face must have looked fierce because Lisa took a step back.

'Can I, Lisa?' she shouted. 'Can I *really* fucking do it?' What a spiteful, hateful voice. But she hadn't stopped there. 'Maybe I could have done it, if just for once … just *one* fucking time in your life you had the brains to let it go!'

Samantha still can't believe that she felt a moment of pure hate for Lisa then. The same girl who only a short time before had comforted her, let her leave a trail of snot and tears down her T-shirt. The girl, who now, more than twenty years on, has taken some of the weight from her pack because she still wants to believe Samantha can do it. The rush of hate had left her as quickly as it arrived and silence crashed in around her, broken only by the heft of her breath.

For all her feistiness, Lisa said nothing. She just looked at Samantha, her face impassive. Unsurprised. She hadn't even looked taken aback or upset. For a while Samantha thought Lisa must have been in the midst of gathering the force to unleash her own anger, but nothing came. It was as though she'd simply allowed Samantha's words to wash over her. Like they were intended for someone else, someone behind or beyond her. But not even this was right. Because in that calm quiet, what Samantha eventually came to realise was that Lisa's silence said, *Yes, I should have let it go*.

Samantha still doesn't know if it was exhaustion or fear that made her say the things she did. Probably a combination of both. Whatever it was though, regret soon took over and she was close to tears again. She turned away from the others and hauled her pack back onto her shoulders. She hadn't wanted them to see just how out of control she was. Just how weak.

'Sorry,' she mumbled to the ground somewhere near Lisa's feet.

Lisa gently pushed her backpack with her hand, propelled Samantha forward. 'You can shout at me all you like if it gets you over this fucking mountain.'

**

The memory of the ascent is still strong to Samantha. 'It doesn't look any easier,' she says to Lisa now.

'It will be,' Lisa says, with the same conviction she'd had last time.

Samantha thinks it was their collective shame that contributed most to the splintering of their friendship. There were too many hateful incidents like that one which had to be put behind them; too many assumptions about their friendship that had to be discarded. How are they to step over the litter of their past mistakes?

At the time, Samantha believed they were acting outside of themselves. That their behaviour was beyond anything they could control. But she knows now that this was an excuse, a poor justification for crossing the line between civility and barbarism.

And poor Lisa. She ended up proving herself capable of taking any measure of abuse for or from either one of them as their control slipped steadily away.

It's EASY NOW FOR LISA TO see how successful he'd been at terrorising them. He gradually took their courage, then their sense of reason and finally struck a blow at the very foundations of their friendship. He played them like puppets. Pulled their strings. Made them dance.

He always had the advantage. Like any good hunter, he observed his quarry. Came to understand something about them. Lisa expects his binoculars were trained on them many times. Saw their confusion when they came to the dead-end trail of his footprints. Probably laughed out loud, especially if he witnessed Samantha's meltdown in the face of it. Saw later how stress and fatigue allowed them to forget who it was they were fighting as they started to fight against one another instead. She imagines he rejoiced at the way things unravelled.

And yet, while he observed all of these things about them, by the third night they still hadn't laid eyes on him since the car park. What a slippery bastard he was.

It takes Lisa a while to adjust to the extra weight of Samantha's gear. Those few items of clothing pushed down on top of her own makes a bigger difference than she expected. Nicole must notice it more. She has Samantha's tent now, secured at the base of her pack along with her own. She's also taken the first-aid kit and Samantha's spare bottle of water. She's jammed both into a webbed side pocket on the outside of her pack.

Samantha refused to give up anything initially.

'I can *do it*,' she said and went to walk on. She held herself tall and proud, and in agony, Lisa expects.

It was Nicole who eventually made her change her mind. She put her hand out to Samantha. Rested it gently on her arm as she went to walk away.

'You did it for me once. Remember?'

Lisa felt an unexpected and inflated sense of happiness at Nicole's words.

Samantha paused. They exchanged a look of understanding, one that spoke deeply about a shared experience. Without saying a word, Samantha lowered her pack onto the sand. Allowed them to separate out some of her gear.

To think back on those disappearing footprints, reminds Lisa of her inability to accept facts. She still marvels at her stupidity in not fully acknowledging the threat of the man, despite all the signs indicating otherwise.

But denial, no matter that the facts placed before her are often damning, is a fault she seems unable to shake. Matt is no better. Neither of them took responsibility for how much they damaged Hannah. They both still suffer the consequences of their neglect.

Hannah's relationship with her mother is on her terms now. Lisa rings her often, but sees her less so.

'I've got exams coming up,' Hannah said during last week's call, when Lisa asked to see her before she came away.

'Not now though? You're not actually *in* exam block now are you?'

'No, but I'm *studying* for them. No good studying for them in the week I *sit* them.'

'No. I suppose not.'

There was a moment of silence in which Lisa didn't bother

to argue against her daughter's logic, only to wonder at the honesty of it.

She hasn't seen Hannah for four weeks now. She misses her. Worries that the time between visits will only get longer.

Lisa's like an awkward boy with a crush on a too-good-for-him girl around her daughter. A boy that's desperate to be noticed but knows that he's punching above his weight.

'When do you finish them?'

'Soon enough.'

Never soon enough. Never enough.

'What's with this walk thing you're doing anyway?'

How to tell her daughter it was for her as much as it was for Lisa?

'It's a stroll down memory lane.' Lisa laughed at her own understatement.

'From where I sit, there's not much of it worth strolling down.'

Hannah didn't sound bitter. She sounded weary, wearier than you'd expect in a nineteen-year-old. And even though she couldn't see her daughter, Lisa pictured her lethargy at their conversation. She imagined Hannah slumped in her chair, maybe she even studied a fingernail while she spoke or doodled on a notepad.

'You wouldn't know this particular lane,' Lisa said. 'It was before your time.'

'Were you different then?'

Lisa didn't answer straight away. She thought about lying. Telling Hannah she was. Telling her about her two dearest, irreplaceable friends, women her daughter has never met. How she believed they brought out the best in her, until they didn't. How she hopes to have the qualities of their friendship returned to her and all the goodness that might come with it if it can be.

'No. If anything, I was probably worse.'

'Jesus. And you wanna spend time with *that* person again?'

'Yes, and I'm going to tell her off. Make her change her ways.' Lisa laughed her silly, trivialising laugh once again.

'Good luck with that.'

This silenced Lisa for a time. Hannah was getting braver with her criticisms. Lisa suspects her daughter's newly found independence has opened her mind to alternative ways of being in the world. There was little that Lisa feared, but the possibility of not being a part of Hannah's life terrified her.

'Listen … do your walk and I'll see you when you get back. Okay?'

Lisa knew the *okay* wasn't a question. It was an assertion. Time was up.

She kept Hannah on the line a little longer though, as long as she could, asked after her boyfriend.

'He's good.'

'Studying too?'

'Uh-huh. The whole house is. It's like a mausoleum. Only we're still breathing.'

Her pretty, witty, scarred girl.

'I love you.' Lisa tells her daughter this every time before she ends their call.

'You too.'

Hannah's witnessed too much. Heard too much.

You selfish bastard!

Bitch!

Fuck you!

The whistle and shatter of cups.

She's seen the ease with which the two people who made her can tear one another apart.

When Lisa looks at Nicole she sees something of her gently guarded daughter. Both are damaged. Both have a loss of faith.

When Nicole said, 'I need spacc,' at the end of this hike last time, Lisa wasn't surprised that she meant permanently. What does surprise her though is how quickly and easily she'd given it to her. But she doesn't think she allowed it out of respect for Nicole. Lisa thinks it was the only way she knew how to hide from her own worst self.

Hannah didn't ask her mother to give her space, she just took it. Now, Lisa has to find a way to encourage Hannah to allow her to fill it again, before the habit of distance effortlessly slides into estrangement.

Before they tackle the climb, they take off their boots and bang them upside-down on rocks to remove the sand from inside. Samantha peels off her socks as well and inspects her feet. The blister plasters have lifted at the edges and sand has worked its way under them. Lisa knows they'll be more abrasive than cushioning. So must Nicole.

'I'll re-dress them.' Nicole takes the first-aid gear from her pack. She kneels down on the sand in front of Samantha.

Lisa sits on a rock away from them and watches as Nicole takes one of Samantha's feet in her hands and wipes the sand from the tops and sides of it with long, gentle strokes. She removes it from between each of Samantha's toes with her finger; runs her flat palm across the sole. She then carefully removes the blister plaster from her heel, clears the sand from the skin beneath it and applies a new one. She rests the foot back on a rock out of the sand then starts on the other foot. She handles each as though it is a precious thing.

Lisa's overcome by the tenderness of this scene. It's more like watching an anointment than someone attending first aid. She's equally moved by the fact that Samantha allows Nicole to do it.

Nicole reapplies the final blister plaster then turns each of Samantha's socks inside out. She slaps them against a rock several times to release the sand caught in the weave. She hands them back to her, turned once more in the right way. She helps Samantha then, who strains against the grip of tight hamstrings to reach forward, to pull each back over her feet.

Lisa feels an uncharacteristic sting of tears as she watches.

She must blink fast to hold them back. She doesn't want the others to notice. But little still gets past Nicole.

'If you're going to cry about it,' she says, not looking at Lisa, 'I'll do yours too.'

Lisa sniffs loudly and shakes her head.

She's not sure what the tears are for. Whether they're for what they've lost or what she hopes they'll regain.

This time the climb takes them through a damaged terrain. Bushfires have ravaged the area and the landscape is deeply scarred. Some trees have blackened hollows burnt into their trunks but despite these deep wounds their canopies continue to flourish. Other trees haven't been so lucky. They are without bark, their wood the colour of old bones, and their barren branches push into the sky like broken swords. Strident saplings fill the gaps now, and the charred branches of older, surviving trees hold up bushy fists of succulent regrowth.

The landscape is parched. Fit only for survivors. *Xanthorrhoea australis* abound. The height of some of these native grass trees indicates their great age. Their bristled, fire-blackened trunks speak of their hardiness. They are indomitable. Sentries to this ancient land.

Small drop-tail lizards scarper across the track, others bravely hold their position and stare up at Lisa from rocks. The gravelly trail is pocked with jumping jack ant nests. She doesn't dare stand for long in the one spot in case these aggressive armies take hold of her with their nasty yellow pincers.

All the headlands they've crossed have been characterised by weathered and fractured granite. This part of the trail weaves between these monolithic boulders. These once molten upsurges push out of the ground like the big blunt heads of sperm whales. The track zigzags between them. The gap between boulders is narrow in places and because she is as deep with a pack on her back as she is wide, there's no turning side on, she has to push through as best she can.

Lisa thinks back to how jittery Nicole was as she walked between these boulders last time. She led as she almost always did, so Lisa saw when she startled, which was often and easily. She looked up regularly. Sometimes she stopped altogether, ear tilted skyward. Attentive.

'What's up?' Lisa asked her at one stage, even though she could guess.

These towering rocks, with their flat spectator platforms and shadowy corridors, unnerved Nicole.

'Nothing,' she had said and moved on.

This time Lisa runs her hand across the rough surface of the boulders as she passes them. She marvels at their longevity. Previously, she'd not considered there to be anything marvellous about them at all. The only good thing was that they'd offered some protection from the wind that gusted on and off all of that day.

Animals go crazy in the wind. Birds hide their heads under their wings. Dogs whimper and go to their kennels. Horses get spooked enough to roll the whites of their eyes, and shy or bolt and get their legs tangled in wire fences.

They were more like horses.

The wind whistled through the tree canopy. It took leaves with it and made branches creak and scrape. Sometimes Lisa imagined words travelling on the wind. *Slut. Cunt. Bitch.* Sometimes the wind laughed.

After a while, Lisa became more like Nicole. She looked up often and startled easily.

Near the top of the headland, the tall boulders are replaced with vast flat slabs of granite. As Lisa walks across them, she wonders how deeply they penetrate the earth. These grey expanses are five, sometimes ten metres across so she pictures them to be like icebergs where the greater part of them is underground, out of sight. Hardy heath and bracken grows right to the edges of these subterranean boulders, despite the shallowness of the soil.

Last time it was a disorientating terrain. As much from

their lack of bushwalking experience as how few people walked the trail back then to keep it worn and easily identified. The granite only added to their confusion. A couple of times they walked round the perimeter of these masses of flat stone looking for where the track began again. Sometimes Samantha panicked during these searches.

'Are you sure this is it?' she asked more than once when they located what was sometimes a poorly defined entry point to the trail again. 'What if it's just an animal trail and we lose the real one altogether?'

To appease her, Lisa or Nicole would walk along it for a way, assess if it petered out or was the real thing.

'Yep! This is it!'

Lisa beamed too enthusiastically at these times, pleased to offer Samantha something reliable. It didn't matter that all she was really offering her was the same shitty trail in the same shitty location with the same creep out there somewhere who was hell bent on tormenting them. But Lisa had to hold on to the fact that it was *their* trail too, and eventually it would take them home.

Except the time when neither Lisa nor Nicole were able to offer Samantha any trail at all.

They reached a stretch of stone that was long and narrow. It curved in a gentle arc from end to end as though mapping the very contour of the earth. Typically the undergrowth grew thick to its edges. The usual heath and bracken mostly, plus scrappy melaleucas and native grass trees, their spiky filaments fanned out like enormous fibre optic lamps. The shaded areas of granite were covered in lacy green lichen and clumps of spongy moss. The vegetation was undisturbed whatever direction they looked.

They walked the perimeter of the expanse of stone trying to find where the trail began again, as they'd had to do in similar situations previously. But they could only find the track from which they'd approached, not the one along which they were to continue.

'It's got to be here somewhere,' Nicole said.

Lisa had felt the frustration she could hear in Nicole's voice. The track's disappearance was as bewildering to her as it would be if someone had tried to tell her that one plus one no longer equalled two.

They walked around that marooned slab of rock several times – clockwise and counter-clockwise – looking for what they thought had to be there. They found what looked like the trail, a narrow worn path that was mostly overgrown with bracken. But when Nicole followed it into the scrub, about three metres in she stood like a half person in the waist-high bracken and raised her arms in a helpless gesture.

'Must be an animal trail,' she said. 'It peters out to nothing.'

'Maybe we went wrong further back?' Samantha suggested. 'And we haven't really been following the right track at all. Maybe we haven't been for ages.'

They'd had to weave their way through so much stone, followed a trail that was little more than a thin strip of gravel in a number of places, but Lisa knew it was undeniably *there*. She shook her head.

'No,' she said. 'We haven't. The track's been obvious to this point.'

And it had been. She was sure of it. She thought back to how the trail widened again once they'd finished going through the last of the tall boulders, how the gravelly line of it clearly curved and crested with the topography. She knew she hadn't imagined any of that.

'It's like his bloody footprints,' Samantha said, and Lisa could hear the panic rise in her voice again. 'It's just disappeared.'

'It has *not*,' Nicole snapped. 'We just need to find it.'

'But we've looked.'

Lisa thought Samantha was about to cry again. For a brief, sickening moment she had a vision of slapping her hard if she did.

'We just need to keep looking.' Lisa tried to keep her voice level, but she could hear the edge to it, the bite of impatience.

Samantha said nothing. Instead, she walked clockwise round the flat stretch of granite again, but Lisa could tell she was only going through the motions of searching. Her gaze was on her feet, whereas Nicole kicked at the scrub that surrounded the rock to see what was beneath. Samantha looked more like a shuffling monk. All she lacked was a prayer wheel.

Lisa felt her temper build. She didn't trust herself not to release it, so she walked back down the track the way they'd come to check if there was something they'd missed on the way up.

The thick bracken obscured the track in parts. It scratched at her bare legs as she pushed through it with her stick. She ran her other hand across the succulent tops as she went.

She could still hear Nicole talking, mostly to herself Lisa assumed, as she couldn't hear Samantha reply. 'This is stupid. It's *got* to be here.'

What was stupid was that they'd allowed themselves to be unnerved so much by the games the man played. What was he really other than an ego-massaging fool? She imagined how he'd probably been laughing at them. She expects he thought himself clever. Superior. But she knew the truth. Or she thought she still knew it then. It was easy to be a clever coward, hidden away as he was. Not ever having to confront anyone over his actions. Everything he'd done to that point had been done on the sly, anonymously. Lisa feared him less because of it. She could pretend he wasn't real.

She stopped and looked around. Hoped to find some clue to where the trail had gone. The tea-tree and melaleucas either side of her were gnarled and twisted and their branches grew off at contorted angles in this higher, exposed ground. Branches had broken off and lay on the ground in untidy twiggy bundles. The papery bark of the melaleucas reminded her of sunburnt skin, the way the creamy bark split and shed from their trunks. She imagined peeling it away, layer by layer, just as she'd peeled the skin from her shoulders as a child.

What a messy place. But then she started to see beauty in the disorder. The way the trees had adapted and rerouted themselves out of necessity. The bends and twists to trunks and branches needed to accommodate the trees standing alongside. Others were forced in new directions by the wind, or their attempts to reach for the sun. It was a landscape configured for survival not aesthetics.

Lisa turned and started to walk slowly back towards the others. She was in no rush. Samantha's panic was tedious. Nicole's Girl Guide diligence wearing.

She cast her eyes around the growth either side of the track. Looked for gaps in the undergrowth. Places where a trail might wend its way between the trees. On her right was a collection of dead branches that had crushed the undergrowth. But she could see that the bracken and heath it covered was still green.

A new fall, she thought. *Very recent*.

She lifted a branch from the top, threw it aside and pushed through the undergrowth a little further to reach the next branch. She threw this one aside too.

Then she thought: *Here is order*.

This was not nature culling its dead wood. This was coward's work.

She walked in further and threw a third, then a fourth and fifth branch aside. She used her stick to lift the bracken crushed beneath to reveal the trail. She walked further in amongst the trees and the trail became obvious again.

She suspected others had been fooled by this subtle veer in the track, walked the fifty or so metres on to the large, flat slab of granite. Created a false trail in the process. She wondered how many before them had lapped that expanse of stone looking for what wasn't there. Wondered if they'd felt as bewildered and disorientated as they had.

Lisa placed her hand on the papery trunk of a melaleuca

and paused before going back to get the others. A gust of wind pushed through the scraggly tree and with it she caught a writhing movement of something hanging from one of the tree's upper branches. The movement startled her. She reared back. Almost fell under the weight of her pack. She backed slowly away from the tree.

It was the bright yellow tent rope that caught her eye first when the wind gusted again. She registered what was tied at the end of it seconds later.

The water dragon was a juvenile. Its spiny scales along its back were still short. Its head and feet were too large for its body. It curled its tapered, muscular tail upwards and kicked furiously with its hind legs in an attempt to free itself. But the yellow cord was tied securely behind its forelegs and in front of its distended belly. It was clearly distressed. Its cheeks were puffed out and its throat was blotched with orange, blue and yellow. It thrashed about again. But its efforts seemed weak.

'Sick bastard.'

Lisa leant her stick up against the tree, took off her pack and rested it on the ground. She reached up to the branch where the other end of the tent rope was tied and released the knot. She lowered the restrained reptile gently onto the ground. Once there it didn't even try to lift its head or run off. It was exhausted. It must have been hanging from the tree for a while. Up close, she could see the rapid flutter of its heart beneath its leathery skin.

The cord was tied round it with a firm reef knot. Tentatively, she tried to loosen it. She picked at it with her fingernail. But it was too tight. She got cross at her timidness, for holding back from this small creature. What could it do to her?

She lifted the hem of her T-shirt and used it to carefully grip the reptile. She could feel its sharp, spiny scales through the fabric, along with the quick pulse of its heart. It fought against her initially, tried to claw her with the long toes on its hind legs. Later, she would notice that it had left a thin, red scratch on her stomach.

She worked at the knot with her free hand till she'd loosened it. She set the water dragon down amongst the undergrowth at the side of the trail then and sat back on her heels and watched it, willed it to run off. But it remained motionless, head and body pressed low to the ground. She couldn't tell if it was injured, exhausted or too terrified to move.

Lisa hid the yellow tent rope deep amongst the bracken, not wanting Nicole or Sam to find it. She hoisted her pack onto her back again, collected her stick and returned to the main trail.

'Found it!' she called, waving at them.

She wouldn't tell them about what else she'd found. Another secret, where previously she'd kept none.

THE TRAIL WENDS GENTLY DOWN, THEN across a flat, exposed region between two headlands. It is a cupped palm of land. Nicole remembers it as the only wide-open space they encountered previously. The trail is easily seen reaching into the distance; it cuts a narrow silver ribbon through the thick, squat scrub and grasses. Every now and again it disappears inside a clump of taller trees, then pops into view again on the other side, whereupon it continues its serpentine course to the next rise. The plain has areas of soft grasses which change colour as the breeze shifts across them like velour stroked against the pile.

Oddly, this section of the trail had calmed Nicole when they reached it last time. She could see all around her. There were no boulders or crests or bends around or behind which someone could hide. The going was easy. The ground was hard but even. She could trot along it if she had to. That calm was hijacked though, about three-quarters of the way across.

Nicole remembers the urgency in Samantha's voice when she called, 'Wait up!'

She turned to see what was wrong, expecting Samantha had stumbled or seen a snake. But Samantha looked back in the direction from where they'd just come, hand over her eyes against the sun, her elbow wide at her side.

'What's wrong now?' Lisa asked.

'I saw him.'

'Where?' Lisa drew the word out on an impatient sigh.

'Back there.' Samantha indicated to a point several hundred metres back. 'I'm pretty sure it was him.'

'Pretty sure?'

Nicole shaded her eyes from the sun as well and scanned the trail all the way back to the hill they'd made their way down only an hour before. She trained her eyes up and down the length of it, paused where it disappeared behind trees, waited to see if someone came out the other side. She couldn't see a soul.

'I saw a tall shape in a dark top,' Samantha said. 'Then it disappeared behind that clump of trees.'

Lisa lost her earlier impatience then. She became animated. 'Okay,' she said. 'Let's find a place to hide and wait for him.' She turned and looked again in the direction they'd been heading. 'There,' she said and pointed to an outcrop of tall, thick scrub not far ahead. 'We'll wait for him behind that.'

'*Wait* for him or *hide* from him?' Nicole asked.

Lisa looked directly at Nicole as she edged past her on the narrow track. '*Wait* of course.' Lisa's stick struck the ground with force as she strode off.

'Are you going to *ambush* him?' Samantha called after her.

'I don't know what I'm going to do.'

'No,' Nicole said. 'You never do.'

Lisa ignored her.

'Maybe it wasn't even him,' Samantha said.

Nicole admired her optimism.

They followed Lisa, but Nicole looked over her shoulder often.

Up until then everything had indicated that he was always ahead of them. But had he been, really? How could they know given this was the first time any one of them had actually sighted him. Ahead or behind made no difference anyway. Nicole felt the threat of him no matter where he was.

'Don't crush the bushes as you walk in,' Lisa said as they reached her chosen hideout. 'Step over them. Let's beat him at his own game.'

Game? Nicole remembers thinking. But that's what it still was to Lisa at that stage. It didn't matter that there weren't any rules.

They made a high-stepped detour off the track till they were concealed behind a line of thick scrub. They took off their packs, laid them flat on the ground out of sight then nestled close to the ground behind the screen of mostly heath, tea-tree and banksia.

They waited.

Well, Nicole and Samantha waited. Lisa spent a few minutes gathering together fist-sized rocks, which she set out beside her. She then pushed peepholes through the branches, which allowed her to see back down the trail. Her stick lay on the ground beside her.

Stillness wasn't normally Lisa's strength. In boring classes at school she fidgeted with trapped energy. She drew intricate geometric designs in her exercise books or sharpened every pencil in her pencil case to a fine point. She could never just sit there. But she mastered stillness this day. She lay on the ground like a sphinx beside Nicole. She pushed her hair behind her ears, maximised the function of those dainty cups. Her breath was calm. Her hands steady. Nicole envied her. Samantha lay at Nicole's other side and pressed in against her. She doesn't know if Sam sought her protection or if being close made her feel braver and stronger than they really were. She felt a slight tremor in Samantha. Or maybe it was Nicole who shook.

It's strange the discomfort an alert body allows the attention to overlook. It was only later that Nicole saw the deep red dimples left on the skin of her knees and elbows from the stones and gravel that dug into them, or the ant-bite on her calf. She had been too preoccupied with sound. The wind created a singsong of auditory frauds. Creaks and scrapes sounded like boots dragging along the trail. The sigh of leaves became the sigh of a man. The uncertainty of these noises jangled Nicole's nerves like the chalkboard scrape of fingernails. The only sounds she trusted as real were those inside her own body, the throb and whoosh of her heart and blood.

'Just let him go past,' Nicole whispered to Lisa.

Lisa ignored her.

'Lisa?'

'Shh.'

When it came there was no mistaking the crunch of gravel. The whispering chafe of trouser leg against trouser leg. Samantha stiffened beside her and Nicole felt how her friend's warm breath came in shallow pants against her shoulder. Instinctively, Nicole pressed lower to the ground. Lisa wrapped her hand around a rock.

They watched him pass. His stride was long. His back was straight under the weight of his backpack, his shoulders squared. He walked with his thumbs casually hooked under the chest straps of his pack. His bent elbows pulsed softly at his sides with each step, like saddlebags.

Nicole knows the three of them walked with the uneven gait of the fatigued. Their shoulders sagged under the weight of their heavy packs. Lisa and Samantha had dark rings under their eyes. The frown lines on their foreheads and the creases in the skin under their chins were filled with grime. It made them appear older, more worn, than they were. Nicole didn't doubt she looked the same. In comparison, the man moved with ease. He seemed fresh and energised and capable.

Nicole rested her hand on Lisa's arm. She doesn't know why she did this any more than she knew why Samantha pressed closer to her. Was it to restrain Lisa if needed, or to take courage from her? Nicole felt both were needed so she left her hand there. She thought the fact that Lisa allowed her to confirmed Lisa's own uncertainty about what she dared do. Nicole foolishly believed that despite her stick and stones they'd reached the limit of her bravado.

The man stopped suddenly about twenty metres further along from where they hid. He unclipped the metal water bottle from his belt, unscrewed the lid and took several sips. He returned it to his belt clip again then hooked his thumbs back under the chest straps of his pack. He was in no hurry to leave. He looked slowly from west to east. His gaze skipped across where they hid and back along to where he'd just come. On his return gaze though, Nicole thought he paused when his eyes reached their position. Just for a single breath, half a dozen rapid heartbeats, nothing more. She wondered if she'd imagined it.

He looked up to the broody sky then and Nicole saw how his beard had come through dark under his small chin. He closed his eyes and smiled up at the clouds.

'Perfect isolation,' he said, loud enough for them to hear.

When he looked down again, it was directly at where they were lying.

Nicole saw then that he wasn't as fresh and at ease as she'd thought. He was dark around the eyes too. Fatigued, she imagined, from his commitment to the long hunt. But his dark eyes shone as they flickered across the line of scrub where they hid and his mouth twisted into an amused line.

He laughed as he walked away, a low, playful rumble.

Then he was ahead of them again. Nicole never doubted that he knew it.

There are no German backpackers at the camping ground this time. Instead, there is a remarkably quiet outdoor education school group, three couples and a family of five, the parents of whom Nicole imagines are trying to de-screen their children by forcing them to go cold turkey in the great outdoors.

Nicole arrived here on low ebb last time. The way things disappeared – her bikini, the tent rope, footprints, the trail

– had been bad enough, shifted her sense of reality in unsettling ways. She no longer knew who or what she could trust – about her friends, humanity, even herself. But then seeing him again had made him real once more.

She supposes all three of them fell apart in their own way. How else to explain that each became unpredictable? A bit wild-eyed crazy. She thinks it probably started when Lisa insisted they arm themselves. Just to hold that stick – that weapon – had put Nicole on guard. Made her view her surroundings with suspicion, to always anticipate the worst. That stick came to symbolise her diminishing faith in the general goodness of people, to include the goodness she'd always believed existed within her. She no longer believed that he, or they, would follow the rules. The world had suddenly stopped working the way she thought it did or should.

The rules are laid out for all to see this time. Written ones. Each campsite has them. There are green tent symbols on timber posts. Some have red lines through them. There are others that read *Keep Out – Area Under Regeneration*. There are signs in the long-drop toilets that ask for organic waste only, for the toilet lid to be left down after use and the door closed upon leaving. There are others again requesting that wildlife not be fed, that fires not be lit, that hikers keep to the track.

Nicole wonders if it would have made a difference had these rules been here last time. Would they have reminded him that he was just one member of a larger, supposedly cohesive social order? In her heart though, she knows that no amount of signage requesting people not do this or that would have made any difference. The only rules he played by were his own.

Each of the campgrounds has square timber tables throughout them now, built low to the ground and with logs pulled up to them for seats. They find one that's free and set their tents up around it.

The campsite looks so civilised compared to last time.

Previously, they laid their wet weather jackets on the ground and sat on them. They levelled their camp stove into the dirt, tried to keep their packets of food out of it as much as possible, and ate from bowls in their laps. Now they set out their individual cooking equipment and packets of freeze-dried food on the table and sit on the logs. It looks communal, companionable. Fun. Except it's not. They are still three people brought together reluctantly. People who are trying to find some commonality, some connection to their past lives.

They are awkward together in a way Nicole remembers being with her first lover. They were both willing enough participants, but it was the gracelessness of the sex that Nicole remembers most. All the parts for which a place had to be found, like a 3D puzzle. There were things to be done with lips and arms and legs and hands. Mostly they crashed and clashed. Teeth knocked. Arms got tangled. Legs closed when they should have opened.

She put little emotion into solving this puzzle at the time, despite the intrigue of it; the way it made boys suddenly cover their groins at the beach or made girls lead with their breasts when they walked. Which is probably why she never found any of sex's rhythm that day. The easy slip, slide and pulse, the conjoined nature of it. For her it was an experience of contrasts. Soft then hard. Tight then yielding. Tidy then messy. Then only awkwardness.

Nicole feels like that post-coital girl again now. Unsure of where or how she fits with others.

The wind had kept up into the evening last time. It blustered through the canopy and tossed leaves and twigs about. The fabric of their tent was pushed inward with each blast, then sucked outward again, liked puffed cheeks, with a ripping sound as the wind eddied about.

They struggled to protect the flame on their camp stove, despite the three of them huddling round it. The flame was pushed away from the pot's bottom and their food cooked slowly and incompletely. They ate in silence. None of them chewed with much enthusiasm or energy; it was just another task that had to be undertaken. Nicole expects each of them was too caught up in their own troubled thoughts, and too mentally and physically exhausted, to talk their way into better ones.

Today has been an altogether different day – sunny, warm and mostly breezeless. The evening now is balmy, still and hushed. It's one of those evenings that usually lifts the spirit, puts Nicole at ease. At home she celebrates such an evening with a glass of wine on her balcony, bare feet up on the edge of her seat, a bowl of nuts or a dip beside her. She has nothing to drink here other than treated creek water and her dinner consists of rehydrated chicken, peas and rice. She doesn't feel celebratory anyway.

Each of them has set up their cooking gear and food on separate sides of the table, so that they sit in a U-shape. They each stir their individual pots, where previously they'd shared everything.

'Where do you think he camped when we were here last time?'

Nicole looks at Lisa. Her directness continues to surprise her. The way she speaks of the past with such ease.

'Not that it matters I suppose,' she adds. 'Given he seemed to be everywhere.'

In some ways Nicole admires Lisa's ability to confront this time in their lives. It's as though she can hold the experience in a glass box in her hand and view it from all sides. It's an objectivity Nicole knows she's never had, so she envies Lisa's skill to be able to examine it at arm's length.

Unable to stop herself, she looks at the thin scar across Lisa's cheek. She's tried not to pay it any attention since they started the hike. But it lures her. It's small but undeniably there, despite the years since the mark was left upon her.

'It *did* feel like he was everywhere, didn't it?' Samantha

stops stirring her pot of food and looks around. 'As much a thing of the imagination as anything else.'

'Till we saw him … on that flat section. Nothing imagined about that.' Lisa glances at Nicole, checking perhaps if she's overstepped the line with their conversation.

'I don't know if that freaked me out more or if his disappearing footprints did,' Samantha says.

'At least seeing him made him real.' Nicole hears the flatness in her voice, and so must Lisa.

'But he's not real anymore.' Lisa looks right at Nicole this time.

Nicole holds her gaze for a moment then looks down to her pot of food again. She thinks about the scar on Lisa's cheek once more, how real it is. And she wonders how Lisa's not forced to remember him every time she sees it. Nicole has no obvious scars, but she still sees him most days.

They eat in silence after that, while darkness rises from the ground up and later is host to a weakening moon.

An assortment of soft glows dapple the camping ground as other campers turn on lights inside tents and at their tables. The occasional laugh rings out from the school group. Otherwise the soft talk of these young people is a distant and indiscernible murmur of differing tones and pitches.

Nicole has set the spaceship light in the centre of their table. Its portholes of soft blue light illuminate beneath Lisa's and Samantha's chins. It gives their faces an eerie glow. Nicole imagines that hers looks no different. It's probably a good thing, not being able to see one another's eyes. It makes them honest.

'Who are your close friends now?' Lisa asks no one in particular.

Nicole doesn't answer and neither does Samantha.

Nicole suspects Lisa has read the silence accurately when she says, 'Neither have I. Not *really* close ones, anyway.'

There was such an intimacy to their friendship. Each

deeply embedded in the life of the other that Nicole never dared to replicate it. Never had the courage to leave herself open to such dependency again, not with women or men.

A man at work has accused her of building walls against friendship.

'Are you coming to work drinks tomorrow night?' he asked her recently.

'Not this time.'

'You didn't last time either. Or the one before that.'

Nicole shrugged. 'I didn't know you were keeping a work social record?'

'It's a personal record. Not a work one.'

He's divorced. The losing party in the break-up supposedly. Although Nicole doubts there are any winners in such an event. He strikes her as a mildly broken man. Not needy or angry so much as fatigued by the thought of starting again. She supposes this is one of the advantages of never having started in the first place.

He has flirted round the edges of pursuing her for a while. She doesn't know why. She hasn't given him any encouragement. She's often wondered if it is a conquest for him, the unattainable made sexier. Either way, he's kept up his pursuit, looked for that small chink of light through which he might enter and stake a claim on her. She doesn't mind him as a person. But caution still tinkles its tinny bell and to this she's always listened.

'Like I said. Not this time.' Nicole turned away, went to head back to her desk.

'You build walls, you know, not bridges.'

He didn't say this unkindly. It sounded more like a thought bubble that accidentally popped out unbidden. When she turned to look at him again, he seemed embarrassed. And because she knew what he said was true, she saved him from his discomfort.

'Walls have a purpose,' she said. 'They hold up a roof. Stop the rain getting in.' She turned away again.

'What if I like rain?' he called after her. 'What if I like getting wet?'

'Go swimming.'

Maybe Nicole's dependency on Samantha and Lisa has never really left her. Maybe that's why Lisa was able to coax her back here. Even though she argued against it in the bar that night.

'It's not going to change anything,' Nicole had said.

'But I *need* to go back,' Lisa insisted. 'It's the only way I know how to fix things.'

Lisa's comment had made her angry. How could she hope to fix something that had already happened? What made her think she even had the right to try after all this time? It was as though she thought she could place a fork under the preceding years and lift them out of their lives, leave bookends of then and now with nothing in between. And yet more than half their lives had been lived during that time.

'Don't you have a therapist to help you do that?' Nicole snapped. 'Isn't that what people do about their hang-ups?'

She knows if Lisa had spoken to her in the same way that night, she'd have picked up her bag and walked out of the bar. But she didn't. She sat there as though what Nicole said *was* the therapy.

'This isn't a hang-up,' Lisa said, voice calm. Nothing like Nicole remembered it being when they were younger. 'It's become a way of life.'

Nicole refused to admit to having similar hang-ups. Told Lisa she'd left it all behind her years ago.

She knows she sounded like a fraud though. What she said was too scripted, too rehearsed, as though she'd been telling herself the same thing for years. She hadn't fooled Lisa.

'We all still hurt,' Lisa said. 'There's no shame in admitting it.' She then went on to say how difficult it was to explain why she wanted to go back when it was more about the doing than the intention of it.

Nicole must have understood something of what she meant though, because here she is after all.

'It's hard to trust,' Nicole says now, breaking the silence.

She sees both Samantha's and Lisa's ghostly chins move up and down.

They had been relieved to see that the German backpackers were at the campsite when they arrived last time. Foolishly they had equated them with safety and protection. Nicole remembers how Samantha hummed while she flattened bracken with her boot to give ground for their tent.

Both men wore their dark hair to the shoulder. They were unshaven and their khaki T-shirts had white stains at the armpits and across their backs and fronts from where perspiration had soaked the fabric then dried. They carried a sharp odour of stale masculine sweat. Nicole expects the three of them carried a female version of the same smell. It is the animal scent of hikers, of those who walk and sleep, walk and sleep, often in the same clothes. Nicole's always liked this smell. It implies effort.

They tried to strike up a conversation with the two men, but they spoke as little English as they did German. Nicole had persisted though, she wanted to find out if they'd seen any other hikers that day, specifically a solo male. She used the only key words she'd retained from her inadequate home-schooled German, realised that in some realms her parents had failed her.

'*Ein Mann?*' she said, and held up one finger. 'Walking.' She mimed the act by using two fingers as legs. She was met with shrugs and confusion.

They set up camp only metres from the Germans. They did this without any discussion. Nicole can't speak for the others, but she knows she was drawn to these other hikers as a cold person is drawn to a flame. The men looked askance at one another as they laid out their tent, then got back on with finishing the set-up of their own. The men ignored them after that.

Proximity to others made no difference in the end. And the

following morning it only served to give the men a close-up example of what female friendships were capable of. Nicole still feels ashamed when she thinks back on it, how these men might still go about their lives believing – and telling others too, quite possibly – that women can treat one another very badly.

The man still came to their tent through the night. Lisa and Samantha slept through it, probably with a newfound complacency due to their campsite companions.

The German men had gone into their shared tent not long before the three of them went into theirs. Nicole listened to the unfamiliar lilt of their accent for a time, then to the sound of their soft snoring. Hearing them must have soothed her because she fell asleep quickly.

There are three certainties for most women till death, or menopause: shitting, pissing and menstruating. They are also the three greatest inconveniences of camping in the wild.

Nicole woke in the night with a familiar rat-gnawing pain deep in her pelvis and an all too familiar stickiness between her legs. She'd got the period she wasn't due to get till the following week.

'Why don't you go on the Pill like every other girl?' Lisa asked her once.

Nicole never had. Partly because she'd had so few sexual partners at that stage and saw no reason to take a drug for the few times she might. But mostly because it sanctioned neither care nor responsibility for the man.

'It's taking *control*, not *responsibility*,' Lisa said, exasperated.

'But they don't even ask. They just *assume*.'

Nicole rummaged around inside her backpack at the foot of her sleeping mat till she found the tampons she'd thankfully packed anyway. She unwrapped one and inserted it in the dark. She lay awake for a while after that. Felt dirty and desperate for the shower she knew she wouldn't get for another two days. She lay on her side, pulled her knees up against the pain, and wished the crotch of her knickers would hurry up and dry so at least that discomfort would be gone.

She tried to work out if it was close to daylight by how dark it was in the tent, if there was any pre-dawn bird chorus. But she couldn't see her hand in front of her face and the wind had dropped off by then, leaving the night hushed and still. The Germans had stopped snoring. Lisa's and Samantha's breath came in soft, rhythmic sighs. All should have been well with the world, except it never was for long back then.

If Nicole were a proper animal, one better equipped for safety and survival with an astute sense of sight, sound and smell, she'd have picked up the scent of him. She'd have heard him shift through the bush. And if she were a real animal in the wild, she'd have recognised the danger of him and taken flight. As it was she froze in her sleeping bag, made her breath inaudible. She listened with her dulled human ears as the pain in her pelvis pulsed.

His tread was soft, slow and purposeful. If one footfall was loud, then there was a pause before the next. It was a cautious, stalking approach. A fox walker. The final soft crack before his footfalls stopped was so close to her head that she was sure if she pushed her hand up against the tent's fabric she would come up against his leg.

There was a whisper of a hand sliding up a cord and then a cutting sound began. A soft, squeaking saw. He used a knife, she decided. Not scissors. They would have made a single *snip* as he severed the cord from their tent. She heard this sawing sound twice and she knew even before she heard his soft footfalls fade away again that when they came out of their tent the following morning, two ropes would be cut from it.

WHEN SAMANTHA THINKS BACK ON THEIR escalating tension, she thinks of it as being like an expanding tumour. It stealthily enlarged inside each one of them until it could no longer be contained by its own perimeters. Then it spewed its vile, ugly contents. How else to explain why they started to fight one another instead of staying united?

The third night was something of a reprieve for her. The German backpackers made her feel safe so she'd slept deeply until dawn. Even so, she still had to force her aching, leaden body out of the tent the following morning.

The two men had already started to break camp. Samantha waved to them. She remembers how she hoped they'd walk in the same direction as them, be at the same campsite that night as well. All she wanted was to sleep easily again and get back to the car the following day.

Little has changed with how she feels this morning, except that her body aches even more than it had previously. But at least this time the ropes on her tent hold it as taut as they did when she erected it yesterday. Last time, their shared tent sagged lopsidedly when they crawled out of it. And Nicole looked to sag along with it.

'Two gone,' Lisa said.

Samantha thought them odd trophies. But she knows now this wasn't what they were to him. They were proof to them that he could get close without them knowing. Except Nicole had.

'I know. I heard him take them.'

Lisa spun round to look at Nicole. 'Why didn't you wake me? I'd have used one of them round his fucking neck.'

'You've just answered your own question.' Nicole turned her back on Lisa and continued to stuff her sleeping bag into its cover.

They'd woken to a cotton wool day of misty drizzle. Samantha's shoes and clothes were damp, and from these the cold ran all the way to the core of her body and made her shiver. They'd pitched their tent on a patch of flattish ground not far from a small creek, so the moisture felt to rise up from the soil as much as drift down from the sky. The sandflies loved it. Samantha could feel them biting her scalp, her neck, her face and hands, any part of her where the skin was exposed. She put her cap on and rummaged for the repellent in a side pouch of her pack.

'I need hot food,' she said. 'I'm so cold.'

'I don't think I can eat anything.' Nicole sat heavily on a rotted log, pressed her half-stowed sleeping bag against her body and rested her head on it.

Samantha could see she looked defeated. Her hair was greasy and hugged the contours of her skull. Her hands were limp around her sleeping bag.

'You have to eat,' Samantha said to her. 'Keep your strength up.'

'You my mother now?' Nicole turned to look at Samantha then, but only so she could glare at her.

'Don't take it out on her,' Lisa snapped back.

'No. You're right. I should save it for you given you got us into this fucking mess.' Nicole stood with renewed vigour then and started stuffing the remainder of her sleeping bag inside its small cover.

'How much longer are you going to play the blame game?' Lisa asked. ''Cause I've gotta tell ya, it's wearing thin.'

Samantha could feel the boundaries of that spiteful tumour bulging, getting ready to rupture. She tried to hold it back. 'C'mon, you two. Don't start.'

In retrospect she knows these weren't her usual words, so in a way she supposes she only inflamed things more.

'Don't *start*?' Lisa shouted. 'From what I can tell I'm the only one keeping this whole shitfest together!'

'What a fucking hero!' Nicole snapped.

'Better to be a hero than a sook like you!'

By this stage, the Germans had stopped what they were doing. Each held a corner of their tent, but they'd stalled in the folding of it. Instead, they watched as this spectacle unfolded before them.

When anger is acted upon and then replayed later in the mind, it always seems to move in slow motion. And in this slow remembering Samantha sees moments in which she might have been able to defuse things, but when considered in real time, she knows the events moved far too quickly for her to have done anything at all. And maybe this was what they were always going to do anyway, attack one another.

Nicole threw her sleeping bag onto the ground and stormed across to where Lisa stood with her back to her, stuffing items inside her backpack. Nicole grabbed Lisa's shoulder with one hand and spun her round to face her. She brought her other hand up and slapped Lisa hard across the face.

Samantha felt emptied and paralysed and broken by this act. She knew no words powerful enough, any which were healing enough, to bring either one of them back from this. So she just stood there, mouth open, and watched as their friendship started to unravel.

Lisa brought her hand up to her cheek. She kept it there while she and Nicole stared at one another for what seemed like minutes but was only seconds. It was time enough though for Samantha to chant inside her head: *Please don't hit her back. Please don't hit her back.*

She doesn't know, even now, why Lisa didn't. But she has remained grateful ever since for this rare act of restraint, for all the good it did their friendship in the end. But who knows, on some subconscious level, maybe this is why Lisa was able to convince Nicole to come back here. Maybe Nicole believes she owes Lisa something.

When Lisa finally took her hand from her face there was blood on it, and it was also smeared across her cheek. Nicole's garnet ring – received with delight from her parents for her eighteenth birthday – had lacerated the skin across Lisa's cheekbone.

Samantha remembers how the German men shook their heads and looked awkwardly at their feet. They finished packing up their gear quickly, shouldered their packs and left soon after. They didn't even look in their direction. They headed out the way the three of them had come in the previous day.

She thinks about how permanent reminders of mistakes that have been made are a torment. Because how do you explain a scar like Lisa's to others? What has she said of it to the man she married, her daughter? What does she tell herself each time she looks in a mirror?

Samantha expects such scars eventually find their place in the repertoire of life's lies. But what a heavy burden it is to be someone who knows the truth.

LISA SENSES MORE THAN FEELS THAT the day will be warm again. There's a kind of lethargy to the stillness, as though the inhabitants of the landscape can't be bothered rousing themselves. She can hear the soft muttering of the creek just behind her tent, but little else.

She feels this lethargy within her body as well – in her calves, back and shoulders. She is reluctant to get going, to start the day's work. And it will be work, as all the days have been so far. To try and navigate a safe way through or around the lines that she has crossed in her past takes its toll.

She lies a while longer, legs pushed into the soft cocoon of her sleeping bag, bare arms up and hands interlaced under her head. She watches the magnified shadow of a fly as it moves across the outside of her tent. It walks in short, rapid bursts then pauses, most likely to dip its proboscis into droplets of condensation. At other times it stops to scratch its hind legs together. She can hear birds now as the day lightens. She recognises the fluid warble of a magpie. She thinks the other sharper call might be a crimson rosella.

It's hard not to think about the day ahead, the days that have already passed. Each footfall has taken her across a mostly unchanged terrain. But it's her hope – perhaps a naïve one – that in retracing the route from years before that she can redefine the contours of it in her mind. She wants to be able to tell herself a different story about what happened out here, build a new future for herself with the reimagining. One not defined by the actions of the man. Or how her actions against him might have precipitated them. This is her hope. Because she's never quite trusted herself since. And she wants to go into middle age at least liking the person she is. Maybe then Hannah will like her more as well.

Hannah never leans in when they sit across from one another at a table. She doesn't speak of her fears or ask advice or whisper secrets.

'Even she sees you for the hateful cow you are,' Matt said one spiteful day. 'No wonder she moved out when she could. Probably worried you'd rub off on her.'

Such an easy shot, to cast those jagged stones of blame against her without once looking in the mirror.

But what if he is right? What if Hannah believes there is something contagious about her; that anger is something passed on like blonde hair or blue eyes?

Lisa knows others have sensed something dangerous about her. To some a single woman carries a nefarious scent.

'She's divorced now, you know? Have to keep an eye on our husbands.'

Lisa heard this said of her. In a school ground. As far as she could tell she was the only divorced woman amongst the dozen or so there waiting for their children to come out, so the woman with the loud whisper must have been speaking about her.

These words had felt like a slap. She'd gone the full circle: once prey, now predatory woman. A still-young divorcee let loose and looking to steal another woman's husband. She decided this woman thought too highly of her partner. Or maybe it was that she didn't think of him highly enough.

She expects there were others who thought she'd let the team of long-suffering women down. She hadn't soldiered on like them, no matter how miserable she was. Others apologised as though she'd suffered a death.

'I'm *so* sorry,' they said, and looked it.

'I've divorced him, not killed him,' Lisa said to one simpering soul.

No one celebrated her divorce. No one gave her high-fives. No one said, *Good for you!* or *Congratulations!* or *Happy days!* No one paused to think that it might be a step towards amelioration. If Samantha and Nicole had still been around, she knows they'd have said all of these things.

In truth, Lisa admires her daughter's decisive and early escape from the home where her mother raged. She must tell her so when she gets back. She can already feel the fullness of pride in her words. 'You're a good person, Hannah,' she'll say. 'I could learn from you.'

Except Lisa wonders if she ever will. She's rarely chosen to run from things she probably should have. And neither is she like those animals that lay low to the ground – water dragons, rabbits, quails – playing dead, playing safe, playing invisible. Mostly, she's stood her ground and taken up the fight. Except for that one time.

She runs a finger across the thin scar on her cheek. This morning it gives her hope. Reminds her of the person she can be.

She would like to bring Hannah here, if she'd come. She could teach her botanical names along the way. Let her hear the enduring complexity of them. She's a bright girl. Lisa thinks she'd pick them up quickly.

But mostly she would like just to walk with Hannah, be present without demands. She can be anyone or no one then, not just mother and memories. And a walker is free to be honest. Stories told to the feet, not the face. She would explain to her daughter that wisdom comes from the gathering of mistakes and that Lisa's stockpile must make her very wise. Maybe Hannah would laugh at that.

And in the hands-wide greatness of this place Lisa would

show Hannah that she does know gratitude. That she can live humbly. That she can live without angry expectation. And if she can make her daughter believe that of her out here, then why not also at home? Why not?

She can hear soft voices amongst the clatter of pots outside her tent.

My turn, she thinks. *I have to face this day too.*

She pushes her sleeping bag off her legs and crawls out of her tent on all fours, then forces her body to stand.

It may as well be an altogether new region Lisa walks through. She can actually see the tubular pink flowers of the common heath – *Epacris impressa*. They offer a vibrant flash of colour either side of the track, as do the yellow flower spikes of the silver banksia. And the tender new growth on the eucalypts lends these trees a halo of lemony-green.

She'd seen no such colours on this day previously. They'd walked through mist. Trees and boulders were blurred as though viewed through a layer of frosted glass; mountaintops were lost from view. Being mindful of places where someone could hide was pointless, given everything was hidden.

Today, little is hidden. Certainly not the escalation in Nicole's disquiet. She looks to be always thinking, thinking. Her earlier gait has lost some of its sure-footed form. She holds herself even tighter than usual; muscles still tensed when they rest, the deep lines across her forehead rarely soften.

But what does she think about mostly? Lisa wonders. How differently things might have turned out if she hadn't stormed ahead that morning? Or does she run through the mathematics of blame, calculating Lisa's greater portion?

Lisa doesn't care about these things. She thinks about their friendship more than anything else. How she'd banked too much on the ultimately false belief that the bond between them was too strong to break, and not enough on the fact that it was something that had to be nurtured and cared for, like a garden.

Last time Nicole had packed up her gear quickly and left the campsite before the blood had even dried on Lisa's cheek.

In the absence of a doctor to give the cut the couple of sutures it probably needed, Samantha cleaned the wound and pulled the edges of it together as best she could with strapping tape.

It stung for most of that morning, and her head ached, so Lisa didn't give much thought or concern for Nicole well ahead, and on her own. When she thinks back on it now, she sees how they played right into his hands.

Lisa remembers how Samantha started to panic.

'Should we go faster?' Samantha said. 'Try and catch up to her?'

'Really? Do you think you can catch up to her?'

Samantha had looked away hurt, but Lisa didn't care. She still had the mindset of the victim. Samantha had pushed past her, changed her pace to something between a fast walk and a slow trot.

'You're gonna kill yourself.'

Samantha stopped and looked back at her. 'She *shouldn't* be on her own,' she said and continued on in her peculiar lock-kneed gait.

But it wasn't sustainable as Lisa knew, and she soon caught up with her again.

Samantha stopped and cupped her hands round her mouth. 'Nicole! Wait!' she called.

Lisa listened half-heartedly for a reply that never came. Samantha called again. Still nothing.

'She'll stop and wait for us eventually,' Lisa said and took the lead once more.

The drizzle distorted everything that day – time, sound, distance, the shape, form and colour of all that was wrapped in it. So when Lisa walked round a bend and up ahead saw a low dark shape against a misty-edged boulder, she thought it was Nicole, sitting on the ground, finally waiting for them.

But as she drew closer, Nicole's backpack took shape. Shoulder straps curved to the sky.

Anger drove how she felt at first. How could Nicole just abandon this thing that held all they needed to survive? *Childish*, she thought. *Attention-seeking*.

But she knows now this was her mind disconnecting her from the truth, softening it with easy outs. Because soon enough the full force of what Nicole's discarded pack meant barged through. About the same time a tremor started in her hands and bile rose in her throat.

When she saw Nicole's stick, that stupid, useless toy of a weapon she'd given each of them, discarded a little further on, the fullness of the truth rushed in. Nicole was left with nothing and no one to help her.

THE GEOGRAPHY THAT NICOLE'S WALKED THROUGH till now has carried elements of familiarity. She's had an impression of having been here before. Now she's in alien land.

Her memory of this terrain has been wiped, if it was ever stored in the first place. The things she sees are the things she expects to see. Granite boulders scattered like giant marbles. Wounded bloodwoods that bleed red sap down their trunks and drip clots of it onto the ground. The trail is still pockmarked with ant nests, although she expects the occupants of them have changed a thousand times over. Birds still call; take flight. Leaves quiver. The undergrowth continues to be alive with mysterious rustles and scrapes. It's all as she's come to expect. But nothing is as she recalls.

Her body feels reluctant today, more than any other so far. She has a sense of holding back. She's pushed herself till now, not so much willingly as purposely. She knows the only way for her to get home is to keep going. But it feels like a Sisyphean punishment.

The one thing that's still crystal clear to her about that day from many years before is how she'd burned hot with shame. Not even the damp air had cooled it.

The thin white line across Lisa's cheek now is a rebuke. But it is a rebuke of Nicole's own making because Lisa hasn't so much as rested a finger on it from what she's seen. Does she at home though? Does she hide it under heavy make-up? Or maybe Nicole's magnified this small wound in her mind, made it wider and longer than it really is. Made it bigger in the way she knows Samantha still sees someone bigger when she looks at herself in a mirror.

Nicole's often wished Lisa had struck her in turn that day. One wound countered with another. But she just stared at her with sad blue eyes. Even to see her angry would have been better than that. When Lisa dropped her hand and Nicole saw the blood, she'd looked away and hadn't been able to look back again. Her shame ran too deep.

It still hurts to realise she's not always been a good person. Sometimes she fears that she hasn't been since.

There is a unique silence all around today. Everything seems stalled and attentive in this un-transmitting quiet.

Nicole wishes an animal would appear to break the stillness. A large muscular one, like a kangaroo. In her mind's eye she sees this animal and her poised in unison as they regard one another in this suspension of sound. Almost as though they stand outside themselves. She studies its features closely. It studies hers. She gets an understanding for the muscles it uses to hold itself still. The right-angled bend of its long muscular tail that keeps it balanced. Its meaty, muscled rump tensed and rippled, ready to leap, but holding back. The droop of its front paws, one slightly higher than the other, purpose stalled. She even sees the patter of its heart in a space between its ribs. The flare of its nostrils.

She thinks about the man and how he might have held his muscles while he hid behind the boulder. She imagines they were tensed and rippled as well. She imagines also that his heart quickened, that his breath whispered in and out in soft pants. She sees him with his left ear turned away from the granite, towards the track, filtering sound. Tuning in to her steps as they came closer, closer.

Without his pack he had sprung quickly and easily. She had no time to react. No time to call out. Too much time to believe she was going to die.

He knocked her to the ground. Lay across her chest to pin her there. Crushed her throat under his forearm, her mouth under his hand. He was close enough for her to see black slugs of dirt caught in the corner of each of his eyes. She pulled and pulled for breath. But never got enough. She fought with her legs. They fought with air. She fought with her hands. Nails. They secured threads of his skin. Not enough. Nothing enough.

'Keep still or I'll break your fucking neck.'

She was a rabbit, a deer, caught in headlights.

She was his.

Was he even nervous about taking her? Or did his belief that it was his right to do so keep him calm? His face, pressed so close to hers, looked excited. His eyes shone. He smiled. Triumphant.

It's easy to use the word blame around these events. But she realises now that she can no longer shift responsibility for what happened. Move it about like a piece of furniture, looking for the best fit in a room, the most convenient position. Blame *is* convenient though, because it gives cause without the need to explore the truth.

In the retelling of her story – if ever she had retold it – she expects some would question why they were even there in the first place. Three inexperienced young women – in life and bushwalking – negotiating the unknown terrain of each. What did they know of hate and sport and the mixing of the two? And how much did they provoke him at his game?

What if Lisa had backed down in the car park?

What if Nicole hadn't got so far ahead?

What if they'd just turned round and gone home instead of stepping over his shit on the second morning?

Nicole still shares her life with this man. He comes for her in her dreams. He clamps his part-animal hand across her mouth and she smells the dirt and grime and sweat of him once more as she wrestles with her sheets and tries to get her breath. She strips the sweat-soaked linen from her bed the next morning. Puts it on a hot wash. Takes fresh sheets from the cupboard. Like the set routes she jogs each day – brightly lit, busy, safe – this is who she is now. She struggles to imagine herself as anyone else.

When Nicole looks back on the girl snatched from this trail, she sees someone she barely knows anymore. This girl's eyes are big and dark and glossy with adrenaline. She lashes out. Boots. Knees. Hands. Nails. Teeth. This girl is a fighter. Nicole admires her. But she squeezes her eyes shut to the memory of her because he was a fighter too. And alongside his greater strength, she proved no rival. He still managed to bind this girl. To gag her. Take her away from her friends.

The worst sound for Nicole that day was when she heard Samantha, then Lisa, call her name. Their voices were so muffled and distant that she didn't believe she'd ever hear them again.

She had sobbed hard then. Her stomach muscles ached with the wailing sounds that were trapped behind the tape he'd put across her mouth. Snot bubbled back and forth in her nose. Tears dripped off her jaw.

He pulled her along at a trot. Their tent ropes served a purpose. He'd jerk her back up onto her feet with them when she fell. The thin nylon cut welts into her wrists. The weight of his pack seemed not to hinder him at all.

And all the while she felt the sodden tampon inside her drag ever downwards.

The breach when it came was sudden. Humiliating. Flooded onto her shorts. Trickled down her bare legs till it became a dirty brown smudge all the way to her knees. Wet, dry, wet, dry as he marched her on.

He seemed angry when he saw it. 'Filthy cunt,' he said and tugged even harder on the ropes that bound her.

Nicole thought her degradation was complete. Then he stopped and made her take off her clothes.

When she thinks back on it now, she wishes she'd walked proud with that menstrual blood staining her legs. Proud of her earthy, metallic smell.

See me, those stains said. *Here is my difference. This is what I can do.*

She doesn't know the purpose of reliving these memories. What does it achieve? Who does it benefit?

Because her experience of memory is that it traps her in a place she no longer wants to be. Reminds her of the person she no longer is. Shows her things she no longer wants to see.

Some days she wishes she could haemorrhage all memory away. Send it into the white light. Lose it entirely and not once grieve its loss.

SAMANTHA FEELS A BOND WITH THE trail now. Place and mind intercept. Thoughts roll out beneath her feet like words on a scroll. History recounts. Geography connects.

When they set out four days ago, she was worried she wouldn't be able to escape her thoughts. Now, she doesn't even try. Because in remembering, maybe this place will give something back to her where previously it's only taken away.

What she's started to realise is that she lives with this landscape nearly every day, but in absentia. Its topography is a part of hers. It's her dips and peaks. Her trudging defeats. Her victories, when she has them. She shouldn't have denied its importance for so long. None of them should have. After all, this place expects nothing of her in coming back. The expectation is all her own. So does this make her a pilgrim? she wonders. She doesn't feel like one. A pilgrim shouldn't know the secrets of the land they cross. And neither should they have abetted them.

She looks down at her feet, to the gravelly ribbon they walk along. This trail has forced rule on the landscape. People travel the threads of it, clockwise or counter-clockwise. Equally, it has forced rules on her life.

***

Does anyone really know how to act in a crisis? Are there people in whom a switch flicks, some mechanism that alerts them instinctively to what they should do? Or do all people do what Samantha did, which was to stop and stare at Nicole's pack, then turn away and vomit?

After Samantha had emptied her stomach, she went and stood alongside Lisa, hand pressed to her mouth. Like Lisa, she looked out across the mist-blurred bushland. Her heart thrashed inside her chest like a trapped bird and her hands shook. She fought to steady her breath.

Lisa cupped her hands round her mouth and called Nicole's name. Samantha saw that her hands shook too.

She remembers the frustration she felt at not being able to see deep into the bush, even though she was terrified of what she might find. She could make out the ill-defined shape of trees and boulders, but nothing much else. She could see enough though to know it was rough, ankle-turning terrain.

'He can't have moved quickly with her if he took her through there,' she said to Lisa.

'No.' Lisa turned to look at Nicole's pack again.

She walked around it much as Nicole had walked round the last of the man's footprints on the beach. Samantha studied the ground too. The gravel was scored with ridges and gouges. From boots she decided, during a tussle. Nicole had fought. She hadn't just taken her pack off and walked away. She'd resisted. Good for her.

Samantha looked beyond the pack. A little further along the trail she saw an arrow drawn in the dirt. It indicated onward.

'Come and look at this!' The urgency in her voice brought Lisa to her side quickly. 'Do you think Nicole's drawn it?'

'I think he probably has,' Lisa said. 'One of his messages.'

'What if it's a trick? What if he's taken her some other way? Or he's hiding her somewhere round here?' Samantha looked about again.

'No. I think he wants us to follow him.'

They unzipped their day bags from their packs then, filled them with a few essentials – a jacket, the first-aid kit, water. They hid the rest of their gear amongst the bracken just off the track, along with Nicole's pack. They tied a tea towel to a branch further along to mark the spot. They did all of this with speed and urgency. There was no discussion. Somehow, they just knew what was needed and what wasn't.

They ran then. Urged on by the adrenaline Samantha had felt weightless. Capable. Up to the demands of their pursuit. But before long she started to fatigue. She tried to pull more air into her lungs – sucking, sucking – but it was never enough. Still she kept running. Her legs worked like pistons – up, down, up, down. Before long a fire burned in her muscles and inside her chest. Soon her side was pierced with a stitch. She tried to run through it. It felt as though she ran with a blade inside her. She ran hunched. She slowed. Lisa pulled further ahead. Why couldn't she do this one thing for Nicole?

Lisa glanced over her shoulder. 'Keep up!' she shouted and pulled further away.

But then Samantha did catch up with Lisa, who stopped suddenly in the middle of the track. Lisa turned as Samantha approached and held up Nicole's beige shorts. There were dark stains on them. Blood. She felt the urge to vomit again, but knew her stomach had nothing left to give.

Lisa rolled Nicole's shorts into a tight bundle and stuffed them inside her daypack.

They ran on.

Samantha still hears the echo of Lisa's command some days, calling for her to *Keep up*. It comes to her anywhere. Anytime. At her desk while she sorts through invoices. The kitchen bench while she slices tomatoes. In the aisle of a supermarket.

Except Lisa doesn't shout it as she had back then. She whispers those words in Samantha's ear, over and over, like a criticism. And when she hears them she finds it hard to catch her breath and her heart quickens. It's like she's running all over again.

WHEN LISA REACHES THE FINAL HEADLAND, she looks out across the ink coloured ocean. Its oily undulations reach endlessly for the shore. At the foot of the rugged peak the sea crashes against the rocky shoreline in a turbulent fury of turquoise and white foam. There is a wrack line of brown, rubbery kelp that shifts backwards and forwards in the wash. Lisa hates the kelp. She hated it last time too. It looks too much like the hair of a drowned woman.

As she gazes around this dramatic point, she can't imagine two more different days. This time it is cloudless and warm. When she finally reached this headland previously her body had quickly chilled inside her damp clothes. Droplets fell from the ends of her hair onto her T-shirt, dripped off the tip of her nose. They rested on her eyelashes, blurred her vision. Her bare arms goose-fleshed. But she hadn't put her jacket on. She didn't want to restrict her movement in any way.

Lisa tries to imagine what his intentions were in leading them to this high, exposed point. Had he felt God-like as he looked down on them from his kingly boulder? She'd wanted to believe there was some kind of certifiable madness to him. Some organic failure of his mind and with this, an understandable reason for his actions. She wasn't looking to justify his behaviour, only to have something by which she could grasp it. But she knows now he was neither mad nor masterful. He was simply a man whose self-aggrandisement meant he never doubted or questioned his right to do whatever he wanted. She recognises this now as the most dangerous man of all.

They must have run for two or three kilometres that day. She hoped to come across Nicole round every bend, over every rise. But she didn't.

The drizzle eased off but the low misty clouds persisted. They shrouded the tree canopy. Made ghostly shapes of their trunks. It was impossible to see the arc of the sun, so time had stalled. Sound was muffled in the damp air. Her breath burned hot in her chest. Mud was flicked up the backs of her bare legs. Later she would find fat black leeches feeding on them.

It was easy going to begin with, round the hip of the mountain. But it didn't last. Before long they had to haul themselves over rocky outcrops again. Risked a turned ankle or a fall on wet, slippery descents.

They had to stop along the way. The first time to pick up Nicole's shorts. Then her T-shirt. Her bra. Finally her bloodied knickers. These they found hanging from a timber sign at a junction in the track which had *Lookout* written on it. Lisa stowed them in her daypack along with Nicole's other clothes. She expects he left this sordid Hansel and Gretel trail not just to shock them or to add to their fear, but to slow them down. All part of the game.

An arrow was scratched into the trail beside the sign. It indicated they head up to the lookout. Lisa bounded over it, strangely relieved. His trail of clues told her that at least Nicole was ahead of them. Not hidden somewhere amongst the scrub behind. She didn't want to think that she was running away from Nicole, only towards her.

The lookout trail became a steep and scrabbly ascent. In her haste, Lisa's feet slipped out from under her several times.

She grazed her knees. Samantha dropped further back. She didn't wait for her.

'Keep up!' she shouted over her shoulder. She didn't want to lose her too.

She was breathless, flushed and uncertain as she neared the top of the headland. What if he'd tricked them with his arrow? What if he'd kept on the main trail instead? Gave himself more time to get further ahead.

But she found Nicole there. Gagged. Bound. Tied to a tree. Naked except for her socks and boots. She sat on the ground, knees pulled up to her chest. Her whole body shook.

All Lisa could focus on when she first looked at Nicole was the red. Different shades of it. Inflamed-red round the black leeches on her arms, legs and torso. Clot-red scratches and abrasions across her body. Brown-red smudged down her thighs. Her hands were tied to a branch above her head with their tent ropes. They were dusky-red.

Lisa gripped her stick firmly in both hands and looked around her. She suspected a trap. That he wanted to see all three of them bound and gagged. But there he was, sitting up high on a boulder.

Lisa went straight to her friend then. Tried not to stare at the blood that stained her thighs, even though the sight of it enraged her. What had he done to her?

She dropped her stick and slipped off her daypack. She knelt beside Nicole and carefully removed the grey gaffer tape from across her mouth. Nicole released the first of many big hitching sobs.

'Thank God,' she breathed, over and over.

Lisa worked to untie her hands next. She struggled. The knots were pulled tight and her hands shook. She watched the man from the corner of her eye as she worked to loosen them.

He sat well above them. The boulder was large enough for him to rest back on his hands, legs stretched out in front of him, ankles crossed. His backpack lay beside him. He was a man relaxed with the world. His dark, damp hair hugged the contours of his skull. His ears poked through it. It added to his lean angularity. Lisa felt a thrill when she saw the red welts across his cheek. Another down his neck. She never doubted Nicole had made those marks. She felt a surge of pride.

Samantha arrived soon after Lisa. She left her to finish untying Nicole, to help her dress.

Lisa picked up her stick and stood with her back to them as she faced the man.

'Learned your lesson yet?' he called from his kingly pedestal.

'This isn't a lesson! It's a fucking crime!'

'You deserved it.'

'*Deserved* it?' Nobody deserves *this*.' Lisa swept her arm behind her to indicate Nicole.

The man shrugged. 'I'd have let her go eventually.'

Was that meant to make it okay? Abduct someone. Strip them. Bind them. Gag them. But at the end of it shrug it off like it wasn't a big deal. Just some kind of life lesson.

'Look at you up there. So tough when you're safe.'

Lisa still believed herself invincible at that stage.

'Lisa,' Nicole pleaded softly.

'C'mon, we need to get out of here. Now,' Samantha said.

But Lisa ignored the quaver in Nicole's voice. The urgency in Samantha's.

'You've been a coward the whole time. And from what I can see you're *still* a fucking coward.'

The man stood with this challenge. Lisa was reminded of how tall he was. She didn't care about his greater size though. Strangely, she felt no fear of him at all. He was just another bully. And she'd fought enough bullies by then to know her capability in the face of them. She widened her stance. Stood as tall as she could. Gripped her stick more firmly.

'Lisa. C'mon.'

Lisa glanced back at Samantha. Nicole stood beside her, dressed again. Samantha had her arm round Nicole's waist. Nicole leant against her. Both were pale. But Lisa could only focus on the shades of red that still marked Nicole's body.

She turned back to the man. 'The three of us could kill you.'

In retrospect she has no idea why she said this. All she knows is that her voice was steady and she meant it.

'Lisa, just shut up.' There was little fight in Nicole's words and she started to cry.

'Yeah, Lisa,' the man mimicked. 'Just. Shut. Up.' He sat down again and bounced his boots in time to a beat of his own making.

'I'm going,' Nicole said.

'Come on, Lisa,' Samantha pleaded. 'Let's just go. *Please*.'

'I love it when women beg,' the man said. '*She* begged. I'd like to hear *you* beg. C'mon, Lisa. Beg for me.'

Lisa hated that he knew her name. It gave him something over her. Something *of* her. Up till then he had nothing but her attention.

'*Please* don't hurt me,' he mimicked in a woman's voice.

'I'd jump off that fucking cliff before I'd beg you for anything.'

'Lisa! Just leave it!' Nicole snapped.

'Ooh, now she's got some fight about her.'

Samantha reached out and gripped Lisa's arm. 'Stop,' she hissed. 'Just. Stop.'

Lisa yanked her arm free.

'What are you *doing*?' Samantha asked.

The man put his hands behind him again and rested back. 'I think Lisa's too stupid to know what she's doing,' he said and laughed.

Lisa wanted to shove her fist in his mouth. Gouge his eyes out with her thumbs. Kick him till blood bloomed purple and black all over his body.

'I'm going.' Nicole broke away from Samantha's side and headed towards the trail.

Lisa took in the stains on Nicole's shorts and thighs again. All the other shades of red. Her grimy, tear-streaked face. The clean square left across her mouth from the tape.

'And just let him get away with it?' Lisa called after Nicole.

Nicole paused to look at her. 'He already has.' She turned and started to walk back down the track.

'But he has to learn he can't *do* this to people,' she implored.

Sam looked as though a rope was tied to each of her arms that were being pulled in opposite directions.

How had she allowed herself to be so reckless? Lisa can only think now that her need to best him went beyond just this moment in time. He was the pinnacle of many moments, the ultimate bully. She'd had enough.

Nicole made her way slowly down the rise. Samantha started edging towards the trail after her.

'C'mon, Lisa,' she said. 'We have to stick together.'

Lisa ignored her. Her attention remained with the man.

'Brave enough to come down off your big rock, little man?'

She felt a trickle on her cheek. She knew without touching it that the wound there had opened up again. She felt no pain from it. She felt very little of anything. Nothing of the aches and strains or fatigue that she'd felt in her body up till then. Not even fear. She was charged. Ready.

Lisa expects the body numbs people to many things – pain, insults, humiliation. The impact of them dulled to a bearable level. How would people survive a lifetime of such assaults otherwise?

Eventually a point is reached though. Too many nerves are rubbed raw. The pain of experiencing them finally crashes home. That, Lisa thinks, is what has brought her back here. Back to this place that once wounded her. Wounded all three of them. She wants to be released from her pain.

She felt pleasure in a deep and satisfying place when she recognised his moment of uncertainty. It emboldened her further.

'Still the coward,' she goaded.

And this must have excoriated his nerves enough to finally bring him down from his eyrie.

WHEN THE ROCKY HEADLAND COMES INTO view it's as though a guardian hand presses against Nicole's chest and holds her back. The path shows her where her natural next step should be, but she's reluctant to take it. She could blame tiredness or overworked muscles or even the weight of her pack for this reluctance. After four days on the trail it's a reasonable excuse. But she'd be lying to herself because she's accustomed to all of these things now.

She looks up at the headland. There's no purity to its form. It's a misshapen and bruised thing. It broods high above her. Down here, where she is now, she feels like she's knelt in prayer at the feet of something great. But this only confirms it as a site her imagination has exalted to a level it doesn't deserve. Sacred but desecrated ground. To attend it again now feels like a blasphemy.

It's fear and shame that holds her back. She knows it. Each had gripped her stomach even before she left the car park. Sometimes she's been barely able to eat. She's tried to deceive and distract both by concentrating on every step. No two have been the same on this complicated and uneven terrain. But despite having tried to maintain an outward gaze, to focus only on the land she crosses, her memories have become something of a landscape too. And she's been compelled to traverse the complicated terrain of them as well.

They were three young women on a hopeful exploration of their capabilities when they first struck out on this trail. This time she feels like a soldier returning to the site of a battle. The ground she walks over is its unmarked grave. And yet the land is utterly indifferent to her. It has no tale to tell. Any story it might have once carried has been grown over, eroded, slipped, subsided. Meanwhile, she's remained trapped by the experiences it was the theatre for.

Nicole can't know what the man was after when he planned his hike. Adventure? Fitness? Isolation? But she suspects his purpose shifted after the incident in the car park. Shifted to something beyond their comprehension. But also to something beyond their combined strength to counter. Let alone for Lisa to try and do so on her own. And yet she stood her ground against him. Challenged their right to be here in the only way she knew how.

At the time Nicole had thought her stupid. Reckless. Equal only to him as the cause of their problems. Now she thinks what a gutsy woman. There have been many times that she's replayed the events that occurred on this cliff in her head and each time she's wished she was as brave as Lisa. Wishes she'd had the courage to stand alongside her friend.

Nicole's hands tingled painfully for a time after Samantha untied her. Then after a while they pulsed hotly as the blood flow was restored to them. Her legs were unreliable. She could barely stand to begin with. She still remembers the strength of Samantha's arm around her. How utterly relieved she felt.

Meanwhile, Lisa had worked on being a figure of torment to the man atop his boulder. Her knuckles white around her stick. Defiant.

Nicole had never been able to put words to her thoughts about what happened to her. Later, she realised she didn't even want to try. All she wanted was to begin forgetting. To put distance and time between her and the headland. Construct a dark and airtight space inside her in which to lodge her humiliation till the feeling of it left her altogether. Except now she doesn't believe humiliation ever leaves the body. That's the power of it. People always define themselves first by those experiences that make them feel less than.

He was right when he said she begged. She did. She submitted. Whimpered. *Please* and *I won't tell* vibrated behind the tape across her mouth.

Lisa would have dropped to the ground. Refused to be led, no matter how much he kicked at her to get up, dragged her along by that tight, cutting rope. She'd have somehow managed to rip the tape from her mouth and scream *You have no fucking right!* She'd have schemed ways to storm him. Wouldn't have mattered that her hands were tied. She'd have found a way – boots, knees, charge into him with her head – till she overcame him. And when he pissed on Nicole – *Give you a wash, eh* – she had looked away. Lisa would have stared right at him and he would have seen the mocking laughter in her eyes.

The attempts Nicole made for freedom were short-lived. She didn't believe or trust in herself to succeed. Survival shows dignity no favours. Once hers was taken from her, everything else that was strong and good about her was taken away as well.

She lost her faith in humanity that day. And she's been unable to restore it since. A hollowed-out place exists inside her where it used to rest. A place that's empty of feeling and kinship. Her humiliation sits like a small, hot stone at its centre.

Who or what might she have been if these things hadn't happened to her? Would she have trusted enough to marry? Gone on to have children? Kept her friendship with Lisa and Sam, instead of believing that discarding it was part of her repair?

Not knowing the answers to these questions sometimes makes Nicole weep.

In moments of stillness she sees him coming down from his high place again. Her mind pictures every detail of him. He makes a slow and self-assured descent. His knees dip softly as he steps from rock to rock. He doesn't pause for balance. Doesn't need to steady himself. When he steps onto the ground he stands with his shoulders back, that weak chin pushed out to make as much of it as he can. Sometimes there is a smile on his lips. Other times a sneer. Always he is taller and broader and more certain than Lisa.

Nicole only faltered when she heard Samantha scream *Run!* She stopped for a moment. Wrestled with her need to leave, to begin forgetting, and her duty to stay and protect. She was paralysed to move back up the trail or down it. It was the beginning of a paralysis that has come to define her life.

THEY COULD HAVE CHOSEN NOT TO take the diversion this time. Turned their backs on this section of their past. Samantha watched as Nicole paused first, then Lisa. Tempted, like her, she supposes, to continue on round to the right. On to their final campsite. Bypass this section altogether. Walk away.

Last time Samantha and Lisa had no option but to come this way. The arrow on the ground indicated the direction they must take. They followed it without question or hesitation.

The trail to the headland weaves and winds between and around the ubiquitous towering granite. Born of liquid fire deep in the earth's belly, Samantha knows what she sees here on the surface are just the crumbs of something larger. This time she stops to observe the grand curves and angles of these great stones. She runs her hand across their roughened surfaces. Feels the heat they trap by day. Marvels at their vulnerability to the patient agents of salt, air and rain. In places, the coarse face of them is eroded into deep crevices and shallow bowls. Many have collected enough soil to become small gardens for everlasting daisies, milkwort and squat tufted grasses. Down at sea level she's witnessed the scouring work of the ocean on this stone to form rock pools. They glint in the sun like sequins on a granite dress. They are home to limpets, turban snails and small translucent blennies that dart between crops of seaweed. A whole different world lives within these eroded bowls. Busy. Unstoppable. Oblivious to what goes on around them.

The shadows cast by the boulders don't bother Samantha as they had previously. Last time they created twilight places used to predatory advantage, as Nicole learned. Back then, fear and the imagination brought a sinister artifice to these dark, secret places. Now though, she notices how the shadows are home to a host of things that thrive in these gloomy areas. Piecrust-coloured toadstools. Plates of brown and orange fungi striped with growth rings. Delicate, dendritic-like lichen. She has no sense for the trickery of the landscape this time. The terrain feels honest.

Samantha tries to apply a similar honesty to her thoughts of the past. What she knows to be the truest of all is that she was more terrified on this headland than she ever had been before or since. She was terrified of the man's capabilities. Terrified of Lisa's apparent disregard for them. Terrified of the isolation and the risk of the three of them being split up once more. Which is why she'd felt so stricken – sickened – when Nicole walked away, while Lisa seemed determined to stand her ground.

Samantha learned something about the survival instinct that day: it's a place people go to in order to make unbearable choices bearable.

A chant had played inside her head as she drew further away from Lisa: *Don't make me choose. Don't make me choose.*

But she succumbed to her lack of courage. She made the unbearable choice bearable. She backed away.

'Lisa! We have to stick together!'

Her impulsive, angry, beautiful friend hadn't even looked at her. Samantha thinks Lisa went to a place of her own that day. Some place beyond all of them. The place she might still go to in order to find the strength to avenge wrongs.

'Some friends,' the man taunted. 'They're leaving you for dead.'

When Samantha thinks about that day now, she doesn't think so much about which friend she chose so much as why they allowed themselves to be put in a position where a choice had to be made. And just as she sometimes hears Lisa's voice inside her head, demanding she *Keep up*, Samantha's often wondered if Lisa hears a voice too, one that whispers *Stick together*. Are they words that have tormented her over the years? Do they cast their own criticism?

On the days when Samantha feels charitable towards herself, she pretends the only reason she chose to follow Nicole and not stay and stand alongside Lisa, was because she believed her leaving would encourage Lisa to do the same thing. She expected her to shout a few more derogatory comments at the man, wave her stick about, but that she'd then back away as Samantha had.

How could she have underestimated her so much?

Lisa had no intention of standing down. She wanted to mark him in some way. To leave him with a scar too, a permanent reminder that he'd picked a fight with the wrong girl. A scar like the one on her cheek. Something he'd also have to invent a story around, rewrite its origins to his family, his friends.

Samantha had paused for a time in her conflicted escape and watched the man as he came down from his grand rocky platform. He was tall, lean and athletic. He negotiated the narrow ledges and long drops with wily self-assurance. He jumped the last metre from the boulder to the ground. Landed as smooth and soft-kneed as a cat. He shifted his long damp hair from his eyes with a quick flick of his head. He grinned at Lisa.

'So you wanna play?' he said.

Samantha recognised instantly and sickeningly that his purpose and pride were far superior even to Lisa's.

'Run!' she screamed, but too late.

The man rushed at Lisa.

Lisa got the first blow in. She swung her stick round with the force of a hammer thrower and struck him across his back. He drew up his arms to protect himself. Drew up his shoulders. Pulled his long tortoise neck in. Made even less of his weak chin.

Lisa swung her stick back, ready to strike him with it again, but he stepped quickly out of reach. When Samantha thinks about it now, she doesn't believe he even considered for a moment that he might come off second best. That he might be in danger. But neither did Lisa.

Samantha's feet were fused to the ground. Only her voice functioned. 'Run!' she screamed at Lisa again.

But the opportunity for Lisa to escape diminished by the second.

Samantha looked down the trail to Nicole, who paused and looked back up at her. She seemed as reluctant to act as Samantha. Fine friends they were.

Samantha's heart stampeded inside her chest. It had a sonar reach up into her neck and ears. Her stomach fizzed.

Where did her lack of courage to act come from, when Lisa seemed to have such an abundance of it? Was it formed by the early challenges and small knocks that defeated her in her youth? Or was it the years of hearing her mother's advice against the dangers in the world: *Don't ask for trouble. Walk away. Turn the other cheek.* Had this instilled her with self-preserving restraint?

The man smiled. 'Look at you,' he said to Lisa, 'with your little stick. Think you're going to hurt me with that?'

He pretended to rush at her, and then quickly stepped back again. He made the same manoeuvre once more, thrust forward, reared back, as sure-footed as a fencer.

Lisa, confused, thrashed her stick before her but it never ended up where it needed to be. Every movement she made had a tormented delay to it. Once again he was playing with her.

Frustrated, Lisa lunged forward, swept the stick in an arc before her. He reared back. Too fast for her again.

He lunged at her then. Grabbed the stick with his hand before Lisa had a chance to pull it away. He wrested it from her. Tossed it to the side where it clattered over the edge of the cliff.

Even disarmed, Lisa didn't run. 'Fuck you!' she screamed.

There was nothing between the two of them then except their panting breath and rage. He dropped one shoulder and charged.

Lisa had her back turned, so Samantha couldn't see her face. But she heard the loud grunt of air that rushed out of her as he slammed into her chest. She reeled backwards. Tried to regain her balance with her arms, but failed. Her head was the last thing to hit the ground. It crashed against a rock with a sickening thud.

Samantha still remembers her split second thought of *Stay down*.

But Lisa didn't. She shook her head groggily then tried to haul herself up again.

The man stood over her. He lifted one giant boot-clad foot and placed it on her chest so that she was pinned to the ground. Lisa, still sluggish from the fall, tried to scramble out from under it, her arms and legs worked like a crab's. He leant forward, placed more pressure on his foot, more pressure on his trophy.

Did he mean to crush her?

Samantha still wonders who that girl was, the one paralysed to act even as her friend looked set to have her ribs crushed in.

'No!' she heard Nicole scream behind her.

Samantha's not sure if it was hearing Nicole close again that finally gave her the courage to act. Or if it was shame. When she finally responded, it didn't feel like a victory blow. It felt like a single convincing stand in the face of many failed ones.

Samantha charged at the man with a lion's roar. She

headbutted him hard in his skinny gut. Her head smashed up against his ribs. She felt them press in then spring out again as she bounced off the drum of his stomach muscles. The shock of the impact travelled all the way from her crown to the base of her spine. Later, she would notice that she had neck pain. It's a pain that still flares up, even now.

She remembers wishing she had horns. Ones sharp enough to gouge him wide open. She wanted to hear him scream with pain. Wanted to see his shock at discovering his spilled intestines. Wanted to smile at his futile attempts to hold the slippery coils in.

She shocked him well enough, that she remembers. And badly winded him too. And she got some of the satisfaction she was after when she saw his confusion and uncertainty as he tried to pull air into his lungs, and how for some time nothing came of his efforts. With all his attention focussed on trying to breathe, he paid no attention or thought for the edge behind him as he stumbled backwards.

Samantha saw it though. And some part of her, that place that still held some sense of goodness, thought to warn him. She's never questioned the fact that she didn't. And she refuses to start now.

He was kept up like a leaf in the wind for a while. His feet held to the edge but eventually his upper body overreached itself. His fear was real then. His breath finally came back to him so she did get to hear him scream. Oddly, it gave her no satisfaction. Only a disgusted sense of involvement in something unnecessarily cruel.

And then he thought he could fly. His flapping fledgling arms were the last things she saw as he disappeared over the edge.

THE HUSHED BEAUTY OF THE HEADLAND makes it difficult for Lisa to conceive that lives were changed by violence here. Previously, clouds sliced off the tops of mountains, made plateaus of them. The ocean thundered against a shoreline that was difficult to see. There was no real horizon to speak of. It felt as though they were marooned on a pinnacle of rock.

In contrast, today is a perfect day – still and clear. The ocean has a placid, metallic sheen beneath a sky that is the kind of blue that draws people outdoors. A day to lie back and hold your face up to the sun, eyes closed.

Not today though. Today Lisa stands rigid on the headland. Her hands grip the barrier that now stretches along the cliff edge. The tubular metal rail is warm and rough with salt and corrosion. The mesh below it is bowed seaward from the feet and knees that have pushed up against it before hers. It did little to stop the vertiginous swoon she'd felt when she first looked down. But it does make her wonder what difference this simple structure might have made to their futures had it been here previously.

Lisa lifts her gaze from the swirling sea at the base of the cliff and looks outward. She expects many have done the same before her. She turns slowly away from the ocean to the mountains that rear up behind her. It's a majestic view. One that people would comment on in awe.

Lisa has no words of admiration for where she stands though. All she can think about is how different her life might have been had she never set foot in this beautiful, treacherous place. Maybe she'd have stood a chance of eventually getting rid of the fight that seems always to live inside her. To set a torch to her quick rage once and for all until it burnt itself out. Instead, she continues to carry the smouldering coals of it. She stokes it often.

'No wonder he wasn't threatened by us.'

Lisa turns and looks up at Nicole. She sits atop the same boulder the man had that day. Her knees are drawn up tight against her chest, arms wrapped round them.

Nicole pushed ahead of Lisa and Samantha once they reached the side trail to the lookout. Her calf muscles bulged as big as ox hearts as she pulled away from them. She looked more machine than human. Someone propelled by rigid cogs and straining pulleys, and not the loose limbs of a walker. By the time Lisa and Samantha reached the headland, Nicole's pack was already on the ground and she was sitting up high.

'From up here we'd have looked insignificant.'

And yet it's Nicole who looks small and withdrawn on her rocky summit.

'He thought we were insignificant no matter where he sat,' Lisa calls up to her. 'That was the problem.'

'I thought the problem was your damaged pride?'

Lisa doesn't reply. She knows she won't be kind if she does. Instead, she looks back to the gentle undulations of the ocean. She imagines the water washing over her. She tries to picture it cooling her anger.

The last four days have been long and hard. She's tired to the bone and the aches and pains run as deep as them too. And now that they've reached this point, she wonders what it was all for. What did she hope to achieve in bringing them back here? Did she really think they could become those young women again? Those three school friends, once united by their differences, only to be dragged apart by them?

But she knows what the real problem was back then, and it wasn't her pride.

'We didn't stick together,' she calls over her shoulder to Nicole. '*That* was the problem.'

Samantha turns and frowns at Lisa.

'What?' she says to her. 'It's the truth.'

What good has it done her to hold down the one thing that has sustained her all these years? Her anger is the single most perfect thing about her, and she's exhausted as much from pushing back against it as she is from doing this hike. Exhausted from pretending to Samantha and Nicole that she's changed.

'Talking about blame does none of us any good.' Samantha says this loudly, so Lisa figures her comment is intended for Nicole as much as it is for her. Sharing the words out, just as she used to. Divvying them up. Equal. Fair. Reasonable. The peacekeeper.

'Don't you *ever* want to shout?' Lisa asks Samantha. 'To punch walls?'

Samantha looks away. She doesn't answer.

Maybe she does, Lisa thinks. Maybe she also pretends she's something – someone – else.

'Why don't you admit it?'

'Admit what?' Samantha asks, looking at Lisa again.

Lisa can see Samantha is genuinely confused and for a split second she hates herself. But obviously not enough.

'That we *all* fucked up. We *all* killed him.'

'We don't know that!' Nicole shouts and Lisa feels the air shift around her as much as hears something whistle past.

A rock clatters down the cliff face. It takes a small shower of stones with it into the sea.

The pain in Lisa's head after the man charged at her and she crashed against the rock was intense. The space before her eyes sparkled with pinpricks of light. Eventually the pain found its rhythm as a deep, dull throb. Later, she found a boggy swelling behind her right ear the size of a toddler's fist. It took weeks to subside.

At the time, the pain was nothing compared to the cold joy she felt as she watched the man's windmilling arms disappear over the cliff's edge. She thought nothing of what he might be falling to, or how far.

She hauled herself up on all fours. She doesn't remember noticing the rocky ground digging into her bare knees or hands. She was wrapped in cotton wool. Not from the low misty clouds all about that day. Her senses were in a fug. Motion slowed. Reality had tipped on an axis so that she no longer held her thoughts straight in her mind.

She remembers the way Samantha looked on expressionless at the space where the man had been. Then wasn't. Her arms were limp at her sides. Lisa expected to see anguish or fear on her face. But she showed neither charity nor concern.

Nicole walked to the cliff's edge with what seemed deliberate slowness. Or was that just the effect of Lisa's fuddled thinking? Because surely she'd have rushed.

She watched as Nicole leant forward at the edge of the cliff and looked down. She turned and walked back, trance-like, to the copse of trees where she'd been tied. With patient force, she worked a broken branch free from the undergrowth, half as thick again as her arm. She dragged it behind her to the edge and lowered the thickest end down. She lay on the ground on her stomach then, head and shoulders over the edge. She gripped the branch in two hands and from there Lisa saw how the small but pronounced muscles in her arms flexed as she shifted the branch about.

Lisa managed to stand. She and Samantha walked slowly towards Nicole as though summoned by a siren song. They lay on their stomachs beside her and peered over the edge.

Two metres down, the man lay unmoving on a ledge the

size of her Datsun. Beyond that was a fifteen-metre drop into the roiling sea.

He lay crookedly. His left shoulder was flung back so she could see all of his unshaven face. His small chin sagged towards his chest. It pulled his mouth open. His long hair obscured his right eye. The other she could see. It was opened no more than a slit. A trickle of blood tracked from his hairline down his left temple and into his ear. Lisa looked down the length of his body. His dented metal water bottle was still attached to his belt. He mustn't have screwed the top on properly after his last drink because it had left a wet stain on the front of his khaki trousers. His right boot was hooked awkwardly under his left calf in a way that would be uncomfortable if he were aware.

Lisa looked back up to his chest. It shifted up and down slowly.

Not dead then.

It felt like a bland diagnosis. One that brought her neither relief nor disappointment.

She remembers thinking *Who am I?* as she looked down at the unconscious man and feeling nothing for his predicament. She also remembers feeling a rare stab of fear at no longer knowing with any certainty.

Nicole hadn't acknowledged them as they lay alongside her. She doggedly kept up her task of trying to wedge the branch under the unconscious man's shoulder.

Lisa looked sideways at her. The girl she saw was a cicada husk of the one she knew, an incomplete version of the real Nicole. That girl wore her righteousness as proud armour. She was someone Lisa relied upon to be her guiding compass and point her away from her own recklessness. But this girl, the one beside Lisa then, was more interested in applying the laws of load and leverage to a lethal task than those of compassion or safety.

Nicole looked neither disappointed nor frustrated by the difficulty of what she was attempting to do. She quietly persisted. Tried different areas along the length of the man's body under which to lodge her branch. She managed to hoist his left leg over his right so that at least his hips were directed towards the edge of the ledge. She set to work on his shoulders once more after that. Got his left arm across his chest briefly, but then it clunked back on the rock behind him again.

The man groaned softly each time she dug the branch under him. Lisa imagined how the sharp, splintered end of the wood must have bruised or broken the skin beneath his clothes.

'Nicole?' Lisa said, finally finding her voice.

She still recalls the gentleness of her tone. And yet she doesn't know what made her think she had to be gentle. Maybe, subconsciously, she remembered schoolgirl tales of the dangers of abruptly waking a sleepwalker. Because surely it was a similar state that Nicole was in? All Lisa knew with any clarity was that she shouldn't startle Nicole. That she shouldn't risk some confused action that could put any one of them on the ledge alongside the man. Or worse – to the place below where she seemed determined to push him.

Nicole ignored Lisa. She kept up her prodding with the branch.

'Nicole?' Lisa said again, but louder. She placed her hand on Nicole's arm.

Nicole looked down bewildered at Lisa's filthy hand with its broken nails and bloodied knuckles. She shuffled away from her a little, as she might if an accidental but unnecessary intrusion on her space had occurred on a bus or a train. A small, discreet repositioning as though not wanting to offend. She returned then, to her deadly but determined task.

It was a selfish thought Lisa recognises now, but part of her had felt a sense of relief at what Nicole was doing. Because while not exonerating the role Lisa had played, it made her feel that at least all three of them were complicit then. That in some way Samantha's, then Nicole's actions reduced her own culpability.

Nicole managed to get a branch-hold under his left shoulder again and with a grunt she pushed him over so that he was fully on his right side. She moved the branch down to his buttocks after that. She pressed it into the soft flesh and pushed.

'No.' Samantha spoke so softly that Lisa could barely hear her.

Then she spoke again and her voice was loud and firm. 'Stop.'

Samantha hauled herself onto her knees and shuffled in closer to Nicole. 'Stop,' she said again and placed her hand on Nicole's arm. 'No more.'

Nicole turned to face Samantha for a moment. Then turned back and looked down at her hands, wrapped round the branch. She frowned at them as though uncertain about whose they were. She carefully rested the branch against the cliff face and gripped the rocky edge of the cliff with both hands. Her knuckles whitened. She opened her mouth wide as though to scream. But no sound came out. Instead, her shoulders hitched in big, strangled sobs while tears streaked through the dirt that covered her face.

They turned their backs on the headland after that. They turned their backs on the man. Left him alone on the ledge. Left him to whatever was to happen to him next. They walked away soiled and bleeding and altered by what happened there.

Nicole pulled away from them on the trail back down. Already working on building the distance between them. Not once did she look back. And as they drew further and further away from the headland, Lisa stopped looking back too. She gradually started to close down that part of her life as well.

How to articulate shame? How to stop it existing only as a deadening of feeling? To give it a face and character, some *purpose*, so that it might be studied from all sides and better understood, used for good?

Nicole has never been able to find the words to describe hers. Even though it lives on in her. It is an experience that's never grown out of, never reconciled. Something that has marked her in permanent ways. It's made its home inside her, but radiates no homely comforts, only cold numbness. It shuts out the forces of warmth and joy and kindness. It tells her she doesn't deserve them. And it has a long tail. One she's learned to live with, but never beyond.

Nicole envies Lisa's apparent lack of it. Maybe if Nicole had her pluck she could have avoided it too. She might have fought more forcefully against the man. Avoided being led like an animal. Not grovelled and pleaded so quickly and easily. As it is, she feels complicit in her abduction. Too willing to comply with the terms of it, as though there was no other option available to her. And when she finally found the courage to exert her will against his, it was only when it was safe for her to do so. Once he no longer posed any threat. In this, Nicole knows herself to be no better than him. They both acted outside of the rules.

From where she sits now, up high on the boulder, she feels as though she's in the balcony seats of a theatre looking down upon a stage. This stage, while unconventional, is no less capable of drama. It's a relatively flat dais of rock. Cushioned in places with low, wombat-nibbled grass. The sea crashes against the shoreline and provides a fitting soundtrack as the waves build into a series of threatening crescendos. And the light and shade of shadows brings shape-shifting life to the boulders that surround it. They take their place as characters in this play, either villain or hero depending on the imagination. The man-made barrier along the cliff edge is the only impurity to this natural set.

Nicole felt a surge of anger when she first saw the barrier. It made the site of her drama look too safe. She stared at it for some time. Felt her hands clench and unclench at her sides. Felt her jaw tighten. This salt-scarred structure would have taken at least one scene away from the performance. It would have allowed her to remain better than the man.

She felt she was owed some kind of explanation for its installation. Stupidly, she looked for a sign that read *Erected because* followed by a list of all the falls or near falls that had necessitated its construction. She could have believed then that what happened here was an avoidable accident. That it had nothing to do with her at all.

She looks down from the boulder to where Lisa stands now, hands on the top rail of the barrier, looking out across the ocean. Even though Lisa seems small from up here, Nicole can still see the signature signs of her rage. It's there – has been all along – in her shoulders, the way the tightness in them forms a gully down her spine, shortens her neck. She's held it in check so well. But Nicole knows the burden of suppressing emotions, be that anger, shame or guilt. It's like wrestling smoke. It's all around, affects the way you see things, but is impossible to hold.

Nicole doesn't feel good about the accusations she's levelled against Lisa along the way. But that's all part of wrestling with something that can't be gripped. Cruel remarks leave the body unchecked. Rocks are thrown. Nicole won't deny that to be able to blame someone else has been a welcome relief from the steady internal monologue of no-good accusations she levels against herself.

Now that she's back here, Nicole realises her return doesn't change or solve anything. The bitterness of this thought surprises her. She must have hoped that she'd find a fix. An easy new beginning. Did she expect to arrive at the headland and it would all be exactly as she'd left it more than twenty years before? All she had to do was tidy up any sign of ever having been here, like picking up the dropped stitch in a knitted garment? Set the place aright and along with it her life?

All she's discovered is that this place holds no trace of what happened to her. It is completely indifferent, thriving even. It's as though she's been told that what happened here was insignificant, unworthy of any record. And that she doesn't matter either.

This realisation hits her like a knee to the stomach.

Nicole drops her head onto her forearms feeling physically winded. She tries to pull air into her lungs but everything inside her feels tight and closed. Or *tighter* and *more* closed, because she can't remember a time anymore when she felt anything but.

She hauls herself up to her feet. She needs to get her breath, but her legs don't feel fit for purpose. She bends forward, hands on knees, and tries to draw in air. She hears a soft animal noise rise up from somewhere. She realises it's coming from her. It builds to a low keen. She doesn't recognise the sound as her own and neither does she recognise the feeling that drives it. But if she were to give it a name then she'd probably call it the sound of wretchedness.

Standing here, stooped over on this grand, aeons old

boulder, Nicole feels such an insignificant and fragile thing in comparison to all that surrounds her. What does she bring to this landscape? This life? What is her purpose? What is her function? And because she can't think of an answer, her keening grows.

'Nicole?'

Samantha's voice is a distant-through-time sound. A call from another era, back when hearing the concern in her voice might have made a difference.

Metres below, Nicole sees them both gaze up at her. Their faces seem dulled. Fragmented. It's like they're disappearing.

She stands tall and forces herself to relax, to let go of muscles she imagines she's held tight for years. She wants to feel softness. She wants to feel something of who she used to be. And with this loosening comes a sense of lightness. An unburdening. She thinks she must be swaying because the two pale faces below seem to drift about like Chinese lanterns on a breeze.

'Nicole!' Lisa's voice cuts through the fug. It's loud, more urgent than Samantha's was. Bossier too. Nicole is momentarily surprised by the familiarity of it.

She senses more than sees a blur of movement below. A brisk shift of arms and legs and then there is just one face looking up. It shifts in and out of focus but she's familiar enough with it again to recognise it as Samantha's.

'Sit down!' Samantha calls. 'Please. Just sit down.'

Nicole doesn't sit. Instead, she thinks about closing her eyes. Closing them to the contours of the land – the mountains, the ocean, the sky. Closing them to the contours inside her. The rise and pitch and plummet of feelings she's navigated all these years.

And because her eyes have to take in so much, must look so far, she does close them. And in the thin darkness that follows her breathing eases. Her throat hushes. And for a moment she thinks she might feel joy.

'Hurry Lisa!'

Nicole wishes she could shut down sound the same way she's shut down sight. Samantha's voice is an intrusion. It's a handwringing sound. One she doesn't want to feel responsible for.

'For God's sake, Nicole! Sit down!'

There's no breeze but Nicole's body sways as if there is. She feels herself tilt and correct on proprioceptive cue. She thinks about how she need only lean forward, push out with her chest to begin with – just a little, just enough – and the rest of her will follow as she tips the balance. Just as the man's balance was tipped. And she'll finally have an end. A hard and beckoning bottom. Just there. Just there in that no longer seen space before her. Not falling. Surrendering.

SAMANTHA DOESN'T BUILD A CAIRN ON the headland. She thought about it. It was going to be a large one if she did. Monumental. Precise. Sturdy. A thing of beauty. Her best yet.

But she doesn't build one, not here. Instead, she edges around the end of the barrier. Squeezes through the gap between rock and mesh, hitches herself up taller, thinner, until she's standing on the precipitous side of the fence.

Lisa sits on the ground a few metres behind. Nicole sits between her legs, resting back against her chest. Their heads touch. Lisa has her arms round her. Nicole shivers still, just a little, even though the day is warm. Samantha knows Nicole's safe in those arms.

There's a fizz in her gut and a blood-thump in her ears from being on this side, the wrong side, of the barrier. No one's forced her to be here. It's her idea.

'I need to know more,' she said to the others.

They didn't say anything. But neither did they disagree.

She holds onto the railing with both hands and tries to channel some of Harry's nerve.

He is always calm in a crisis. He never gets flustered or angry or shouts. He thinks clearly, practically. Slips into whatever man he needs to be to suit the situation. Samantha thinks she sensed this protective calm in him when they met. Maybe this is what she fell in love with first, his ability to absorb fear or worry so that she didn't have to. Sponged it up like a water spill. Kept her on her dry pinnacle. Safe. That he could do this and love her back had seemed more than she deserved at the time.

Samantha rests her forehead on the top bar of the barrier. She stays like that for a moment until her breath steadies. Then she looks down to find her first foothold.

Lisa doesn't call for Samantha to be careful. Neither does she come and watch her progress, advice at the ready. Samantha is pleased about this. She wants her faith, not her guidance.

She looks down, but doesn't let her gaze travel all the way to the crashing waves fifteen metres below. She tasks her eyes only with finding a spot where she can place her foot. There's a shelf just below and she lowers her right leg down to it, gripping the mesh with clawed fingers.

Her boot slips. The shelf is covered with ball bearing-like gravel. Her heart tumbles in her chest. She pauses to steady it, carefully clearing the surface of gravel with her boot. She hears it patter against rocks as it falls.

Samantha tests that the shelf has the design to hold her. She gradually increases the load on it. The wire cuts into her fingers as she eases her body down till her leg bears all of her weight. It holds.

She imagines any one of her sons making this two-metre descent with quick ease. Fearless. Agile. One, two, three steps and they'd be down. They'd trust the rocks they stepped on to bear them. Trust their ability to choose them well. Once on the ledge below, she imagines how they'd sit with their legs over the edge of it, feet swinging. As calm and at ease as a Pacific gull taking a breather.

Samantha takes an unreasonable amount of time to decide where to place her foot next. She tests one spot, then another, but she's too cautious to trust any of them. *Just pick one!* she thinks. And so she does.

Her fingers go red from gripping firstly the mesh then once it's out of reach, they go red from gripping rock ledges. She must trust all four points – hands and feet. It's a descent of faith as much as one of nerve.

She concentrates so hard that she doesn't notice the thump of fear again till she's reached the ledge. Once there, she doesn't trust her legs so she gets down on all fours. She crawls back from the edge of it and sits with her back pressed up against the cliff face.

'Made it,' she calls as agreed.

'Okay,' Lisa calls back.

Not *Well done* or *I knew you could do it* or *Be careful*. Samantha appreciates Lisa's restraint.

She rests her head back against the cliff face, eyes closed, till her breathing and heart steadies. She opens them again after a time and looks out across the ocean.

Silver gulls are suspended on thermal currents before her. They hang there like a child's mobile. Some are almost at eye level. She can see their red legs pulled up into the white undercarriage of their bellies. Their wings are spread wide and are mostly still as they hold their bodies aloft, except for the tips of their feathers, which quiver in the soft breeze. They change course with slight tilts and dips. Others flap vigorously past, a destination in mind. Beneath them, beneath her, is a vast body of silken water. There's a tanker in the distance. Red. The size of a paperclip.

Now that she's here, Samantha welcomes the solitude. Her muscles finally relax and her back moulds into the rock face behind her. She stretches out her legs. They don't quite reach the edge. She places her hands flat beside her. She feels the long history of scars on the stone beneath them. She can think about Nicole now that she's here, cry if she wants. There's no one to see her quick blinks or quivering bottom lip, which in front of Nicole earlier, she'd had to pinch between thumb and finger to keep steady.

To think of Nicole is to think of the kind of trust Samantha needed of herself just now to reach this ledge. Not being able to trust in others is one thing, but to realise you can't trust in yourself is something else altogether. Because who are we left with, if not ourselves? Who pulls us back from the edge? Who's the last one to stop us falling, if not ourselves?

Lisa has stopped Nicole for now. She wrapped those thin, strong arms around her, pulled Nicole back from the edge of herself. The same arms that always fought for them, always had their backs regardless of whether or not the recklessness of them was the reason she needed to act. Then Harry took Lisa's place for Samantha.

She thinks back to the conversation she had with him as she was leaving for this hike. Her backpack still smelt shop-bought on the back seat of her car, not the filthy sweaty thing it is now.

'Do you ever think about when we first got together?' she asked him.

Harry rested his forearms on the frame of her open car window. He picked at a spot of dirt on his arm, tried to scrape it off but didn't have the fingernails for the job. 'Not really,' he said.

Samantha looked ahead over the car's dash. 'I do. I think about how you called me after that first night and asked if we could do it again ... the meeting one another ... but sober.' She turned to look at him. 'Do you remember that?'

Harry didn't pause to think. He nodded straight away. It surprised her.

'Yeah. I remember.'

'I think we need to try that again,' she said. 'The meeting one another.'

'But I know you now.'

'No, you don't. You have an idea of who I am, but it's built on what you expect me to be.'

'What if I don't like the new you as much?' he joked. 'Can I get the old one back?'

'This is serious, Harry. Our marriage is failing.'

He finally stopped picking at the dirt on his arm and looked at her. For the first time this safe, reliable and predictable man showed Samantha his fear.

'Is it?' he asked.

She thinks of the quiet way he has of diverting disputes. His softly spoken, *I've got this*, said with a steady hand to a shoulder, almost as if he hopes to take up the person's tension through his palm. But in that moment beside the car, Samantha saw that he didn't have this. This was something beyond his control or ability to mop up. In fact, she doesn't expect he even knows where to begin.

So it's down to her. Has she *got this*? Is she prepared to keep *him* safe? Safe with her?

They're both imperfect, but he's always accepted her as good enough, something she's never accepted of herself. Maybe each of them is being the best they know how to be? Maybe they're as good as they'll ever be?

Half her life has been spent with him. And while he doesn't always see her, she expects this is because he trusts he could put his hand out, even if they were to live in complete darkness, and know it would find her. Maybe she's being childish in still wanting – expecting – the first flush of a new relationship after more than twenty years. Maybe what they have now is what the intense and complex emotion of first love subdues into. Something that in truth might be more beneficial to the longevity of a relationship – contentment in belonging.

She takes this time now to cry. Not big hitching sobs. She expects they'll come later. Her tears are mostly silent. She cries for all their losses. Their innocence. Their courage. Their friendship. She cries for what could have been.

After a while, she dries her cheeks on the hem of her T-shirt. Takes some deep breaths. She's ready to start her search.

She doesn't know what she's looking for. What could still be here after so many years? Stupidly, she expected to see the branch still up against the cliff face when she first looked over the edge. A callous reminder of how unhinged they were. But of course it would have rotted away or rolled into the ocean long ago. It will be in a million tiny, scattered splinters by now.

She shifts along the ledge on all fours. She still doesn't trust herself to stand. She runs her hand across the cliff face as she goes, studies its grey surface. She scours the ledge. She looks for what? Bones? Teeth? *Die cunts* gouged into the rock?

She finds no tufts of dark hair. No dented water bottle wedged into a crevasse. No scraps of khaki fabric. No wristwatch or buttons or zips.

There's litter: a soft drink can, a faded muesli bar wrapper, a desiccated apple core. Bird shit. Leaves. Twigs.

And there are loose stones. She gathers together as many suitable ones as she can find.

It's a small, imperfect cairn. It's not sturdy or precise or beautiful. But it's here on this secret-keeping ledge. And she built it.

THEY SET UP THEIR TENTS AT the final campsite but decide not to sleep in them. Instead, they lay their sleeping mats side by side on the ground. Together, they've decided to sleep under the stars.

They hadn't stopped here last time. They'd rushed back to their packs as quickly as their shaken, battered bodies had allowed. Nicole hadn't even argued against it when Lisa and Samantha took some of the weight from her pack. They walked through the night, following the weak beams of their torches. They walked in silence. The air was damp and carried the medicinal scent of eucalyptus oil. The trees dripped moisture; it rained down upon her if any breeze caught their leaves.

Lisa walked behind the other two. She wanted to be the first one he came across should he follow. If he even could.

She saw them stumble. She saw them fall. She helped them up.

The night was rich with sounds – the strangled, vibrating growls of possums, the grating chirr of nightjars. Cricket orchestras played. There were whistles and warbles and shuffles in the undergrowth. Lisa startled often. She expects the others did too. Paired lights shone down on her from branches or through the scrub – eyes that were red, white, amber. Mostly they disappeared as quickly as they appeared. By dawn, her nerves were as raw as a wound scoured by a wire brush.

They didn't talk about the man they'd left behind on the ledge. They didn't talk about the fact that she had wanted to throw his backpack from the cliff into the sea. Leaving him with nothing.

Samantha stopped her. 'Don't!'

The force of her voice had startled Lisa enough to make her drop his pack back on the ground.

Nicole wouldn't look at them, let alone tell them what he'd done to her. This was – still is – left for them to imagine.

The detail seems immaterial now. How Nicole's world looked afterwards is all that matters.

Lisa knows Nicole's disconnection began that night. She eased away from them step after step. Moved to the other side of something. A place where neither Lisa nor Samantha could follow her or hope to pull her back from.

By the time they reached the car park just before sunrise, the Nicole that Lisa had known for years had gone.

Lisa likes the unfamiliarity of tonight's campsite. It's lack of history.

It's a pretty site. Inland. A shallow creek runs beside it, so the grass is lush and spongy underfoot. The water is cold and clear and a balm for worked feet. The trees are at rest. The afternoon sun is kindly. After the heavy burdens of the day, she feels lightness now for having arrived here. For having made it.

There are three other tents set up in nearby clearings. A comfortable chatter comes from each. Lisa feels like they're a part of something more. She wonders at the difference it would have made if the area had been as frequented by hikers then as it is now. They could have walked, camped, with others. Found civility in company. Been less susceptible to the animal actions of an individual. Become less like animals themselves.

But she's not here to find excuses or to reimagine what could have been. She's here to forgive the person she was back then. The one she's been since. It's a big ask. She knows she's not even close yet to achieving it. But at least her older self has started a conversation with the younger one. They might yet become friends.

A buttery moon nudges up from behind the crown of a tree. It looks like one half of a broken biscuit. It also looks close enough that Lisa could reach out and pluck it from the night sky.

'I kept an eye on the newspapers afterwards,' Samantha says.

Lisa feels Nicole nod beside her. 'So did I.'

They lie on their backs in their sleeping bags. Nicole in the middle. Lisa had held back laying out her sleeping mat. She felt like someone playing a game of three cups. She watched for where the one with the stone landed.

'I'm okay,' Nicole said when she settled in alongside her.

Lisa liked that she hadn't sounded embarrassed.

It's cooler now the sun has set. But it's cosy in her downy sleeping bag. With hands under her head, Lisa looks up and admires the vapour trail of stars that make up the Milky Way.

'I never found anything though,' Samantha continues. 'No reports of a rescue. Or a missing person. Or of a body being found. Nothing.'

Lisa doesn't admit that she didn't even look. It's not that she forgot about him, because she never has. It's just that she didn't care enough about him to want to know his fate.

'I thought about driving back here a few weeks later,' Samantha says. 'See if his car was still in the car park.'

'Did you do it?' Nicole asks.

'No. I didn't have the guts.'

The half-biscuit moon lifts slowly above the tree.

'Does it matter what happened to him?' Lisa feels Samantha and Nicole turn in her direction. She doesn't know why they do. There's nothing for them to see in the dark. She takes it as a sign of their disapproval. 'Because I guess he's still out there anyway,' she adds.

'Do you think so?' Samantha sounds young, hopeful.

Lisa doesn't answer. Instead she watches a satellite blink across the sky. Before long she loses it amongst the litter of stars.

EPILOGUE

NICOLE HADN'T INTENDED TO TAKE THE side trail up to the headland. She'd planned to walk right past the detour. But her feet shifted to the right as though they were in charge. *No shortcuts*, they said, where obviously her mind was prepared to allow them. Before long she was back on the rocky point.

There are more clouds today. They bring new shadows to the theatre. Dark curtains fall across the surrounding boulders and then lift quickly away. There is a strengthening wind too. She thinks about how different things could have been in a breeze like this, that moment when she teetered with the dissonance of being grounded and not. This breeze then could have been the hand to her back that took away choice.

But there are choices this place has taken from her. Her world was made smaller because of her experiences here. She pulled in the parameters of it, pruned it back like a rose bush, but unlike the rose, she didn't grow stronger or fuller for the treatment. No, she pruned her life back so hard she no longer knew how to blossom at all. Was she meant to be a partner to someone? she wonders. A mother? It's easier to think not than to think that she had cut this branch from her life. But if not a mother, then she might at least have been a godmother.

Hannah is everything and nothing like Lisa. When Nicole

first met the girl, she was thrust back to her school days. Here was the skinny blonde girl who patched her knee that day, the girl who claimed her. She'd almost wept upon their introduction, had to look away from her youthful, innocent face. *Be careful* she wanted to warn her. *We don't always control the rules of our future.* So in truth she thinks she would have probably made a terrible godmother, taught the girl to acquiesce, where Lisa has taught her the power of choice.

When Nicole met Samantha's sons she hadn't known how to speak to them. It made her realise what little she understands about the lives of young men, how inexperienced she is in socialising with them. Samantha does it with natural ease. She calls them out but gives them rein as well; a seamless juggling act of holding on and letting go. Each of her boys is in the image of himself but the whole is taken from the features of each parent – shoulders, hair, height. They are young men but playful still, almost childlike in their torment of one another. And Harry, a monolith of a man in any room, seemed proud and bewildered in turns by the family before him, as though disbelieving his good fortune in being part responsible for its making.

Nicole doesn't allow herself to try and conjure the image of the child she might have had. She looks away from the white light left by this child's absence. Instead, she looks to the flat, grey granite she must cross to reach the barrier at the cliff's edge.

She hadn't wanted to go near the barrier previously. But today she does.

Progress already.

She steps over lacy lichen, cubes of scat and tufted grass that has found opportunity in slim gaps. She places her hands on the guardrail when she reaches it and looks down to the ledge. She is immediately surprised by its lack of familiarity. She recalls nothing of its contours and angles, its colour and texture. Nothing of its width or length.

She tries to picture him lying there, but can't.

She can't picture the young woman who lay on her belly and tried to push this man from the ledge either. She's just as foreign to her. Did she really even exist? In a way Nicole doesn't think so. It wasn't her.

But because of her, Nicole left this place with two new truths held in the palms of her hands. Her degradation rested in one, her capacity for cruelty in the other. Rarely has Lady Justice balanced one with the other.

None of them ever questioned their duty or failure to report what happened here. Nicole suspects for Lisa this was because she didn't care; Samantha, because of her culpability.

For Nicole it was because she had nothing to show for it. No physical signs beyond a few scratches and leech bites. There was only a girl's account. A doctor can't hold a stethoscope to the soul, put a stitch to shame.

But it's enough to say this place has possessed her ever since.

She's back again though, and in her hands she now carries hope.

She will cross the mountains in reverse this time. Confront the opposing hardship of them. She will turn old, difficult climbs into new, easy descents. Each of her steps will cover the same ground but in a different way. The geography unchanged, but her vision of its contours renewed.

ACKNOWLEDGEMENTS

THANKS AND GRATITUDE TO MY PUBLISHER, Madonna Duffy, for her ongoing support of new voices in the Australian literary landscape, and for including mine. Special thanks to my editor, Jacqueline Blanchard – I still can't believe my good fortune at being teamed with not only a talented editor but also a keen bushwalker who connected with this story beyond the page. I would also like to thank Varuna, The Writers' House for the space and uninterrupted writing time provided while working on this book.

This is a story about friendships and of mine I would like to thank Kris Olsson for the many talks and walks we've shared; and Annah Faulkner and Cass Moriarty for their encouragement with this slippery craft we've embarked upon. Heartfelt thanks to my sister, Kerri, as well as Julie, Alison, Louise, Dave, Sue, Caroline, Lynda and my Tuesday friends for their unwavering support and faith in my work. Thanks also to the many readers and booksellers I've met through my writing – your passion for books and words is a lifeline to this often threatened social and cultural necessity.

Finally, thanks to my family, John, Aaron and Liam – your unconditional love sustains me.

COME VISIT US AT
WWW.LEGENDPRESS.CO.UK

FOLLOW US
@LEGEND_PRESS